## A STRUGGLE FOR LAW AND JUSTICE...

**LUKE TRAVIS:** T................................ for county sheriff ................................ taking over. ................................ and Abilene is headed for trouble . . .

**CODY FISHER:** Quick with his fists and quick to spot trouble, the deputy is the first to find out what Travis's rival is up to—and the first to pay the price . . .

**MASON KINCAID:** The brash Eastern land agent is in Abilene to make his fortune. Now he's the moving force behind a new sheriff, a man he believes he can control . . .

**JOHN HENRY DAWES:** With his dark hair and waxed handlebar mustache, he's the very image of a no-nonsense lawman. But once the election is over, Dawes has brutal plans of his own . . .

**LIN ROGERS:** The young man is part of Dawes's gang. But when he falls in love with an Abilene lass, he sees his boss for what he really is, and knows that he must act . . .

**FAITH HAMILTON:** A beautiful woman with a wounded heart, she's a newcomer in Abilene— on a secret vendetta against Mason Kincaid. Now her bitter scheme is leading her into a liaison with a killer . . .

**MIKE WHITSON:** With his band of outlaws he's burning a swath of destruction outside of Abilene— and opening the way for Dawes to take over the town . . .

**Books by Justin Ladd**

Abilene Book 1: The Peacemaker
Abilene Book 2: The Sharpshooter
Abilene Book 3: The Pursuers
Abilene Book 4: The Night Riders
Abilene Book 5: The Half-Breed
Abilene Book 6: The Hangman
Abilene Book 7: The Prizefighter
Abilene Book 8: The Whiskey Runners
Abilene Book 9: The Tracker
Abilene Book 10: The General
Abilene Book 11: The Hellion
Abilene Book 12: The Cattle Baron
Abilene Book 13: The Pistoleer
Abilene Book 14: The Lawman

Published by POCKET BOOKS

Most Pocket Books are available at special quantity discounts for bulk purchases for sales promotions, premiums or fund raising. Special books or book excerpts can also be created to fit specific needs.

For details write the office of the Vice President of Special Markets, Pocket Books, 1230 Avenue of the Americas, New York, New York 10020.

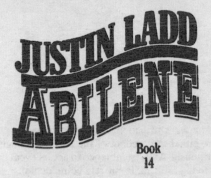

# JUSTIN LADD
# ABILENE

Book
14

# THE LAWMAN

™ **BCI** Created by the producers of
**Wagons West, Stagecoach,
White Indian, and San Francisco.**

*Book Creations Inc., Canaan, NY · Lyle Kenyon Engel. Founder*

**POCKET BOOKS**

New York   London   Toronto   Sydney   Tokyo   Singapore

This book is a work of fiction. Names, characters, places and incidents are either the product of the author's imagination or are used fictitiously. Any resemblance to actual events or locales or persons, living or dead, is entirely coincidental.

An *Original* Publication of POCKET BOOKS

POCKET BOOKS, a division of Simon & Schuster Inc.
1230 Avenue of the Americas, New York, NY 10020

ISBN: 0-671-69313-1

First Pocket Books printing June 1990

10 9 8 7 6 5 4 3 2 1

POCKET and colophon are registered trademarks of
Simon & Schuster Inc.

Printed in the U.S.A.

# Chapter One

————◆————

THERE WERE DAYS, DEPUTY CODY FISHER REFLECTED AS HE strolled down the boardwalk of Abilene, when it felt downright good to be alive.

This crisp autumn afternoon was a sterling example. A fresh breeze wafted in from the northwest, and large, puffy white clouds sailed through a deep blue sky. The sun was pleasantly warm but not hot. All in all, it was a day made for a picnic with a pretty woman or a leisurely few hours on the bank of a pond with a cane pole in hand.

Somebody had to keep the peace in Abilene, though, and Cody was one of the men entrusted with that duty. Not that there was any trouble at the moment. Everything was pretty quiet.

Cody paused and leaned against the railing along the boardwalk. His keen eyes missed little as he surveyed Texas Street, Abilene's main thoroughfare. He was a young man, a few years past twenty, although sometimes he appeared older. Cody had seen a great deal of violence in his life, and that aged a man. The faint scar across his left cheek—souvenir of a knife fight back in his stormy past—gave him a naturally grim look, which, however, was quickly dispelled when he smiled. He had black hair and favored dark clothes, from his flat-crowned hat to his well-worn boots. In the carefully oiled holster on his hip was a new Colt Lightning. The revolver was a double-action model, unlike the single-action Colt Army that Cody had carried until recently. The caliber of the new gun was a little smaller, .41 instead of .45, but from what Cody had seen so far, it would make up for that in speed of use. Not having to pull back the hammer with his thumb between each shot might save him fractions of a second in a tight spot. And Cody knew from experience that those little shavings of time could prove to be mighty important.

He nodded greetings to people who passed him on the boardwalk. There was quite a bit of foot traffic, and most of it was moving toward the eastern end of town. His curiosity aroused, the deputy straightened from his relaxed pose and followed the crowd.

As Cody drew near the Dickinson County Courthouse, he saw that the people were gathering on its front lawn, facing the steps that led up to the big double doors of the main entrance. Cody frowned in puzzlement. He had not heard about any meeting or rally at the courthouse today, and his boss, Marshal Luke Travis, had not mentioned anything about it, either. Travis usually knew about everything that was going on in town. Still, these folks had clearly come here for a reason.

That reason became apparent a moment later. As Cody watched from the back of the crowd, the doors of the courthouse opened, and two men emerged to stand at the top of the steps. One of them was a burly individual in late middle age, wearing brown pants and coat, white shirt, and string tie. His belly was prominent and his wide shoulders sagged a bit, but looking at him one sensed that he had been a powerful man at one time. His battered white Stetson was shoved back on thinning, reddish-gray hair, and his broad ruddy face was wreathed in a grin.

The other man was considerably younger, thirty perhaps. Unlike his companion, whose clothes were storebought and ill-fitting, this man's expensive dark suit and vest seemed tailored just for him. Perched on his dark hair was a black felt hat, and his boots were made of soft leather. He had a quick, easy smile, which several of the ladies standing next to Cody were returning. With his sleek, handsome good looks, he certainly seemed to have charmed the womenfolk of Abilene. Most of the men were looking at him with admiration that was tinged with envy.

Cody knew both of them. The big, redheaded man was Roy Wade, the veteran sheriff of Dickinson County. The other man—the one who looked like a city slicker, in Cody's opinion—was Mason Kincaid, one of Abilene's prominent businessmen and a member of the town council.

Cody had a grudging respect for Roy Wade, not because of the man he was now but because of the lawman he had once been. Mason Kincaid, on the other hand, was nothing but a smooth-talking snake in the grass. Luke Travis and his deputies had clashed with Kincaid more than once in the past.

Kincaid held up his hands for silence, bringing to an expectant end the chatter among the people in the crowd. He grinned at them and said, "My friends and fellow citizens of Abilene . . . I'm very glad you came to hear my little announcement today. It's good to see all of you taking such an active interest in the affairs of our community."

Announcement? What the devil was Kincaid talking about, Cody wondered.

"As all of you know, this man standing here beside me

has served Dickinson County faithfully and well for many years," Kincaid went on. "Sheriff Roy Wade has been the top lawman in these parts for a long time, and we've been lucky to have his experience and courage on our side, on the side of law and order."

Cody did not doubt Sheriff Wade's experience, but the man's courage was more questionable. A few months earlier, when Nord Madden and his ruthless gang of outlaws had been on a rampage in the county, Wade had left it up to Travis and Cody to deal with the desperadoes.

"But all good things must come to an end, as the old saying goes." Kincaid's deep, resonant voice carried well. "Sheriff Wade will be retiring shortly, and even though it will be difficult, the citizens of Dickinson County must begin to consider who will replace him. In approximately two weeks an election will be held, and a new sheriff will be chosen."

That was not news to Cody; he had known about the upcoming election for quite a while, just like everyone else in town. But he had been busy and had not thought much about it. He supposed the same thing could be said of many other townspeople of Abilene.

Kincaid continued, "So far, no candidates have announced their intentions to seek this office. Well, that is about to be remedied, my friends."

Cody caught his breath. Surely Kincaid was not going to announce that *he* was running for sheriff. The land agent had no experience as a lawman, and Cody had seen enough of Kincaid to know that he had no idea what frontier law enforcement was all about.

Kincaid's next statement dispelled that worry. "I've taken the liberty of contacting a man named John Henry Dawes." A murmur of surprise rippled through the crowd until Kincaid lifted his hands again to quiet it. As the spectators became silent, Kincaid went on, "Most of you have heard of Mr. Dawes and know him to be a fine, upstanding law officer who has served as marshal and sheriff in some of the toughest places in the West. Mr. Dawes has generously consented to come to Abilene to run for the office of sheriff, and I am here today to tell you that I will enthusiastically support him!"

Cody frowned. He had heard of John Henry Dawes. As Kincaid had said, Dawes had a good reputation as a lawman. But that was not what concerned Cody. He instinctively distrusted Mason Kincaid, and anyone who would throw in with Kincaid merited that distrust as well. That attitude might not be fair, but he could not help it. Kincaid had done too much to make life miserable for Abilene's marshal, and there was no man whom Cody admired more than Luke Travis.

Travis would want to hear about this. Cody slipped out of the crowd and turned to walk toward the marshal's office. He could hear Kincaid's voice talking behind him, but Cody paid no attention to what he was saying now. The important announcement had already been made.

As he strode along the boardwalk, Cody suddenly wondered if this election was going to be more important than most folks in Abilene suspected.

Most lawmen—those who managed to live long enough—developed a sixth sense that told them when trouble was brewing. At least other longtime peace officers had told Luke Travis that. But the marshal of Abilene was not sure he agreed. He had been wearing a badge for over twenty years, off and on, and he had learned that all hell could break loose when you least expected it.

Today, for example, looked about as peaceful and quiet as anybody could want a day to be. He stepped out of his office onto the boardwalk, hooked his thumbs in his shell belt, and glanced up and down Texas Street.

Travis was a tall, lean man in a black coat, brown pants, and high black boots. He wore a flat-crowned tan hat, which at the moment was pushed back on his sandy hair. A full mustache drooped over his wide mouth. On

5

his hip was a Colt single-action Army, a gun that had gained considerable fame under its nickname—the Peacemaker. Travis was better with a pistol than most men, but he preferred finding other ways to deal with problems. In the marshal's opinion talking to a man was considerably more productive than shooting him.

Suddenly he heard the sound of cheering and clapping, and he cocked his head, trying to determine where the commotion was. It seemed to be coming from the courthouse lawn, and when Travis looked that way, he spotted Cody Fisher, an urgent expression on his face, hurrying toward him. Travis stiffened; trouble might break out today after all.

The marshal stepped forward and met Cody at the corner of Texas and Cedar streets. Cody paused at the foot of the steps leading up to the boardwalk, and Travis asked, "Something going on up the street?"

"There's a rally on the courthouse lawn," Cody replied. "Mason Kincaid and Roy Wade are talking to the townspeople about the election for sheriff. Did you know anything about Kincaid bringing in somebody to run for the job, Marshal?"

Travis's forehead creased in a frown. "I hadn't heard anything about it, no. I knew he and Wade had been thick as thieves, though. This must be something they cooked up together. Kincaid mention any names?"

"John Henry Dawes."

The frown on Travis's face deepened. He lifted a hand and rubbed at his jaw for a moment, then grimaced and dropped his arm.

Cody was watching Travis's reaction. "Looks like you've heard of him, too," he said.

"I know about Dawes," Travis replied curtly. He came down the steps into the street and started across the intersection toward the boardwalk on the far side.

Cody fell in beside him. "Going down to hear Kincaid?" he asked.

"If there's anything left to hear." Travis shook his

head. "I don't know how he managed to keep this quiet. Was there a good crowd to hear his announcement?"

"There were quite a few people. I wondered the same thing. Kincaid must have passed the word about the rally to certain people and told them to tell their friends. Maybe even told folks *not* to tell you."

Travis was not sure about that. Kincaid and he had had more than their share of trouble in the past, but he did not want to be too quick to see scheming where there might be none. It was possible he simply had not heard about the rally.

By the time Travis and Cody reached the courthouse, the crowd was breaking up, and Kincaid and Wade were nowhere to be seen. As the spectators walked past Travis, he nodded to several men and touched the brim of his hat as he greeted the ladies. Most of the people were talking excitedly among themselves, and there was still a feeling of anticipation in the air, as if something important were about to unfold. Travis rested a hand on the boardwalk railing and looked at the courthouse, figuring that Kincaid and Sheriff Wade were probably inside.

A heavyset man wearing a bowler hat came across the street and climbed onto the boardwalk, puffing slightly as he did so. He nodded to Travis and his deputy and greeted them with a polite "Good afternoon, gentlemen."

"Mr. Croft," Travis replied. "I hear your partner made an announcement today."

"Yes, sir, it's a fine day for the county," Eugene Croft said. He frowned slightly. "I was not aware that the business relationship between Mason and myself was already so well known, though."

"I try to keep up with things," Travis said dryly.

Croft was one of Abilene's leading attorneys and a friend of Mason Kincaid. Travis was not surprised when he learned that the two men had joined forces in a land development business. The marshal had no idea what they had in mind for their joint enterprise, but given what he knew of both men, he was sure it would be lucrative.

Croft nodded again. "Well, I must be going. Business to attend to, you know."

He lumbered off, and as they watched him go, Cody said, "What do you think he and Kincaid are up to?"

"Don't know, but I wouldn't worry too much about it. Croft and I don't always see eye to eye on things, but I reckon he's an honest man."

"What about this Dawes? If he's tied in with Kincaid . . ." Cody did not voice the rest of his suspicions, but Travis knew what he was implying.

"How much do you know about Dawes?"

Cody shrugged. "I've heard of him. Supposed to be a good tough lawman. He was a deputy up in Bannock, marshal of a couple of towns in the Dakotas. Cleaned out the outlaws in Iron Mountain, then carried a badge in Texas and New Mexico for a while. He's been in some mighty rough spots, I'd say."

"That's right," Travis agreed. "Dawes has always played it straight, as far as I know—but he's quick to use a gun. Maybe he's had to be. Sometimes you have to meet violence with violence. And to give the man his due, he's usually been hired to clean out some outlaws' nest and bring law and order to a place where there wasn't any. So he's had to be fast with a gun. But Dickinson County isn't like that. We've got our share of problems, but it's not the same as it was ten years ago."

Cody chuckled, but there was little humor in the sound. "Strange, isn't it? I mean, here's Kincaid backing a man like Dawes when all he's done since he got on the town council is complain about how you and me and Nestor are too old-fashioned and use our guns too much."

That irony had occurred to Travis as well. Mason Kincaid was quite progressive and wanted Abilene to be even more civilized than it already was. One of the first steps on that road, in his view, would be to abolish the marshal's office and establish a uniformed police force, just like the ones back East. The days of old-style Western lawmen like Luke Travis were over, he had said on more than one occasion.

Cody went on, "What are you going to do about Dawes?"

"It's none of my business." Travis shrugged. "I'm just another citizen when it comes to this election. Kincaid can support anyone he wants to."

Cody shook his head. "It still doesn't seem right."

"I know what you mean, but politics are like that. There's a lot of truth in that old saying about strange bedfellows."

Travis turned and started back toward his office, ignoring the puzzled look that Cody gave him.

By the next day Travis had put Mason Kincaid and the upcoming sheriff's election out of his thoughts. He had plenty of other things to worry about.

He was in the office with Cody and Nestor Gilworth, the massive former buffalo hunter who now served as a part-time deputy. Nestor was also the handyman for the orphanage at the Calvary Methodist Church. Reverend Judah Fisher, Cody's older brother and pastor of the church, ran the orphanage jointly with Sister Laurel, the strong-willed Dominican nun who had brought a band of homeless children to Abilene several years earlier. More recently Judah and Sister Laurel had taken Nestor under their wing. He had been a troublemaking drunk before they showed him he could be a useful member of the community. Since then the big bearded man in the buffalo coat had become Travis's friend and a trusted aide.

At the moment Nestor's bulk was sprawled on the old broken-down sofa that sat against the front wall of the room. Hooch, the scruffy yellow tomcat that had started to hang around the marshal's office a few months earlier, was curled up on the other end of the sofa, asleep.

Gesturing broadly to emphasize his points, Nestor was spinning a yarn about his days as a civilian scout with the Army.

"So there we was, surrounded by Shoshone," he said. "They'd done killed all the patrol 'cept for me, a major, a couple of privates, and Cap'n Pryor an' that Mexican feller who rode with him. They had us pinned down good an' proper and was figgerin' on waitin' us out. But there was a storm comin', a reg'lar blue norther. Soon as I saw it was headed our way, I told the boys that was our chance to get out o' there."

"You mean the Indians would leave rather than stay around until the storm hit," Cody said. He was cleaning his new pistol. Travis was at the desk, doing paperwork and pretending not to listen to Nestor. He had heard enough of the big man's tall tales to know where this one was leading.

"No, that ain't what I mean at all," Nestor replied. He grimaced at Cody, then resumed his story. "Them Injuns was bound an' determined to get us, but we'd already downed a bunch of 'em, so they was too leery to charge us again. That's why they was waitin'. You see, we didn't have no food an' water, and they knew it."

"I think I'll modify these grips," Cody said, turning the Colt Lightning over in his hands.

Nestor demanded, "You listenin' or not?"

"Yeah, I'm listening, Nestor. The Shoshone were trying to starve you and your friends out."

"That's right. They might've done it, too, if it hadn't been for that blue norther. Dropped the temperature a good forty or fifty degrees in less'n a half hour. By nightfall it was below zero out there on the plains. So we just got on our horses and rode back to the fort."

"Wait a minute." Cody looked up at Nestor and frowned. "I thought you said the Indians had you surrounded."

"They did."

"And they didn't leave when it got cold."

"Nope, they stayed right where they was. I told you, they was powerful mad at us."

"And yet you were able to ride right past them?"

"Sure. There weren't no moon that night, and it was so dark, they couldn't see us."

"But they would have heard your horses," Cody pointed out.

"Yep. They sure would have." Nestor grinned. "But it was so cold the sound froze 'fore the Shoshone could hear it."

"What?" Cody sounded disgusted.

"It's the gospel truth," Nestor said solemnly. "Why, it just so happens I was ridin' by that same place the next spring, when ever'thing started thawin' out, and durned if I didn't hear them hoofbeats we'd made the winter before, just cloppin' along as nice as you please."

Cody rolled his eyes and started to mutter, and Travis had to chuckle. He could have warned his deputy what was coming, but folks had to learn some things for themselves.

The opening of the office door made Travis look up, and he smiled when he saw the woman who was coming in. "Morning, Aileen," he said, a little surprised to see her but nonetheless glad she was paying him a visit.

Usually at this time of day Dr. Aileen Bloom was in her office seeing patients. There was not a better doctor to be found west of the Mississippi, as far as Luke Travis was concerned, and that opinion was not influenced in the least by the fact that Aileen was an attractive woman. Still, her beauty could not be denied. Her rich brown hair, her slender figure, her fair skin and lovely features . . . Add in her intelligence, courage, and determination—Travis had thought more than once that some man would be mighty lucky to marry her one of these days.

As long as it was not Mason Kincaid. Travis still remembered all too vividly the night he had accidentally seen Aileen locked in Kincaid's embrace. That memory had stayed with him and rankled him no matter how hard he tried to banish it.

"Good morning, Luke," Aileen said with a warm smile as she came into the office. "Are you busy right now?"

He shoved the paperwork aside. "Never too busy for you," he replied honestly.

Two men entered the office behind Aileen, and Travis was equally surprised to see them here at this time of day. Both gentlemen were bearded and brawny, but the resemblance ended there. The first man had dark hair and wore a conservative dark suit. He was tall and broad-shouldered and carried himself with a grace unusual in such a big man. His name was Leslie Gibson, and Travis knew him well. A former prizefighter from the East, Leslie now taught some of the children in Abilene's two-room schoolhouse. A strange occupation for a man with his background, some had said when Leslie first came to town, but it suited his gentle nature, and he was genuinely devoted to his students.

His companion was more than a head shorter and at first glance gave the impression of being as wide as he was tall. Shaggy, rust-colored hair shot through with gray topped his large head, and a bushy beard of the same shade covered his strong jaw. The sleeves of his red-checked shirt were stretched tight over his muscular arms. Like the other man, he was hatless.

Travis regarded both of them and said, "Playing hooky from school, Leslie? And what about you, Orion? You're usually still asleep at this time of day, aren't you?"

"Dinna be joking wi' us, Lucas," Orion McCarthy replied. The owner of Orion's Tavern, which was next to the building that housed Aileen's medical practice, the burly Scotsman was Travis's oldest friend in Abilene. He went on, "We be here on serious business."

"I managed to get some time off this morning, although Mr. Simpson wasn't too happy about it," Leslie added.

Travis was not surprised to hear that. Thurman Simpson, Abilene's schoolmaster, was rarely happy about anything, to judge by his perpetually sour expression. Travis pushed back his chair and stood up, saying, "This must be important. Come on in and tell me about it."

He remained on his feet until the visitors were seated, Aileen and Leslie in chairs that Cody pulled up in front of the desk, Orion on the sofa with Nestor. The weight of the two big men made the old couch sag dangerously.

Aileen leaned forward in her chair and began, "I suppose you've heard about the election for sheriff, Luke."

"Sure. For a while I didn't know if anybody was going to run for the office. Looks like our friend Mr. Kincaid's seen to that, though."

"That's why we're here," Leslie said. "The news is all over town that Mason Kincaid is bringing in this man named Dawes to run. Some of us are a little concerned."

Travis frowned. "About Dawes? From what I've heard, he's an honest peace officer. Maybe a little too rough sometimes, but . . ." The marshal shrugged.

"That's not it," Aileen said. "For all we know, Mr. Dawes would make an excellent sheriff. But it doesn't seem right that no one's running against him. And it certainly isn't right that we should seek out a stranger when we have someone right here in town who would make an outstanding sheriff."

"We do?" Travis asked.

"You, Luke," Aileen replied quietly.

Travis sat back in his chair, eyes widening in surprise. "Me?" he exclaimed. "But I'm the marshal."

"That's no reason you can't run for sheriff," Leslie said. "Aileen has looked into the matter."

As Travis swung his startled gaze back to the doctor, Aileen said, "That's right, Luke. I know women haven't won the right to vote in Kansas—yet—but I don't see any reason why we can't take an interest in politics. So when I heard about Dawes coming to town to run for sheriff, it occurred to me that you might be an even better choice. I went to the newspaper office and went through their files, trying to find a precedent—"

"Thought you wanted him to run for sheriff," Nestor put in.

"She said precedent, not president," Cody told him. The deputy was grinning broadly, clearly pleased with the idea of Travis becoming sheriff.

Aileen smiled. "As far as I've been able to determine, there's nothing in the state laws to prevent a man from being town marshal and county sheriff at the same time. It's been done several times before in Kansas, most notably by Mr. Hickok before he came here to Abilene."

Travis nodded, recalling that Wild Bill had indeed been the marshal of Hays and the sheriff of Ellis County at the same time. And according to Aileen, there were other instances of one man holding both offices. But he had never seen himself as a sheriff. He had been the marshal of Wichita for years before coming to Abilene, and although Roy Wade had not until recently kicked up any fuss about Travis occasionally enforcing the law outside the town limits, Travis had always focused his attention on the town that hired him. To be responsible for an entire county, to have to answer to the county commissioners and also, ultimately, to the voters . . . He was not quite sure that appealed to him.

" 'Tis a good idea, Lucas," Orion spoke up. "Ye know th' county, an' ye know th' folks who live here. An' 'tis no' a fairer man t'be found hereabouts."

"It sounds like a fine idea to me," Cody said. "I don't know what Kincaid's up to, but I reckon this would make him think twice about it."

Travis frowned again and glanced at Aileen. He was not sure how serious her relationship with Kincaid had gotten, although he had not seen them together lately. Still, he did not want Cody saying anything to upset her. As Aileen met his gaze, however, her expression was calm and level. Clearly she was waiting for his decision.

"Please give it some serious thought, Luke," Leslie urged. "I think it would be good for the whole county to have the benefit of your experience, not just those of us here in town."

"Me'n Cody'd be glad to give you a hand, too," Nestor rumbled. "Would that make us sheriff's deputies, as well as marshal's deputies?"

"It would," Travis said. "And I might have to hire some more men, with the whole county to cover."

"I'm sure the commissioners wouldn't object to that," Aileen assured him.

Travis drew a deep breath. He had never carried a badge for the personal power it might give him. He had become a lawman because he was good at the work, and he remained one because it gave him opportunities to help people. Maybe as sheriff he could do even more good.

And try as he might to be fair, he still instinctively distrusted Mason Kincaid. If Kincaid's handpicked man became sheriff, there might be more trouble down the road. "All right," Travis said, hoping he was not making the worst mistake of his life. "I'll do it."

# Chapter Two

—————◆◆◆—————

Accompanied by Aileen, Leslie, and Orion, Travis went to the courthouse later that morning, paid the small filing fee, and had the county clerk enter his name in the election for sheriff. It was as simple as that. He was a candidate.

As the little group emerged from the courthouse into the autumn sunlight, Travis turned to the others and said, "All right. What do I do now? I've never run for office before."

"You'll need someone to manage your campaign," Aileen told him. "I think Leslie would be a good choice for that."

"Me?" Leslie said in surprise. "I thought asking Luke to run was a good idea, but I don't know a thing about managing a campaign."

"Maybe not," Travis replied with a grin, "but you

helped get me into this. It's fitting that you get to do some of the work now."

"But what about Orion?"

The big Scotsman shook his head. "'Twould no' look right. I be nothing but a saloonkeeper, while ye, Leslie, be a schoolteacher, a highly respected member o' th' community. 'Twill make Lucas's chances o' winning better t'ha' ye running his campaign."

"And I think it's a good idea as well," Aileen added, smiling at Leslie.

The teacher took a deep breath and then sighed. "All right," he agreed. "I'll do it. How difficult can it be? I'll arrange for you to make some speeches, Luke. We'll visit the various groups here in town, then make a swing through the county."

"Speeches?" Travis asked dubiously.

"Of course. How else are you going to let the voters know what you stand for?"

Travis grimaced. He had given a speech during the Fourth of July festivities a few months earlier, and he did not have particularly fond memories of that day. Getting up in front of a crowd and talking made him about as uncomfortable as anything he had ever done.

"You'll do just fine," Aileen assured him. "You have nothing to worry about, Luke."

"It's just that I'm not sure it's necessary," Travis said. "Folks around here know me. They know what I stand for, as Leslie put it."

"Not all of them. There are new people moving into the county every day. Most of them probably *don't* know you, Luke." She put a hand on his arm. "I'm sure you won't have any problems."

Travis was not certain of that at all, but there was no point in complaining now. He had gone into this with his eyes open.

When they reached the marshal's office, Leslie grabbed his hand and shook it. "I'll get right to work on your schedule," he promised, "as soon as school is over today.

I'll let you know where and when the first speech will be. Congratulations, Luke."

"I haven't won yet," Travis pointed out.

Orion pumped Travis's hand next. " 'Tis only a matter o' time," the Scotsman told him heartily. "I'll see ye at th' rallies . . . Sheriff."

Aileen was the last to take her leave. "I'm really glad you're doing this, Luke," she said. "Abilene has needed a new sheriff for a long time. I don't have anything against Sheriff Wade, but he should have retired some time ago."

"I wish he had, too," Travis murmured. "Then maybe somebody besides me would've gotten roped into this."

Aileen laughed softly. "It won't be that bad," she assured him.

"We'll see," Travis said pessimistically.

By the next morning, word had gotten around town that Travis was running for sheriff. During the short walk between his rented room and the marshal's office, more than a dozen townspeople must have stopped him to shake his hand and tell him that they thought he would make a fine sheriff. While Travis accepted the plaudits graciously, he wanted to get to the office, and the continual delays irritated him.

They came with the territory, he thought. Glad-handing was part of being a politician.

Cody was waiting for him when Travis came into the office. The young deputy was just taking his hat from a peg beside the door. "Morning, Marshal," Cody said. "I was just coming to look for you."

"I had to stop and talk to some of the voters," Travis said dryly. "What's up?"

"I stopped by the railroad station earlier. Harve Bastrop told me that John Henry Dawes was due in on the eastbound this morning. Kincaid's planning to be down there with a band and everything to welcome him."

Travis frowned. "Making quite a fuss over the whole thing, isn't he?"

"I reckon he wants to get the campaign off to a bang-up

start. Thought you might want to go over there and take a gander at the big welcome."

Travis shook his head and hung up his hat. As he went behind the desk, he said, "It's none of my business what Kincaid does as long as he doesn't break the law. There are no laws against a band playing a song while he shakes hands with Dawes."

Cody looked surprised. "You mean you're not curious about Dawes? Don't you want to see what he looks like?"

"I imagine I'll run into him during the campaign," Travis said, and began to shuffle through some reports on the scarred desktop.

"Well, if that doesn't beat all . . ." Cody muttered, shaking his head.

Travis studied his young deputy for a moment, then said quietly, "Look, I think you, Nestor, Aileen, Leslie, and Orion are taking this election business a lot more seriously than I am. I don't particularly want Kincaid's man to win, but I still have duties to attend to here, and so do you. I don't intend to get so busy campaigning for another job that I neglect the one I've already got."

Cody looked abashed. "Sorry, Marshal. Reckon you're right." He was still holding his hat. Now he put it on and continued, "I'll go over to the Alamo and find out what the damages were in that fight there last night. Then we can fine those cowboys we hauled in and cut 'em loose."

"Good idea," Travis agreed. He could hear snoring coming from the cellblock, where three ranch hands were sleeping off a drunken binge. They had started a brawl at the Alamo Saloon and smashed some tables and chairs before Travis and Cody arrived to break up the fight. Once the Alamo's owner had given Cody an estimate of the damages, Travis could assess the fine for disturbing the peace, plus damages, and let the cowboys go sheepishly back to their ranch. Business as usual, Travis thought, election or no election.

Cody went out, and Travis tried to concentrate on the reports in front of him, but his thoughts kept straying to the Kansas Pacific depot. He knew the railroad's schedule fairly well, and if the eastbound was on time, it would pull in at about ten-fifteen. Travis glanced up at the pendulum clock on the wall. Nine-thirty. He looked over at the sofa, where Hooch was lying in his usual spot, carefully washing a paw. The cat gave Travis a smug look.

Travis sighed and went back to his paperwork.

At ten o'clock he gave up and pushed the reports aside. Cody still had not returned from the Alamo, and Travis knew he was probably having trouble getting the owner to give him a realistic figure. Every time a brawl broke out in his saloon, the man tried to exaggerate the amount of damage. It was only fair that the cowboys who had gotten drunk and caused the trouble pay for what they had broken, but Travis was not going to fine them unfairly.

Travis stood up, stretched, and looked into the cell-block to check on the cowboys. All three of them were still sleeping soundly. Travis shook his head and walked toward the door, bending down on the way to scratch Hooch behind the ears. He grabbed his hat, then settled it on his head as he went out. He was just going to take a turn around the town, he told himself. But within a few moments he was approaching the railroad depot.

Travis had to grin sheepishly as he stepped into the big, high-ceilinged, redbrick building beside the Kansas Pacific tracks. After lecturing Cody about tending to business, here he was himself, for one reason and one reason alone—to get a look at the man who was going to be his opponent in the election.

It seemed that a few other folks had had the same idea. The waiting room of the station was packed with people standing shoulder to shoulder as they awaited the arrival of the eastbound train. Travis's height enabled him to gaze over the heads of many in the crowd, and he could see the town band outside. Also on the platform were a group of ladies in elegant dresses and stylish hats. They were all members of what passed for high society in Abilene, and Travis knew their leader well: Mrs. Eula

Grafton, a handsome, middle-aged woman with gray hair. At the moment Mrs. Grafton was talking to one of her companions, an attractive young blonde. She wore an expensive pale blue dress with white lace at the collar and cuffs. A hat of darker blue sat on her curly hair. Travis frowned slightly at the sight of Faith Hamilton.

Faith had been in Abilene for several months, but Travis had never been able to figure her out. She was from somewhere back East and had obviously known Mason Kincaid before he came to Abilene, but Travis had no idea what the connection between the two of them had been. Lovers, perhaps? It was possible; Faith was a beautiful young woman. Now, though, Kincaid seemed to avoid her as much as possible. In the meantime, Faith had become a part of Mrs. Grafton's society circle. She was young and pretty, dressed well, and evidently had money, so she was welcome at the teas and other events held by the ladies. Even though she was still staying at the Grand Palace Hotel, where she had kept a room since her arrival in Abilene, she was becoming a fixture in town.

An impeccably groomed Mason Kincaid was standing at the edge of the platform, gazing toward the west. In his hand was his watch, and he kept flipping it open and looking at it. Travis glanced at the big clock on the depot wall. It was not quite ten-fifteen; the eastbound train was not late, but Kincaid was clearly anxious. His reputation as an influential man in Abilene could be riding on the outcome of this election, and Travis knew it. He wondered just how much his own decision to run had been based on that very knowledge.

"Quite a turnout, eh, Marshal?" a voice asked beside him.

Travis turned and saw Thurman Simpson smiling up at him. The expression looked somewhat ludicrous on the schoolmaster's pale, narrow face. Simpson was short and slender, with thinning hair. He ran his classroom with an iron hand. Students who wound up in Leslie

Gibson's class instead of Simpson's always considered themselves extremely lucky.

"Appears that folks are interested in getting a look at John Henry Dawes, all right," Travis said to Simpson.

"Is that why *you're* here, Marshal?" asked the young man who was standing on the other side of Simpson. His voice was eager, and he held a notebook and a pencil in his hands.

Travis summoned up a smile for Emmett Valentine, a reporter for the Abilene *Clarion*. "I'm as curious as the next man, Emmett," Travis said. "John Henry Dawes has quite a reputation as a lawman, and that's the business I'm in, after all."

"And the fact that the man is going to be your opponent in the upcoming election has nothing to do with your presence here, I'm sure," Valentine said sardonically.

Travis shrugged. "Like I said, I'm curious." Wanting to divert Valentine, he turned to the schoolteacher and went on, "I'm a mite surprised to see you here, Mr. Simpson. School is in session this morning, isn't it?"

Simpson sniffed. "Gibson requested some time off to pay a visit to you. I thought it only fair that he watch my class this morning while I came to see the next sheriff of Abilene."

"Then you'll be supporting Dawes in the election?"

"No offense, Marshal," the schoolmaster responded in unctuous tones. "I don't know a great deal about this man Dawes, but anyone who has the support of a fine, upstanding citizen like Mason Kincaid can count on my vote. Besides, I'm not sure it's a good idea for one man to be both marshal and sheriff."

Travis hated to agree with Thurman Simpson, but to a certain extent he had that same reservation himself. If he did win this election, he might have to give some thought to resigning his position as marshal. There were other men who could handle the job—like Cody Fisher.

The shrill whistle of a train cut through Travis's musing. A palpable stir of excitement and anticipation went through the crowd. The eastbound was coming into town.

Mason Kincaid turned and gestured sharply to the leader of the band. As the uniformed men broke into a patriotic tune, the people inside the depot surged forward. Emmett Valentine pushed through the crowd, scribbling on his pad as he went.

Feeling a bit foolish, Travis craned his neck for a better view and moved toward the front of the crowd. He spotted Roy Wade on the platform next to Kincaid, and a faint rueful smile touched his lips. To Travis, the scene suggested a passing of the torch, the old sheriff preparing to welcome his successor.

The rumble of the big Baldwin locomotive momentarily drowned out the band as the train pulled into the station. With a squeal of brakes and a hiss of steam, it came to a stop alongside the platform.

Several people disembarked and looked surprised at the crowd and reception committee. Harvey Bastrop, the stationmaster, quickly led these passengers around the group waiting on the platform.

Then a tall, broad-shouldered man sporting an impressive waxed and curled handlebar mustache stepped off the train. In his boots with fancy stitching, brown suit, and broad-brimmed, cream-colored hat, he cut a dashing figure. When he saw the crowd, he swept his hat off, revealing a full head of dark hair, and waved it in greeting. The crowd responded to the gesture by breaking into enthusiastic applause, and he accepted the applause and cheers with undeniable aplomb. Mason Kincaid stepped forward and spoke to him, and the man extended a hand to Kincaid and shook with him. After Roy Wade introduced himself, Kincaid took the newcomer's arm, turned to face the eager crowd, and gestured to the band to stop playing. As soon as it did, Kincaid raised his voice and said, "Good citizens of Abilene, allow me to introduce the next sheriff of Dickinson County, John Henry Dawes!"

A fresh wave of cheering and clapping went up as the

band broke into another song. Dawes lifted his hands, acknowledging the welcome and asking for quiet at the same time. The gesture lifted the tails of his coat, and through a gap in the crowd, Travis caught a glimpse of the pearl-handled revolvers Dawes wore.

Those were probably the same guns Dawes had used to clean up the Randall gang in Iron Mountain, the Colts that had put an end to the San Saba County War down in Texas. Dawes was fast on the draw, or so Travis had heard. If the man was elected sheriff, no doubt Travis would get an opportunity to witness his gun-handling skill sooner or later.

As soon as the crowd had quieted down again, Dawes smiled and said in a booming voice, "Well, I surely do thank you for that welcome, folks. There's nothing that makes a man feel better than a big howdy from the people who are going to be his new friends."

That brought more applause. Dawes waited for it to die away, then continued, "Mr. Mason Kincaid here told me that Abilene was a mighty friendly town, and I can see now that he wasn't exaggerating. I'm right proud to have been asked to come here and serve the folks of Dickinson County as your sheriff. Providing, of course, that the voters see fit to bestow that honor on me."

"I don't think that's going to be a problem, Mr. Dawes," Kincaid said enthusiastically. "Is it, folks?"

Another ovation welled up from the crowd, and several people pressed forward, eager to be introduced to Dawes. Among them was Mrs. Eula Grafton. With practiced charm Dawes shook hands with her and several other society ladies, then paused and said with a big smile, "And who is this?"

Travis saw the sudden tension on Kincaid's face as Faith Hamilton stepped up. "Hello, Mason," she said.

"Faith," he replied tightly.

"Well, aren't you going to introduce me?"

"Yes, by all means, introduce this enchanting young woman, Mason," Dawes said.

Grudgingly Kincaid made the introductions. "This is

Miss Faith Hamilton, John Henry, an . . . old friend of mine. Faith, John Henry Dawes."

For a second Travis thought that Dawes was actually going to lean over and kiss Faith's hand, but he settled for shaking it instead. "I'm very pleased to meet you, Miss Hamilton," he said. "Any friend of Mason's . . . Well, you know how the old saying goes."

"Indeed," Faith murmured. "I've heard a great deal about you, Mr. Dawes. It's said that you will restore law and order to Dickinson County."

"Oh, I'll do my best to see that the lawless elements don't get out of hand. At times it's an unpleasant job, but someone has to do it."

"I'm sure you'll be equal to the task, Mr. Dawes." Faith turned to Kincaid. "Mason, I was wondering when you and I were going to have dinner again."

Travis thought Kincaid looked as though he wanted to say *When hell freezes over,* but the land agent never got the chance.

"It just so happens," Dawes said quickly, "that Mason and I are going to have dinner together tonight, Miss Hamilton. We'd be honored to have you join us. Wouldn't we, Mason?"

Kincaid took a deep breath, and a forced smile curled his lips. "Certainly. Won't you join us, Faith?"

"Why, I'd be delighted! If you're sure I won't be intruding. I mean, you two gentlemen undoubtedly have political matters to discuss."

"Nothing that can't wait," Dawes assured her.

Kincaid took Dawes's arm and started to steer him toward the entrance to the station. "Mr. Dawes has had a tiring journey, Faith. I'm sure we don't want to keep him from his rest."

"Of course not." She smiled at Dawes again. "Good day, Mr. Dawes. I'm looking forward to dinner."

"Good day to you, Miss Hamilton. I'll be awaiting our engagement with great anticipation, too."

Travis had seen enough. He edged toward the back of the crowd and the door of the depot. He supposed he ought to feel a little insulted by the way the townspeople were greeting Dawes. After all, he had put his life on the line more than once to protect most of these folks.

But that was not the way being a lawman worked, Travis told himself. The people had a right to their opinion, and Dawes was something of a celebrity, after all. When the excitement died down a little, some of those same people who were cheering now would realize that Dawes might not be the best choice for sheriff, despite his reputation.

At the moment Travis just wanted to slip away and get back to his work. He should not have come, he realized. This was Dawes's moment—Dawes's, and Kincaid's— and Travis had no right to intrude on it.

But as he reached the door of the station, he glanced back and saw that the crowd had parted to allow Dawes, Kincaid, and Roy Wade to enter the building. At that moment Kincaid's eyes looked across the big room and met Travis's. The marshal saw something that he could not quite identify in Kincaid's gaze.

"Wait a minute, Marshal!" the land agent called out.

Travis bit back a curse. This was turning into an even bigger mistake than he had thought. He briefly considered ignoring Kincaid but decided against it when he realized how it would look to the crowd. Besides, he was still curious about Dawes.

Kincaid brought Dawes up to Travis, trailed by Wade, Thurman Simpson, and Emmett Valentine. The young reporter was still writing furiously on his pad.

Kincaid was smiling smugly as he said, "Mr. Dawes, this is Luke Travis, the town marshal of Abilene. He'll be running against you in the election." Now that he had gotten Dawes away from Faith Hamilton, Kincaid was less concerned about the candidate's fatigue.

Dawes grinned and stuck out his hand. "Mighty pleased to meet you, Marshal. I didn't know who my opponent was going to be. Glad to see it's another fine lawman such as yourself. I've heard a great deal about you."

"Same here, Dawes," Travis replied, forcing a smile as he returned the firm handshake. "I'm surprised you've heard of me. I've never been to as many places as you have."

"Oh, yes, indeed. You helped corral that renegade Kiowa, Buffalo Knife, a while back, then put a bunch of rustlers behind bars up Cheyenne way. You tracked down Nord Madden and his gang, too, unless my memory's playing tricks on me. Which it sometimes does, when a man gets to be my age." Dawes laughed heartily, and Kincaid and the other spectators joined in the laughter.

"I've heard a few stories about you, too, Dawes," Travis said. "You've tamed some pretty rough towns."

Dawes gave him a self-deprecating smile. "Just doing my job. I'm sure you know all about that, Marshal."

Emmett Valentine spoke up. "Do you mind if I ask you a question, Mr. Dawes? I'm Emmett Valentine, from the *Clarion.*"

Dawes turned to the reporter. "Not at all, Mr. Valentine. Ask away."

His pencil poised, Emmett asked, "What makes you think you would make a better sheriff than Marshal Travis here?"

Kincaid started to bristle a bit, and Travis frowned, but Dawes boomed out another laugh and waved a finger at Emmett. "Oh, no, you don't, son," he said cheerfully. "I just got into town after a long train ride, and I'm a mite tired. You're not going to get me to make a speech right here and now. But I will say that I never claimed I'd make a better sheriff than Luke Travis. All I promise the voters of Dickinson County is that I'll try my utmost to be the best sheriff I can be. And with that, ladies and gentlemen—" He lifted his hat again, waved it over his head, then said to Kincaid, "Mason, I think you were going to take me to the hotel?"

"Yes, of course," Kincaid replied quickly, leading Dawes out of the depot. The crowd trailed behind them.

Travis waited until most of the people had gone, then sighed and shook his head. Dawes had been friendly enough, and he certainly knew how to get an audience in the palm of his hand. Like it or not, Travis had to admit that the man had impressed him.

Sensing that someone was watching him, Travis glanced up and saw Faith regarding him from across the room. As Travis met her gaze, she started across the lobby toward him.

He doffed his hat and said, "Miss Hamilton, isn't it?"

"That's right, Marshal," she answered, her voice cool. "I see you were on hand for Mason's latest triumph." Her tone held a mocking note.

Travis shrugged. "I reckon I was curious," he replied, his fingers idly turning his hat. "I wanted to get a look at John Henry Dawes, just like everybody else."

"So did I. And I must admit, I was impressed. It looks as if Mason may have made the right choice . . . this time."

"Dawes seems to be a good man," Travis said. "I've heard he's a little quick to use his guns, but maybe he's looking for a place where he won't have to."

"He's killed a great many men, has he?"

Travis thought that was a strange question for a lady to ask, but he replied, "Dawes has downed his share of desperadoes, I reckon. It's nothing for a lawman to be proud of."

"But it does impress the voters, I imagine." Faith smiled sweetly at him. "Well, good day, Marshal. I have to be going."

Travis nodded to her. "Good day, ma'am." He watched her walk out of the railroad station, feeling as though he had missed about half their conversation. Then he realized that that was usually the way he felt after talking to Faith Hamilton.

As Mason Kincaid ushered Emmett Valentine out of the hotel room and closed the door, he was feeling quite pleased with himself. He turned to the tall man with the handlebar mustache and said, "I'm sorry about that,

John Henry. You know how determined newspaper people can be."

Dawes tossed his hat onto the bed. "Don't worry about it, Mason. I'm used to reporters and dime novelists and folks in general being curious about the great John Henry Dawes."

Kincaid stiffened, the satisfaction he had enjoyed only seconds before evaporating. He could not tell if Dawes was serious. After a moment he said, "Of course, it *is* important to get the press on our side. If the *Clarion* supports you, that will go a long way toward helping you win the election."

"I thought you said the outcome was a foregone conclusion," Dawes replied as he took off his coat and loosened his collar and tie. "After all, Travis may be a good man, but he's not nearly as famous as I made him out to be when I was talking to him."

"I know that. Still, there's no point in taking chances." Kincaid's hands clenched into fists. "Besides, I want you to beat Travis as badly as possible."

"Had some run-ins with the man, have you?" Dawes grunted. He lifted one of his carpetbags onto the bed and unfastened the buckles holding it closed. Then he reached inside and brought out a squat brown bottle. Holding it up, he asked Kincaid, "Drink?"

Kincaid shook his head and frowned. "It's a bit early, isn't it?"

"There're only two good times to drink whiskey," Dawes told him with a grin. "Night . . . and day." He pulled the cork with his teeth, spat it into his other hand, and lifted the bottle to his mouth.

Kincaid's frown deepened. He had not known that Dawes was a heavy drinker. That might turn out to be an advantage—a drunk was sometimes easier to control than a sober man—but it might turn against him as well.

"It probably wouldn't be a good idea to let the public see you doing that," he warned.

Dawes lowered the bottle. The level of the liquid inside

had descended a couple of inches. "Don't worry, Mason," he said casually. "Whiskey doesn't muddle me. And if anybody knows how to give the public what it wants, that man is John Henry Dawes."

Kincaid was not completely reassured, but he nodded, then gestured to the basin and pitcher that sat on the dresser. "I'll let you freshen up and rest a little now. We'll be having lunch with the mayor and the town council in a while. That'll be your first official public appearance. I'll come by to get you."

"Right," Dawes replied absently, then he turned to Kincaid, his eyes snapping with interest. "Before you go, tell me a little about Faith Hamilton. She's a lovely girl."

Kincaid averted his face and grimaced. He was certain Faith's surprise at the dinner invitation had been feigned. That had probably been her objective when she came to the train station with Mrs. Grafton and the other ladies. She would go to any lengths to embarrass him, he thought bitterly.

"I knew her for a while back East," he told Dawes, trying to keep his tone nonchalant. "As I told you, we were friends. That's all."

Dawes took another drink of whiskey. "Then you won't mind if I take an interest in the lady."

"Mind?" Kincaid shook his head. "No, John Henry, I won't mind at all."

That was a bald-faced lie. Kincaid did not want Dawes to have anything to do with Faith Hamilton. She was too much of a threat, considering everything that had happened between them in Philadelphia. But it would not do to tell Dawes about the smoothly planned seduction, the engagement, the unannounced departure in the middle of the night with a large sum of money that had belonged to Faith's father . . .

And then, after he had used that money to establish himself in Abilene, she appeared out of nowhere, holding her knowledge of his past over his head like a sword, holding it but maddeningly doing nothing to exact her revenge on him—if revenge was truly what she was after.

Even now, as he thought about her, his fingers closed as if he was about to slip them around her neck and choke the life out of her—

Kincaid took a deep breath and tried to bring his fury under control. Maybe killing her *was* the best idea, he thought—only that would throw suspicion on him. Quite a few people in town knew that they had been acquainted back East. Surely there had to be some way to dispose of her.

Kincaid was certain of one thing: He would not let Faith Hamilton ruin his plans. Big things were going to happen in Abilene. Once John Henry Dawes was in office—owing a good-sized debt to Mason Kincaid for getting him elected—those things could start to happen.

This was just the beginning, Kincaid thought, and Faith would either stay out of his way—or die for her trouble.

"I'll see you later, John Henry," Kincaid said, forcing his voice to remain calm and level.

Dawes lifted the bottle again. "I'll be here," he replied.

# Chapter Three

———◆———

IN ALL THE YEARS LUKE TRAVIS HAD BEEN IN ABILENE, THERE had never been a hotly contested election. The selection of Aileen Bloom for the town council had been controversial; women did not have the right to vote. But the doctor was so well respected—having overcome the community's initial resistance to a female physician through her talent, hard work, and determination—that she had readily won a seat on the town's governing body.

This campaign for sheriff was going to be different, though. Travis sensed that right away.

He made his first speech to the local temperance society, which was led by Mrs. Eula Grafton. On more than one occasion Mrs. Grafton had urged Travis to try to close down the many saloons in Abilene. Since Kansas law permitted the sale of liquor, Travis had been able to resist the pressure. If he was elected sheriff, she and the people who shared her views would want him to do something about the roadhouses and taverns outside the town limits as well. But as he stumbled through a short speech in which he promised to do his best to uphold the law, he could sense their skepticism. He tried not to glare at Leslie Gibson, who was standing in the rear of the group gathered in Mrs. Grafton's parlor. Leslie seemed to be avoiding meeting Travis's eyes.

"You did just fine," he assured Travis after the speech. "The ladies were all impressed."

Travis snorted, not believing it for a second.

The next day he heard that Dawes had also spoken to the temperance society and promised that if elected he would throw his influence behind the growing movement to make liquor illegal in Kansas. Until such legislation was passed, of course, he could do nothing but enforce the laws as they were written, he told them regretfully. That report came from Judah Fisher, who, as a member of the society, had attended the meeting.

After a few more days passed, Travis knew why he had never considered running for office before: It was too much work. Frustrating work, at that. Every time he turned around, Emmett Valentine seemed to be underfoot, scratching on that pad of his with a stub of pencil. Travis tried to ignore the reporter as he shook hands, smiled a lot, and spoke to several more organizations: the Grange, the Masonic Lodge, and the Tuesday Afternoon Ladies' Literary Circle, of all things. It was important to get his message across to the women, Leslie told him enthusiastically. They might not vote, but they had considerable influence over their husbands.

Travis smiled some more, sipped tea, ate dainty sandwiches that were smaller than his thumb, and wished to hell that he was trading lead with some outlaw instead.

And everywhere he went, John Henry Dawes seemed to have been there first.

Dawes had met with the mayor and the town council, the county commissioners, and everyone else who had any influence in Abilene. Travis had not heard any of his speeches, but people were more than happy to tell him what Dawes had said. It was a simple platform—Dawes was promising to enforce the law fairly and efficiently, no more, no less. That was exactly what Travis was pledging to do. But Dawes was an orator, able to stand in front of a crowd and make it feel as though it was hearing something special. Travis could do nothing but set out his ideas in plain, simple talk.

By the fourth day of the campaign, Travis stopped reading the *Clarion*. Emmett Valentine was very impressed with Dawes, and his articles reflected that.

Cody must have known what prompted Travis's sigh as he pushed the newspaper aside on his desk without looking at it that morning.

"I wouldn't worry about what Emmett has to say, Marshal," Cody told him. "He doesn't understand what carrying a badge is really like."

"Neither do most of the voters," Travis replied glumly. "But they'll decide the outcome, won't they?"

Cody could do nothing but shrug. Travis was right, of course.

Travis was coming to a realization, too. He had entered this race so that Mason Kincaid's candidate would have some competition. But he was discovering now that he wanted to *win*.

And the reason for that was probably that everywhere he saw John Henry Dawes, he also saw Kincaid, and the land agent was already wearing a smug smile of triumph.

Travis told himself to go back to work and forget about Dawes and Kincaid. He was doing his best. That was all any man could do.

Mason Kincaid walked into the Alhambra, one of Abilene's best restaurants. There was a tense expression on his face, an expression he tried to disguise as several of the diners greeted him. Behind him came John Henry Dawes and Faith Hamilton, arm in arm, talking and laughing.

A waiter came up to Kincaid and said, "Good evening, sir. The usual table for the three of you?"

Kincaid nodded a little more brusquely than he had intended. He noticed the slight surprise in the waiter's eyes and knew that he was going to have to keep a tighter rein on his temper.

Dawes had been in town less than a week, and already people were accustomed to seeing him with Faith and Kincaid. They were a regular threesome, had been ever since that first night when Dawes invited Faith to join them for dinner. She and Dawes had gotten along splendidly. Dawes insisted on bringing her every time they went out to eat, and she attended most of his speeches as well.

Which meant that Kincaid saw her several times a day, and each time was a particularly annoying burr under his saddle, as these Westerners phrased it.

The three of them settled down at their regular table. The Alhambra boasted polished wood floors, crystal chandeliers, and potted plants scattered around the room. It could hardly compare with the fine restaurants Kincaid had frequented back East, but for a frontier town like Abilene, it was high class. In his booming voice Dawes ordered a bottle of wine.

"Are you sure it's a good idea to eat here every night, John Henry?" Kincaid asked. "It might make the common folk believe that you think you're too good for them."

"Not much danger of that when I take my other meals at lunch counters, bunkhouses, and chuck wagons," Dawes replied with a chuckle. "A good sheriff has to be able to go anywhere in his county, Mason, from the fanciest places to the plainest."

Kincaid grimaced. Dawes had a point, but being lectured by the man rankled. Before Kincaid could reply, Faith said, "I think the Alhambra is very pleasant, Mason. I certainly enjoy coming here with the two of you."

"And we appreciate your company, my dear," Dawes said gallantly. "Don't we, Mason?"

"Of . . . course." Kincaid swallowed the bile that was rising in his throat.

The wine arrived, and he concentrated on that for a

moment, savoring the taste and the bouquet. Nothing special, but again, the best Abilene had to offer. Kincaid took a deep breath. Faith was enjoying her little game, but so far she had not done any harm. The campaign was going very well. Everywhere he went, people talked about what a fine sheriff Dawes was going to make. Support for the man was widespread, and while nearly everyone seemed to like and admire Luke Travis, the marshal just did not inspire people to vote for him, especially not over a man like Dawes.

The election was all but won, Kincaid decided, sipping his wine. Once that was behind them, he would deal with Faith Hamilton.

The meal went fairly smoothly. Kincaid was able to repress his unease at Faith's presence to discuss the campaign with Dawes. When they had finished eating, Dawes lit a cigar and leaned contentedly back in his chair.

"Mighty glad you got in touch with me about this sheriff's job, Mason," he said. "I think I'm really going to like it here in Abilene." He looked at Faith meaningfully as he spoke.

"I've been wondering about that, Mason," she said, turning to Kincaid. "How did you happen to invite John Henry to come here and enter the election?"

Kincaid downed the last of his wine. "There was no happenstance about it, Faith," he said. "I knew that Roy Wade was retiring and that a new sheriff would be needed, so I investigated and found that the most qualified candidate was John Henry Dawes. You can go over to the *Clarion* anytime and read about his exploits in their files."

"Now, I don't know that I'd call them exploits," Dawes added modestly. "Just a man doing his job."

"You're not making a speech now, John Henry," Kincaid replied, a slight edge to his voice. "You don't have to play to the crowd."

For a moment Dawes's eyes hardened as he gazed at

Kincaid. Then he smiled and said, "You're absolutely right, Mason. We're among friends." He turned his attention to Faith. "At any rate, my dear, Mason sent me a telegram asking if I'd be interested in the job, and it just so happened that I was looking for another position. I had just resigned from the marshal's job in Ysleta."

Faith frowned. "Where?"

"Ysleta. It's a small town in Texas, on the Rio Grande downriver from El Paso. Quite a thriving community in some ways, but outlaws tend to congregate there because it's close to the border. Sometimes the river changes course, too, which can make for some interesting jurisdictional disputes. Upshot of it is, there're places where neither the United States nor Mexico claims the land. No-Man's-Land, some call it, or Hell's Half Acre. I've even heard the term Outlaw Island used. Quite a colorful place."

"It sounds like it," Faith said, her eyes sparkling with excitement.

Dawes shrugged. "I'd done what I could to bring law and order to those parts. I was ready to move on. But from what I've seen so far, I might not mind settling down here in Kansas. It's a fine land, and the people are . . . very interesting." He was giving Faith that look again, and she was returning it.

Kincaid bit back his anger. They could make calf eyes at each other all they wanted, and it would not bother him. What they did was their own business—as long as it did not interfere with his plans.

After the men had brandy, Dawes rose and escorted Faith out of the restaurant, leaving Kincaid to settle the bill. He caught up with them on the boardwalk outside. The three of them headed toward the hotel where Dawes was staying.

"No speeches to make tonight, Mason?" Dawes asked.

"No, there'll be a rally tomorrow morning on the courthouse lawn. There should be plenty of people there, since everyone who lives in the area comes into town on Saturday for supplies."

Dawes nodded. "I'll be ready."

Might as well attempt to be civil, Kincaid thought. He turned to Faith and asked, "Can we walk you back to your hotel?" She was staying at the Grand Palace, he recalled, which was neither grand nor palatial as far as he was concerned.

"Why, that won't be necessary," Faith replied. "You see, I moved out of the Grand Palace this afternoon. I'm now staying at the same hotel as John Henry."

Kincaid glanced at Dawes. The man was smirking under his handlebar mustache.

Taking a deep breath, Kincaid told himself to remain calm. Dawes could be infuriating, but Kincaid was convinced they both had the same objective—Dawes's election as sheriff and the power that went with it. He could not afford to anger Dawes at the moment.

"Well, that's fine," he heard himself say to Faith.

Dawes and Faith continued to chat as they made their way to the hotel. Kincaid said very little, and his silence did not seem to bother them. When they reached the hotel, he went up the stairs behind them. Dawes was still arm in arm with the beautiful young blonde.

As Dawes unlocked the door of his room, he said to Kincaid, "No need for you to see me in, Mason."

"But . . . I thought we could go over what you'll say at the rally tomorrow."

Dawes waved a hand. "Don't worry about that. I've given hundreds of speeches. When the time comes, I'll say the right thing, you can count on that. And the people will eat it up, just like they've been doing."

Kincaid shot a glance at Faith, concerned that Dawes was revealing his cynicism to her, which he usually kept carefully concealed. But Faith did not seem surprised by Dawes's comments.

Maybe she already knew the man better than he did, Kincaid thought suddenly.

"I'm pretty tired," Dawes went on. "Think I'll turn in early."

"Me, too," Faith said. "Bed sounds wonderful." But

she made no move to go to her own room. Dawes reached out and took her arm.

A sneer tugged at Kincaid's mouth. Let them act that way if they wanted to, he told himself. He could not blame Dawes for succumbing to Faith's charms. He remembered all too well the passion she had aroused in him. The warmth of her silky skin, the sweet taste of her mouth, the urgency with which she clasped him to her . . . All those memories flooded Kincaid's mind.

With his face a taut, expressionless mask, he said, "Good night, then," and turned to stalk away down the hotel corridor.

Kincaid lit another cigar as he emerged from the hotel onto the boardwalk. He drew deeply on the tightly wrapped cylinder of tobacco and stood there for a long moment, trying to quiet his raging emotions. His turmoil might not be visible on his face, but inside he was seething.

Was it possible that after all this time he was jealous? He considered that for a few seconds, then abruptly discarded it. He might have good memories of making love with Faith, but that was the extent of it. No, he was angry because of the way she and Dawes were flaunting their relationship. Dawes would soon be the top law enforcement officer in this county; he needed to be more discreet in his affairs. That was the only reason Kincaid was upset with them.

He turned and started down the boardwalk. As he lifted his gaze, he saw Aileen Bloom coming toward him. The doctor was just passing through an oblong of light that spilled through a doorway, and she looked lovely this evening. But then, Kincaid thought, Aileen always looked lovely.

As they met, he smiled and said, "Hello, Aileen. Out for an evening stroll?"

She returned the smile. "No, I'm on my way to Northcraft's Drugstore to pick up some medical supplies."

"Why don't I accompany you, then?" he asked. It did not make sense, Kincaid told himself, to worry about Faith Hamilton when he was friends—maybe more than friends—with a woman such as Aileen.

She hesitated slightly, then said, "All right. That would be fine, Mason."

He fell in step beside her as she continued toward the drugstore. "I haven't seen much of you lately," he said. "I suppose your practice is keeping you busy."

"Yes, it is. There's always an increase in cases of grippe and croup at this time of year. I've been seeing quite a few children every day, and some adults, too." She glanced at him. "But you've been busy, too, I imagine, what with your land business and this election campaign."

Kincaid smiled in self-satisfaction, his earlier bad mood gone now. "That's true. There are quite a few demands on my time. But it'll all be worth it."

"Once the election is over, you mean."

"Of course." A thought occurred to Kincaid. "Listen, Aileen, there's going to be a rally for John Henry Dawes at the courthouse tomorrow morning. I'd like you to attend as my guest."

Aileen's footsteps slowed. She stopped and turned to face him. "I can't do that, Mason," she said.

Kincaid frowned. "Why not? We were just saying how busy we both are, and we haven't spent any time together for quite a while. I just thought this would be a chance . . ."

She was shaking her head. "I'm sorry, I really am. But I won't be going to that rally."

Kincaid's voice hardened as he said, "Because of Travis."

"That's right. It's no secret I was one of the group that persuaded him to run against Mr. Dawes. I just don't think it would look right for me to attend a rally for an opposing candidate."

"Why, that's . . . that's nonsense!" Kincaid exclaimed. "I've seen people who support Travis at John Henry's speeches. I've even seen Orion McCarthy at some of them."

"What Orion and other people do is their business. I just wouldn't feel comfortable."

Kincaid put a hand on her arm. "I thought you and I had something special, Aileen. That night when I kissed you—"

"I'd rather we didn't discuss that, Mason. I . . . I think it was a mistake for us to become involved with each other. While we agree on some things, there are too many other things that we feel differently about."

"Luke Travis, for example," Kincaid shot back, his voice bitter now. Anger was building inside him again. "Travis is the real reason you don't want to see me anymore, isn't he?"

"I don't know," Aileen answered, and she sounded sincere. "I really don't. I've never been certain how Luke feels. . . ."

"I suppose you're right," Kincaid said in brittle tones. "Perhaps it would be better if you and I didn't see each other anymore." He took his hand off her arm.

"I'm sorry, Mason. I didn't want to hurt you—"

"That's all right," he said abruptly, forcing a laugh. "Don't worry about me, Aileen. Why, there are dozens of women in this town who would be glad to be seen with me."

"I'm sure that's true." Aileen's tone was rather stiff. "I must get to the drugstore now, Mason. You don't have to walk with me."

"That's fine. Good night, Aileen."

"Good night." She turned and went down the board-walk.

Kincaid watched her for a moment, then dropped his cigar to the planks and crushed it savagely. What he had said was true—there *were* plenty of women in Abilene who would be thrilled to be the object of his attention. But the only two *he* had ever wanted had turned their backs on him.

# Chapter Four

**T**HE EASTBOUND TRAIN CLATTERED THROUGH THE EARLY morning mists that lingered over the prairie. Out on these flat, straight stretches, it was easy to let the speed build up unintentionally. An engineer needed an alert, watchful eye and a steady hand on the throttle. At the moment Charlie Basserman had neither.

Charlie was not asleep at the throttle, but he was groggy after the all-night run. The fireman, a middle-aged, sullen half-breed called Chickasaw Dave, was in much the same shape. Both men were veteran railroad workers, and they were relying on instinct and habit to take the train into Abilene, some twelve miles to the east.

Basserman yawned and rubbed his eyes as he sat on the engineer's seat. The locomotive was running just fine; his ears would detect any irregularity in its rumbling rhythm, and an alarm would sound in his brain. Chickasaw Dave had the fire well stoked and was sitting on his

haunches on the other side of the cab, leaning against the
iron wall.

The engineer yawned again and tilted his head so that
he could look out the cab window and down the tracks in
front of the train. The rails stretched smooth and unbro-
ken up ahead.

Howling a curse, Basserman lunged for the brake lever,
grabbed it, and hauled it back with all his weight. Dave
slammed forward against the front wall of the cab and
yelped in pain. The brakes squealed and screeched as
Basserman attempted to bring the massive iron leviathan
to a halt.

"What the hell!" the fireman shouted as he scrambled
to his feet.

"Something on the tracks!" Basserman cried in reply,
all his drowsiness gone.

A sudden spurt of flames had attracted his attention.
Someone had piled brush and scrub timber on the
railbed and then, from the looks of the black smoke
billowing up, poured kerosene on it and set it afire.
Basserman kept leaning on the brake as the train shuddered and slowed. The gap between the engine and the
obstruction was closing up too quickly. The frantic
engineer did not know if he would be able to stop the
train in time.

If the barrier was only a stack of brush, the locomotive's cowcatcher would plow right through it without
any trouble. The fact that the brush was on fire was an
added hazard; the flames might spread to some of the
cars that passed over it. But the biggest danger was that
the blaze concealed something. If whoever had set the
fire had pried up a rail on the other side—

At the thought of a derailment Basserman felt a cold
ball of fear roll around in his belly. "Give me a hand!" he
called.

Chickasaw Dave flung himself across the cab to grasp
the brake lever and add his weight to Basserman's. The
lever almost bucked right out of their hands, but they
held on for dear life. Gradually the train slowed and

shuddered to a halt less than ten feet from the blazing barrier.

Peeling his fingers off the brake lever, Basserman lunged for the pistol he kept on a shelf beside the throttle. There was only one reason anybody would start a fire on the tracks—to stop the train and hold it up.

Basserman saw men on horseback gallop out of the smoke and haze, and he swung his pistol toward the leader. Before he could fire, though, smoke and flame and noise exploded from the gun in the rider's hand. Basserman cried out in pain as the bullet struck him in the shoulder and flung him to the floor of the cab. Frantically Dave thrust his hands in the air to show he was unarmed and would not put up any resistance.

Gritting his teeth against the agony of his bullet-shattered shoulder, Basserman pulled himself to a sitting position and looked around the cab for his fallen gun. He spotted the revolver and awkwardly reached for it with his left hand.

Someone vaulted into the cab, and a booted foot kicked the pistol out of Basserman's reach. He let out a little sob and looked up into the barrel of a Colt. The menacing weapon was held by the man who had just leapt from his horse into the cab of the locomotive. The outlaw was not wearing a mask of any kind. He had a narrow, pockmarked face and intense, deep-set eyes that stared down at Charlie Basserman. His lips were twisted in a humorless smile as he said, "Leave it be, old man, and you'll live through this. Nothing to get excited about, just a little holdup."

This was the man who had shot him in the shoulder, Basserman realized, the one who had led the outlaws' charge. The other desperadoes were galloping along the sides of the train now, some of them swinging off their mounts to enter the cars, no doubt to strip the passengers of their valuables. Basserman winced as he heard more shots; somebody had unwisely resisted. A moment later there was a muffled explosion.

The bandit who was holding his gun on Basserman and

Dave grinned. "That'll be the safe in the express car. Hope you're carrying enough to make this worthwhile, mister."

"You'll hang for this, you son of a bitch!" Basserman ground out.

"Oh, I don't think so. The law would have to catch me first, and none of the star packers around here're smart enough to catch Mike Whitson."

So that was his name, Basserman thought. Like a lot of outlaws, this man was too arrogant to conceal his identity. He was *proud* that he held up trains.

Carefully Basserman noted every detail of Mike Whitson's appearance, from the black hat with its taut chin strap to the black vest, red shirt, and black chaps. The outlaw was a little under medium height and slight, but what he lacked in stature he made up for in ruthlessness. The cold, hard look in those reptilian eyes made that clear. Basserman suddenly realized he was very lucky to be alive. Whitson would have enjoyed putting more slugs in him.

In less than fifteen minutes, the train had been efficiently looted. Basserman was light-headed from shock and loss of blood, but he thought he would be able to get the train into Abilene if he got the chance.

The outlaw directed a hard look at both the engineer and the fireman and said, "Don't try anything stupid. Wait until we're gone, then get out of here. And when you get to Abilene, be sure and tell folks Mike Whitson and his men stopped you."

"Sure, mister," Dave said with a gulp. "We'll tell 'em."

With his gun still in his hand, Whitson swung down out of the cab and mounted the horse that one of his men held for him. He wheeled the animal and galloped away, the rest of the outlaws trailing behind him.

Chickasaw Dave dropped to his knees next to Basserman and said anxiously, "You all right, Charlie?"

"Hell, no, I've been shot, you idiot," Basserman snapped. He winced as he pulled his engineer's coat aside to check his shoulder. It was broken, all right, he thought as a fresh wave of pain washed over him. He went on, "Tie it up so the bleeding will stop, then start stoking the fire again. Get some of the passengers to clean that mess off the tracks. It'll be burned down enough by now for 'em to do that. And check on the express messenger . . . even though I reckon there's a good chance those owlhoots killed him. Come on, Dave, get busy."

"Take it easy, Charlie," the fireman advised as he began to tear strips off his shirt to bind up Basserman's wound. "Them outlaws are long gone. There's nothing we can do about it now."

"We can notify the law in Abilene," Basserman said sharply. "They can track those bastards down."

Dave chuckled. "You're forgettin', Charlie," he said. "Roy Wade is the sheriff in Abilene."

Basserman closed his eyes and sighed. Dave was right. They were about to elect a new sheriff in Abilene, or so Basserman had heard, but that was a few days off. Roy Wade was still in charge, and there was little chance of him tracking down anybody.

"We've still got to carry the news into town," Basserman said. "Maybe *somebody* will do something."

But even as he said it, he knew the chances of Whitson being caught were awfully slim.

John Henry Dawes was going to have another good audience, Luke Travis thought as he stood on the boardwalk in front of his office and watched the people heading toward the courthouse.

Buckboards and saddle horses lined both sides of the street. The usual Saturday crowd was in town. And it appeared that most of them were going to hear Dawes's speech. Travis could hear the band playing from the courthouse lawn. With just a week to go until the election, Dawes and Kincaid were still campaigning actively.

Cody Fisher came down the boardwalk and joined Travis at the railing. "Going to the rally?" the deputy asked.

"Don't reckon I'd be very welcome there," Travis replied dryly. "Wouldn't want to steal any of Dawes's thunder."

Cody chuckled. "He does seem to be mighty fond of hearing himself talk." His tone became more serious. "Some folks seem to think the election's already over."

"Maybe it is," Travis replied. "Dawes has run a good race. He's told the people what they want to hear, and he's got a reputation to back up what he says. Could be he'll make a good sheriff."

Cody glanced sharply at Travis. "I'm not used to hearing you give up, Marshal," he said.

Travis shook his head. "Didn't say I was. I'll be in the race until it's over. But there's no point in ignoring the facts, either. Chances are Dawes is going to win, and then we'll have to work with him. I'm just hoping he'll be an improvement over Roy Wade."

"Couldn't be much worse," Cody muttered.

"I wouldn't say that," Travis commented. "We'll just have to wait and— What the devil?"

Travis had spotted Harvey Bastrop, the stationmaster at the Kansas Pacific depot, hurrying down the board-walk toward them. The man had a frantic look on his face.

"Luke!" Bastrop called out. "Have you seen Sheriff Wade?"

"I imagine he's down at the courthouse for that rally," Travis replied as Bastrop came up to them and stopped to mop perspiration off his forehead with a handkerchief. The stationmaster had evidently run all the way from the depot and was out of breath. Travis went on, "What's the trouble?"

"The eastbound that was due earlier this morning just limped in," Bastrop said. "It had been stopped and held up, Luke! The engineer was wounded pretty bad, and the express messenger was killed!"

Travis stiffened. "Anybody else hurt?" he asked sharply.

"A couple of the passengers have gunshot wounds. I've

already sent somebody to fetch Dr. Bloom and take her over to the station. The outlaws cleaned out the train, lock, stock, and barrel."

"Anybody recognize who it was?" Cody asked.

Bastrop nodded. "The leader of the gang called himself Mike Whitson. According to Charlie Basserman, the engineer, this Whitson behaved as if he *wanted* credit for the holdup. He told Charlie to be sure and tell everybody he stopped the train. Have you heard of him, Marshal?"

Travis shook his head and looked at Cody, who repeated the gesture and shrugged. "Don't reckon we have," Travis said, "but that doesn't mean anything. Outlaws drift into these parts from all over. We can check our reward dodgers and see if there's one on Whitson. In the meantime you'd better let Roy Wade know about this."

"I guess so," Bastrop replied with a frown. "I don't know if it'll do any good, though."

"Come on," Travis said, taking hold of Bastrop's arm. "We'll go find Wade."

With Cody trailing behind, Travis and Bastrop joined the people heading toward the courthouse. When they arrived, they found a large crowd had already gathered on the lawn and was listening to the band music. A speaker's platform, draped with red, white, and blue bunting, had been erected. The chairs on the platform were empty at the moment.

Travis made his way through the mass of people, uttering a few sharp commands to open a path for himself, Bastrop, and Cody. There were several puzzled glances directed his way, along with a few openly resentful ones. When they reached the front of the crowd, Travis spotted Thurman Simpson standing nearby.

"Have you seen Sheriff Wade, Mr. Simpson?" Travis asked.

The schoolmaster shook his head. "I imagine he's in his office, Marshal," he replied, lifting his voice over the music.

Travis nodded and said, "Thanks," then turned toward the courthouse. Wade's office was inside.

Before they reached the front doors, Sheriff Wade emerged with Mason Kincaid and John Henry Dawes. A loud cheer went up from the crowd. Dawes grinned and waved.

Then Kincaid's gaze fell on Travis, and he tugged at Dawes's sleeve and indicated the approaching trio. Wade saw them, too, and frowned.

"Somethin' wrong, Marshal?" Wade asked as Travis came up to them.

"Harvey has some bad news," Travis said, stepping aside so Bastrop could move forward.

"Well, spit it out, Harve," Wade told him.

Quickly Bastrop repeated what he had told Travis and Cody. Wade's frown deepened, and Dawes appeared concerned. When Bastrop was finished, Dawes spoke up before Wade could say anything.

"This is an outrage!" the candidate said. "These outlaws have to be taught that they can't strike with impunity in this county!"

"Damn right," Wade agreed, hitching up his pants under the swell of his belly.

"Then you're going after them, Sheriff?" Bastrop asked.

Wade clapped him on the shoulder. "Can't right now, Harve. But as soon as this rally is over, I'll mosey out there and take a look around. Could be I'll pick up the trail of them murderin' skunks."

Travis's eyes narrowed. "You're not starting now, Sheriff? That gang already has a big lead."

"That's right, Marshal, so I don't reckon a little while longer'll matter much. A sheriff's got a whole heap o' responsibilities, and one of 'em is keepin' his word. I promised I'd introduce John Henry here 'fore his speech, and I intend to do just that."

Travis's expression became even more bleak. He remembered all too well how Roy Wade had handled things when the Madden gang ran roughshod over the area. Wade had already set his sights on retirement, and chasing an outlaw gang had seemed too risky to him. That had been the occasion of Travis's first serious clash with Mason Kincaid; the town councilman insisted that Travis not violate his jurisdictional boundaries. The whole situation had led to a lot of unnecessary bloodshed and heartbreak. And now it looked as if the same thing was about to happen again.

"Nestor and I can ride out and try to track Whitson's gang," Travis said. "Nobody around here is better at reading sign than Nestor."

"That's all well and good, Marshal," Kincaid said sharply. "But this crime occurred in Sheriff Wade's bailiwick, not yours. I believe you should defer to his professional judgment."

"We've tried that before," Cody said, his voice hot with rising anger. "It never got us anything but—"

"Take it easy, Cody," Travis broke in. "I'm sure Sheriff Wade knows what he's doing."

Wade flushed at the palpable scorn in Travis's tone, but he said, "Damn right I do. And right now I'm goin' to get this rally started." He stumped toward the steps leading to the speaker's platform.

Kincaid followed him, saying, "Come on, John Henry."

Dawes hesitated, looking at Travis. The marshal met Dawes's gaze, and after a few seconds Dawes said, "Sorry to hear about this, Marshal. Lawlessness hurts everybody."

Without further comment Dawes turned and followed Kincaid and Wade onto the platform. Another cheer greeted him.

Travis sighed and said to Bastrop, "Come on, Harvey, let's go over to the station. I want to talk to that engineer if he's up to it."

With Cody and Bastrop behind him, Travis skirted the crowd while Sheriff Wade stood up and began introducing Dawes. Before Travis reached the street, however, he heard Dawes's voice cut into Wade's opening remarks, calling, "Marshal! Marshal Luke Travis!"

Travis stopped and looked back in surprise. Dawes was motioning to him to come up to the platform. The candidate turned toward Wade and said, "Excuse me for interrupting you, Sheriff, but I believe the marshal has important news."

Travis exchanged a glance with Cody. The deputy shook his head, indicating that he had no idea what Dawes was up to.

Dawes beckoned again and said, "Why don't you tell the people what's happened, Marshal?"

Several men in the crowd cried out their agreement. Travis sighed, made his way to the platform, and climbed the steps. Dawes was waiting for him and led him over to the center of the structure. Travis felt foolish, as he always did standing before a large group of people. He had given his Independence Day speech from a similar platform.

The crowd quieted down as Travis looked out over them. He cleared his throat and then in as few words as possible told them about the train holdup. There were shouts of outrage when he mentioned the wounding of the engineer and some of the passengers and the killing of the express messenger.

As soon as Travis finished, Dawes moved in smoothly. He clenched his right fist and pounded it into his left hand as he said, "This is what happens when peace officers don't do their job! Outlaws feel that they are free to ride where they please, to rob and rape and pillage!" He glanced at Roy Wade, whose face was turning even redder than usual. "I'm not saying that Sheriff Wade has not done an exemplary job," Dawes continued. "He has served the citizens of this county very well for many years. But no one would deny that he has earned a chance to rest, to enjoy the years of his retirement. It's time to place your trust in someone else, to look to a new sheriff to protect you from lawless brigands like this Mike

Whitson and his gang! And that's exactly what I'll do if I'm elected sheriff of Dickinson County! I give you my solemn word that I will track down Whitson and his men and make them pay for this atrocity!"

As Travis listened to Dawes's speech, he did not know whether he should be impressed or angered. The man certainly knew how to seize an opportunity. Dawes's ringing pronouncements had the crowd cheering and clapping again.

"What about you, Marshal?" Mason Kincaid suddenly demanded, coming forward to stand next to Dawes. "If you're elected"—Kincaid's tone made it clear that he doubted such a thing could ever happen—"what do you intend to do about this band of desperadoes?"

Travis frowned. So far he had managed to avoid direct confrontations or debates with Dawes. He knew all too well that Dawes's flamboyant style went over better with the public than did his plain speech. Having to address such a critical issue right after Dawes's stirring statements would only highlight their differences.

He had to answer honestly, though. He gazed at the crowd, which looked back at him expectantly, and began, "I'll do my best to arrest anybody who breaks the law, just like I've always done as marshal. That's all I can promise, folks—"

"I'll personally supervise the pursuit of this gang," Dawes cut in, somehow making it seem that Travis had interrupted him, rather than the other way around. "We'll get as many deputies as we need, and we'll bring Mike Whitson to justice!"

Another lusty ovation swept over the platform. Travis sighed. Cody Fisher and Harvey Bastrop were just about the only sympathetic faces he could see.

As the crowd continued to cheer John Henry Dawes, Travis walked off the platform. Dawes could campaign all he wanted to. Travis still had a job to do.

# Chapter Five

————◆————

NESTOR GILWORTH WAS HAPPY TO RIDE OUT TO THE SITE OF the train robbery with Travis. They found the spot quite easily because Travis had questioned Charlie Basserman, the engineer, who was recuperating from his bullet wound in one of the rooms Aileen Bloom used for bedridden patients. The train's fireman, the half-breed known as Chickasaw Dave, added a few more details.

Finding the tracks left by Whitson's gang was no challenge for Nestor, but the trail played out several miles north of the Kansas Pacific tracks on a stretch of rocky ground. As the two men drew their horses to a halt, Nestor pushed back his battered hat and said, "Looks like them fellers knew what they was doin', Marshal. We could still scout 'em out, but unless we was real lucky, it'd take a dozen men and a week or so."

Travis sighed. "We don't have the men or the time.

Come on, Nestor, we're going back to Abilene. Dawes can deal with this after he's elected."

"You sound mighty sure that's what's goin' to happen."

"You didn't see and hear that crowd this morning, Nestor," Travis told him. "I did."

Nothing happened over the next couple of days to alleviate Travis's pessimism. Word reached Abilene that the Whitson gang had struck again, hitting a bank in a small settlement called Briar on Saturday, then raiding a church service and stopping a stagecoach on Sunday. "Mighty busy bunch of owlhoots," Cody muttered in disgust when he and Travis heard about Whitson's latest depredations.

Whitson was not only raking in the loot, he was providing John Henry Dawes with plenty of fuel for more speeches. Dawes spoke from the balcony of his hotel on Saturday night, then appeared at services at the Baptist and Lutheran churches on Sunday. Each speech was marked by passionate promises to run down Mike Whitson and any other outlaw foolish enough to set foot in Dickinson County.

"To hear Dawes tell it, he could track down Frank and Jesse James and the Youngers all by hisself," Nestor groused as he sat in the marshal's office with Travis on Monday morning. "It's a wonder there're any outlaws left anywhere west of the Mississippi!"

Travis grunted and tried to concentrate on the wanted posters spread out on his desk. He had already been through them once, looking for information on Mike Whitson, but the search had been fruitless. He was checking the dodgers again now just to make sure he had not missed something, but he did not expect to find anything. Whitson could have come to Kansas from anywhere between Texas and Canada or Missouri and California. There was no way a lawman could keep up with every bandit in the West.

It was an overcast fall day, with a chilly wind out of the

northwest. The weather matched Travis's mood. He was not surprised when Cody came in a few minutes later and said, "More bad news."

Travis glanced up. The deputy was carrying a folded copy of the Abilene *Clarion*. "That today's paper?" Travis asked.

Cody nodded. "I know you quit reading Valentine's stories about the election, Marshal, but I thought you'd better see this." He placed the paper on the desk so that Travis could read the story featured in a prominent box on the front page.

"What is it?" Nestor asked. "More o' that young whippersnapper's slobberin' over Dawes?"

"Not this time, Nestor," Travis told him. "It's the paper's official endorsement, by the editor. And he's saying that folks ought to vote for Dawes." Travis's mouth quirked. "According to this editorial, Dawes is the law-and-order candidate."

"Law and order!" Nestor exploded. "What about *your* record? You're the one who found out who was poisonin' that whiskey last year an' killin' off all them folks!"

"And you're the one who kept the lid on the whole town when everybody was about to riot over that Confederate general," Cody added. He leaned over the desk and went on, "Seems to me it's time you went over to the paper and set a few things straight."

Travis pushed back his chair and stood up. "There's a part of me that wants to do just that," he admitted. "But it doesn't work that way. The paper has a right to say whatever it pleases, and so does Dawes, as long as they're not trying to hurt anybody or break any laws. I don't have to like it, but there's nothing I can do about it."

Cody stared at him for a long moment, and Travis could see the anger and confusion in the young man's eyes. Cody's late father had been a judge, and Cody himself had been a deputy for quite a while now, but despite that, there was still a wild streak in him, left over from the days when he had been a gunfighter. That part of Cody still favored direct action when confronted with a problem. And Travis could certainly sympathize with him.

"All right," Cody finally said with a sigh. "If that's the way you want it, Luke."

"It is," Travis said firmly. "However the election turns out, I want to win or lose fair and square."

"You think Dawes can say the same thing?" Cody asked.

"That's his business, not mine."

But Travis found himself pondering that question and others as the day went on. Now, with the *Clarion* solidly behind him, what else did John Henry Dawes need to win?

There were no raids by the Whitson gang for a couple of days, and Travis began to wonder if they had moved on for parts unknown. The fact that they had struck so many places in such a short period of time might indicate that they had been trying to put together some traveling money. If that was the case, it was unlikely that they would ever be brought to justice for the crimes they had committed in Dickinson County, no matter what promises Dawes made. But sooner or later, the law would catch up to them somewhere, Travis thought. And like nearly all outlaws, Mike Whitson and his men would meet their ends with the aid of a bullet or a rope.

Leslie Gibson still had Travis making speeches from time to time, but the marshal's outlook had become even more pessimistic. He saw the way the townspeople greeted Dawes when they passed him on the street. Dawes had won them over completely. For a while Travis had thought that the settlers who lived out of town might support him in enough numbers to swing the election, but Dawes had done his work well, paying visits to ranch houses, farming communities, and small churches scattered throughout the county. His emphatic pledges to run down any rustlers who tried to operate in the area brought the ranchers over to his side. Hunter Dixon, the owner of one of the area's biggest spreads and as such an influential man, had come out in support of Dawes, and it was a virtual guarantee that many of the smaller ranchers would follow his lead.

For the first time since he had known Luke Travis, Cody Fisher saw the marshal give up, and it did not sit well with the deputy. At least, that was Cody's view of what Travis was doing. Travis, however, insisted that he was merely being realistic.

On Thursday evening, while Travis was making his nightly rounds, Cody and Nestor were in the marshal's office. Nestor was sitting on the sofa playing with Hooch, dangling a string in front of the cat's face and then jerking it back whenever Hooch swatted at it. Cody was behind the desk, his chair leaned back and his booted feet resting on the desktop.

"It just doesn't seem right," Cody said, a frown on his face. "Dawes has got the marshal stampeded."

Nestor glanced up from his game with the cat. "I wouldn't bet on that. Luke Travis ain't the kind of man who stampedes."

"Then why hasn't he tried harder to win this election?" Cody demanded.

Nestor's forehead furrowed in thought, his attention straying from Hooch. A second later, he let out a yelp and jerked his hand back, bringing a long, bleeding scratch to his mouth. After sucking on it for a moment, he exclaimed, "That durned animal clawed me!"

Hooch was licking his paw in satisfaction. Cody chuckled, then became serious. "It's almost like Marshal Travis doesn't want to win."

"I reckon he does," Nestor said. "But he just ain't the same kind of man as that Dawes feller. Folks look at Dawes, and they see some sort of dime-novel hero, shootin' it out with desperadoes and charmin' all the ladies at the same time. That ain't the way Luke Travis is. The marshal just does his job and goes on about his business. Ain't nothin' fancy about him. So folks overlook him and don't never stop to think that it was fellers like him who made this here frontier a safe place to live. Leastways it is part of the time, which ain't bad considerin' less'n twenty years ago there was still a heap o' Injuns and bad men hereabouts." The big man stroked Hooch's back, the scratching incident forgiven, and went on, "So it ain't hardly fair to ask Travis to be like Dawes. The marshal just ain't got that in him."

That was one of the longest speeches Cody had ever heard Nestor make, at least concerning something serious and not some whopper. The deputy said bitterly, "Too bad folks can't seem to see what the two candidates are really like."

Nestor shrugged his massive shoulders. "Reckon that's politics for you. Common folk who run for office have always had a hard time gettin' voters to take 'em seriouslike. One feller who managed to was that Colonel Crockett. Now, I knew ol' Davy when I was just a younker back in Tennessee. Fact is, we went coon-huntin' together once, and the gol-durndest thing happened . . ."

Cody grinned, knowing that Nestor was launching into another yarn. The big man did not get very far into the story, however, because at that moment hurrying footsteps thumped on the boardwalk outside. The door was thrown open, and a townsman stuck his head in the office.

"Big fight over at the Bull's Head!" he cried.

Cody and Nestor were on their feet instantly. "Come on!" Cody rapped. "We'd better see what's going on."

He grabbed his hat as he and Nestor went out the door. By the time they reached the boardwalk, the man who had brought the news was running down the street, spreading the word of the brawl. Cody scowled. The more people who showed up at the saloon, the worse the fracas was liable to be.

Cody had no idea where Travis was at the moment, but he was confident that he and Nestor could handle the disturbance. The two deputies ran across Texas Street to

the Bull's Head Saloon, the establishment once owned by
Ben Thompson, a gambler and enemy of Wild Bill
Hickok, during Abilene's most violent period many years
earlier. Thompson had left Abilene long ago, heading for
Texas, and Hickok had met his end up in the Dakotas,
but the Bull's Head was still there. Occasionally it tried
to live up to its wild past.

A few feet in the lead, Cody entered the saloon first,
slapping the batwings aside and then ducking frantically
as he saw a chair spinning through the air toward him. It
flew over his head and crashed into the wall. Nestor
crowded through the entrance, took in the scene, and
grinned. Cody saw his excited expression and knew what
Nestor was thinking—this was a fight worthy of breaking
up.

The tavern was filled with brawling men. Fists flew,
tables crashed to the floor as men landed on them, bottles
shattered, and poker chips scattered. The saloon girls in
their gaudy, low-cut dresses had retreated to the second
floor, where they hung over the balcony and shouted
encouragement to the battlers below. From time to time
one of the bartenders would poke his head up and
venture a look over the bar, then duck back down to
avoid another missile. Miraculously the long mirror
behind the bar had not been shattered. Across the room
the piano player, with his gaitered sleeves and pomaded
hair, was perched atop his instrument, trying to stay out
of harm's way. Top-hatted gamblers in frock coats scurried around the floor on hands and knees, gathering up
the money that had spilled from overturned tables where
poker games had been in progress. The cacophony of
shouted curses, fists striking flesh, and the grunts of
struggling men punctuated the bedlam.

Cody and Nestor hesitated, trying to sort out the
combatants before they plunged into the melee. The
Bull's Head was frequented by cowboys from the local
ranches, and Cody recognized most of the men who were
fighting. After a few moments, though, Cody pointed

toward a knot of struggling men in front of the bar. Three strangers who were fighting side by side were at the core of that battle. If he and Nestor could get to the bar and break up that fight, the other skirmishes might stop as well.

A man came staggering across the floor toward the deputies, knocked in their direction by a punch. Nestor grabbed his collar and tossed him through the batwings into the street. Cody nodded and said above the din, "Let's go!"

They waded in, flinging men aside, blocking punches, throwing some of their own. Nestor went first, clearing a path with his bulk. He grabbed men, cracked skulls together, then shoved the limp cowhands out of the way.

One cowboy snatched up a chair and whipped it toward Cody's head. The deputy caught one of the chair legs with his left hand and drove his right fist across the cowboy's jaw. The man's legs buckled, and he dropped to the floor. Cody tossed the chair aside and moved on to the next opponent.

Cody knew he and Nestor could have stopped this brawl by drawing their guns and firing a couple of slugs into the ceiling. Compared to the damage the saloon had already suffered, a pair of bullet holes would not have amounted to much. But going about it this way would allow him to work off some of the frustration that had been building in him during the past week. He might not be able to fathom the game called politics, but he could sure knock a few drunken brawlers on their backsides.

Cody grabbed the shoulder of another cowhand, spun him around, and dropped him with a hard right cross. Nestor was still laying waste to the men around him. Cody reached the bar, found a spot where beer had not been spilled on the hardwood surface, then put a hand on it and vaulted up.

"Hold it!" he shouted at the top of his lungs as he stood above the battling men. He drew his gun and moved behind the three strangers. His heart was pounding heavily, and he decided he had had enough of this. The

Colt Lightning cracked wickedly as he squeezed off a shot into the ceiling.

The shot made some men dive for cover, and others froze, fists cocked back for the next punch. Nestor shoved a few of them aside and stepped up to the bar, turning to put his back to it as he pulled the big Dragoon from its holster. He was to the right of the three strangers, so Cody hopped down on the other side, flanking them and facing the roomful of angry cowboys.

"I don't know what started this," Cody said in a loud voice, "but it's over, right here and now."

"They started it, Deputy!" one of the cowhands shouted, pointing at the men beside Cody. "Them three bastards right there!"

Cody glanced over at them. "What've you got to say to that, mister?" he asked the nearest one, a man in his forties with a lined, leathery face, blue eyes narrowed in a perpetual squint, and scruffy reddish-brown whiskers.

The man spat on the floor and said, "We was just enforcin' the law, Deputy. You damn well better get used to it."

For a long moment Cody stared at the man in surprise, wondering if he had heard right. He turned to the other two and saw the hostile gazes being directed toward him. The second man was a heavy-featured, gray-haired individual about the same age as the first one. The third man was quite a bit younger than either of his companions, no more than twenty-five. Even though he was slender and of medium height, he had been giving a good account of himself. His hat had been knocked off, revealing brown, slightly curly hair. He glared at Cody as he said, "That's right, mister. Anybody who causes trouble around here is going to have to answer to us."

Completely baffled, Cody said sharply, "Hold on a minute. Just who the devil are you?"

"Name's Buff Cotter," the red-bearded man replied. He jerked a thumb at the gray-haired man and went on, "This here's Jim Geraghty, and the young fella is Lin Rogers."

One of the cowhands spoke up, saying, "They came in here and started bustin' the place up, Cody! It wasn't our fault!"

Cody looked around in confusion and spotted one of the bartenders peering over the bar. Leaning across the hardwood, Cody grasped the man's collar and pulled him upright. "All right, Wilson," he said. "I don't seem to be making much sense of all this, so you tell me what happened here, and give me the straight of it!"

"S-sure thing, Cody," the bartender quavered. "What do you want to know?"

"Who really started this?"

The bartender swallowed. "Well, some of the boys from the Turkey Track were arguing with the hands from the Diamond J. You know how those two bunches are. . . ."

Cody knew all right. Glancing around the room, he saw quite a few punchers from the ranches the bartender had mentioned. This would not be the first time a fight had broken out between the two crews.

"We were just funnin'," a Diamond J rider put in. "It didn't mean nothin', Deputy. And it wouldn't have amounted to much if those hombres hadn't come hornin' in!"

Cody glanced at Wilson. "So the fight had already started before these men got involved?" He nodded toward Cotter, Geraghty, and Rogers.

"That's right, I guess," the bartender admitted.

Cody turned back to the three strangers. "So how did you get mixed up in it?"

"Done told you," Cotter replied, his tone surly. "We seen that brawl and moved in to break it up. We figured to arrest the ones that was fightin'."

"Arrest 'em?" Nestor echoed. "Seems to me that's a job for a lawman."

"That's exactly what we are," Lin Rogers said tightly. "We work for Sheriff John Henry Dawes."

Understanding began to dawn on Cody. "You mean you used to be deputies for Dawes?"

"No used to be about it," the one called Geraghty said, speaking up for the first time. "We're John Henry's regular deputies. Just got into town on the train and were headin' down to the courthouse when we saw this fight goin' on. Figured it was our duty to break it up."

Cody felt a surge of anger and tried to force it down. "Maybe you boys didn't know it," he said pointedly, "but the election isn't until next Tuesday. Dawes isn't the sheriff yet."

Cotter waved his hand. "Hell, that don't mean nothin'. He's goin' to be."

"He's so sure of winning that he already sent for you, is that it?" Cody asked.

"Reckon you could say so. What difference does it make?"

"The difference is that you didn't have the authority to break up a fight, and you sure as hell didn't have the authority to arrest anybody!"

"That's right!" one of the cowboys called. "Why, when they come in here and started talkin' about arrestin' all of us, well, we sort of put aside our differences to set 'em straight. Ain't that right?"

The punchers from the Turkey Track and the Diamond J nodded.

Cody leveled the Colt Lightning at Cotter. "It seems to me you three are the reason a little ruckus turned into a brawl. That sounds like disturbing the peace. You'd better come along to the jail. Maybe a night behind bars will teach you a little about following the law yourselves."

Cotter sneered. "Not hardly," he scoffed. "You're nothin' but a town deputy. You ain't goin' to throw us in jail just for tryin' to keep the peace." Then he began to laugh; it was an ugly sound. "Looks like that's somethin' you boys don't seem to be able to do."

"We'll see about that, mister," replied a new voice.

The words crackled in the air, and people stepped back hurriedly as Luke Travis strode into the saloon, his gun drawn. He came over to the bar, nodded to Cody and

Nestor, and went on, "I heard there was trouble over here. Looks like you two have got it under control, though." He turned to the other three men. "I heard what you were saying. You don't have any legal authority, so I reckon it'd be best if you came along peacefully."

Lin Rogers said, "You're Marshal Travis, aren't you?"

"That's right, son."

"Don't matter to us who you are," Geraghty said harshly. "We're not goin' anywhere, 'specially not to some two-bit jail."

"Damn right," Cotter growled.

Cody tensed. Cotter, Geraghty, and Rogers were all armed, and from the stubborn, hostile looks on their faces, it was clear they were not going to cooperate. People in the saloon suddenly began to move back as the threat of gunplay materialized, hanging heavily in the air.

The three strangers had called the turn. It was up to Luke Travis, Cody knew, to call their bluff, if bluff it was.

"Hold on a minute!" someone cried from the doorway of the saloon.

"John Henry!" Rogers called out, relief sounding in his voice.

Cotter grinned and said, "Howdy, John Henry. How 'bout tellin' these local star packers they can't arrest us?"

Dawes walked into the Bull's Head, a solemn expression on his handsome face. He looked at the men and nodded to each in turn. "Hello, Buff, Jim, Lin. Good to see you. I'm glad you got my wire and came right on." Dawes sighed. "I suppose that makes this mess my fault, Marshal Travis. I sent for these men. I wanted to have everything in place—just in case I win the election, you understand."

"You can send for whomever you please, Dawes," Travis said tightly. "But that doesn't give them the right to cause trouble in my town."

"Not much longer—" Cotter began.

Dawes cut him off. "You're absolutely right, Marshal. I apologize for my associates. You go ahead and do whatever you have to do."

"What!" Geraghty exclaimed. "You're tellin' him he can arrest us, John Henry?"

"That's exactly right, Jim," Dawes replied. "I haven't been elected yet, so the three of you had no authority to get involved in a fight."

Travis frowned at him. "How did you know what happened here, Dawes?"

"The word is getting around town already," Dawes said with a smile. "I heard the commotion and started to stroll over, and I ran into a man on the way who told me what to expect when I got here. Again, I'm sorry for my part in this, Marshal, inadvertent though it was."

"But you are saying I should arrest your deputies?"

"They're not actually my deputies right now, just my friends. And while I don't particularly want to see them in jail, everyone has to obey the law, even men who may soon be enforcing it."

Dawes's ringing tones filled the saloon, and as Cody glanced around, he saw men nodding in agreement. Suddenly Cody realized that Dawes had taken what had been an ugly incident that should have reflected badly on him and turned it into something that made him appear to be fair and impartial. The man was a master at making himself look good.

"All right," Travis said, and Cody could tell that the marshal had come to the same realization. Travis turned to Cotter, Geraghty, and Rogers. "You men come up with the money to pay for these damages, and I reckon a night in jail will take care of any charges of disturbing the peace."

Cotter flashed a furious look at Dawes. "John Henry . . . ?"

"Do what the marshal says," Dawes ordered.

Cotter sighed and began to dig in his pocket for money. Geraghty and Rogers did the same. Within a few moments they had put together enough funds to cover the damage that had been done to the Bull's Head. After handing the bills to the saloon's owner, they trooped out, followed closely by Travis, Cody, and Nestor. The three

lawmen still had their guns drawn, but it was clear that
the prisoners were not going to give them any trouble. As
the little group started across Texas Street toward the
jail, people crowded around Dawes to shake his hand and
commend him on his masterful handling of the matter.

Cody heard what was going on behind them and shook
his head in disgust. He was not the only one to notice.

Buff Cotter glanced back over his shoulder and with a
sly smile said, "Reckon things're goin' to be a hell of a lot
different around here next week."

"Just keep moving," Travis said flatly.

Cotter was probably right, Cody thought gloomily.
Things *were* going to be different. And he had a feeling
the change would not be for the better.

# Chapter Six

CODY AND NESTOR WERE ALREADY IN THE OFFICE WHEN Travis arrived the next morning. The marshal hung up his hat and went to the desk. Cody had turned one of the chairs around and was straddling it, while Nestor stood near the open cellblock door and peered through it. As Travis sat down, the big man shut the door, then lumbered over to the desk. In what passed for quiet tones, he said, "I been tryin' all night to figger out where I seen that Cotter feller before, Marshal, and I think I've finally remembered."

Travis leaned back in his chair and looked up at Nestor. "You know Cotter?" he asked.

"I know of him. Seen him a few times down at Fort Griffin when I was still huntin' buffler. That was what finally made me recollect where I knew him from, that nickname of his."

Travis nodded, remembering that the man was called Buff Cotter. "He was a hunter, too?"

"That's right. I never rode with him, but I heard he was a mighty good shot. Must've been, 'cause every time I saw him in Fort Griffin he had plenty o' money. And he weren't shy about spendin' it, neither. He was right fond o' gals and booze, the way I remember it. 'Course, he weren't the only one." Nestor rubbed the back of his hand across his mouth. Not very long ago Nestor had been a drunkard himself. Travis knew he must be remembering those times. After a moment Nestor went on, "If my memory ain't playin' tricks on me, Cotter got in a few scrapes with the law while he was down there in Texas, too. Had a run-in one night with a big feller on a sorrel hoss, and I heard later that the man was a Ranger. How somebody like that wound up bein' a deputy hisself, I just don't know."

Travis shook his head. "It's not that unusual. Plenty of men have been on both sides of the law at one time or another in their lives. As long as Cotter's still not wanted anywhere—and I can't find any record that he is—it doesn't matter what he's done."

Cody spoke up. "Are you going to let them go this morning?"

"I suppose so," Travis said and nodded slowly. "They paid the damages, and I said one night in jail would be enough of a fine for what they did." He opened the desk drawer, took out a ring of keys, and stood up. "Have they had any breakfast yet?"

"No, we haven't gotten around to it," Cody replied.

"They can fend for themselves, then," Travis said. He started toward the cellblock.

At that moment the front door of the office opened, and Leslie Gibson stalked into the building, his face dark with anger. He brandished a folded newspaper and asked, "Have you seen this?"

"Well, good morning, Leslie," Travis said dryly. "Have we seen what?"

"There's a story in today's *Clarion* about a fight in the

Bull's Head last night," Leslie explained, opening the paper to the front page and dropping it on Travis's desk. "The paper makes it sound like Dawes broke it up all by himself while you, Cody, and Nestor stood by helplessly."

Cody got up and hurried over to the desk. "Let me see that," he said hotly. He turned the paper so that he could scan the columns, and after a moment he looked up at Travis. "Leslie's right, Marshal. Emmett Valentine doesn't even say that it was Dawes's men who started the blasted fight in the first place!"

"What really happened, Luke?" Leslie asked, making a visible effort to calm himself.

"Dawes got a little ahead of himself," Travis told him. "He sent for the men who are going to be his deputies, and when they saw a little ruckus in the saloon, they tried to break it up and arrest the cowboys who started it. That turned a small fight into a big one." He went on to tell Leslie about Dawes's part in the affair.

When Travis finished, the schoolteacher sighed heavily. "The man is a master," Leslie said with grudging admiration. "I've never seen anyone like him."

Travis inclined his head toward the cellblock. "I'm about to let his men go," he said. "Hadn't you better get on to school, Leslie?"

"I suppose you're right," Leslie replied. "I am going to be a little late." He grinned sheepishly. "That's not a very good example for a teacher to set. I'll see you later, Luke."

"So long," Travis said, and Nestor and Cody echoed the farewell. When the door had closed behind Leslie, Travis turned to the cellblock; he did not even glance at the newspaper still spread out on the desk.

Cotter, Geraghty, and Rogers were all in the largest cell, which had four bunks. Geraghty was sprawled on one of the bunks, his hat pulled down over his eyes and a cigarette dangling from his mouth. Cotter was standing at the barred window, peering out at the cool autumn morning, while Rogers was sitting on another bunk, whistling a tune. Rogers stopped short and stood up as Travis strode to the cell door.

"You letting us out?" the young man asked.

"I said I was going to this morning, didn't I?"

"How the hell did we know you'd keep your word?" Cotter growled.

Travis thrust the key into the lock and twisted it. "I generally do," he said, letting it go at that. He did not want to be drawn into an argument. He swung the cell door open and stepped back so that they could file out.

Rogers came first, followed by Cotter and then Geraghty, who seemed a bit groggy, as if he was having trouble waking up. As he walked out of the cellblock, he rubbed a hand over his face and said, "I need an eye-opener."

"Just see that you don't cause any more trouble," Travis snapped. He went to the cabinet where the prisoners' guns had been stored, opened it, and handed over the coiled shell belts and holsters.

"We're not here to cause trouble, Marshal," Lin Rogers said as he buckled his gun belt. "Once that election is over, we'll be stopping it instead."

Cody stepped up to Rogers and fixed him with a level stare. "Not inside the town limits," he said. "That's up to us."

"We'll see," Rogers replied coolly. Anger sparked in his brown eyes as he met Cody's belligerent gaze.

Cotter caught Rogers's arm. "Come on, kid," he rasped. "We've spent enough time in here. I want to get out and get the stink out of my nose." He directed a meaningful glance at Nestor, who as usual was wearing his thick buffalo coat.

"Reckon you ought to be used to the smell of buffler, Cotter," Nestor said as the three men started toward the door. "You shot enough of 'em and sold the hides down there in Texas."

Cotter stopped short, his eyes growing narrower than they already were. "You know me, mister?" he demanded.

"Seen you around," Nestor replied. "I spent some time down at Fort Griffin, too, and all around the Staked Plains."

"Then you know I ain't a man to cross," Cotter snapped.

Nestor snorted. "Then how come that Texas Ranger put the run on you?"

Cotter paled. "You son of a—"

Geraghty grabbed his arm, just as Cotter had pulled Rogers away from Cody a moment earlier. "Let's go, let's go," Geraghty said impatiently. "I need a drink."

"Yeah, sure." Cotter let himself be led out of the office, but he glared over his shoulder at Nestor as he went. Rogers and Cody were exchanging similarly hostile looks.

Travis sat down behind the desk and sighed. He had thought that once the election was over, things would settle back to normal. He was going to make an honest effort to work with Dawes and get along with him. But with sheriff's deputies like those three around, the election could be just the beginning of Abilene's troubles.

Lin Rogers drew a deep breath as he paused on the boardwalk outside the marshal's office. It felt good to be out. Spending a night on the wrong side of a cell door had bothered him more than he expected it would, more than he cared to admit. He had never been in that situation before.

"Come on, kid, let's get a drink," Jim Geraghty said.

"Better not go back to the Bull's Head," Cotter added. "Let's mosey down to the Alamo instead. I've heard about that place."

Rogers had heard of Abilene's famous Alamo Saloon, too, but he was not in the mood for a drink. Hunger gnawed at his belly; food sounded much more appealing than whiskey.

"I think I'll get some breakfast," he said to his two companions. "You fellas want to come with me?"

Geraghty shuddered. "Bacon and eggs and flapjacks on an empty stomach? No thanks."

"Me, neither," Cotter said.

"Well then, I guess I'll see you back at the hotel later." Rogers grinned. "I guess we shouldn't have checked in. We never got to use the rooms except to leave our gear there."

"Don't worry about it," Cotter told him. "John Henry said the rooms were on him till after the election. We can find another place then."

"You really think John Henry's going to win?"

Cotter and Geraghty looked at each other and grinned. "Kid," Geraghty said, "I can guarantee it."

"I thought so," Rogers replied, returning the knowing smile. He lifted a hand. "Well, I'll see you later."

Cotter and Geraghty were still grinning as he turned away and began looking for a place to eat. A building on the other side of Texas Street caught his eye. Painted on its large curtained window were the words SUNRISE CAFÉ. That sounded promising. Rogers started across the street toward it.

Abilene looked like a nice town, he thought, glancing up and down the broad avenue with its one- and two-story frame buildings. Businesses were already open for the day. Customers were bustling in and out of the stores, and wagons were rolling down the street. Rogers paused to let a buckboard pass and smiled at the man and woman on the seat. They returned the smile, the man nodding pleasantly. Yes, sir, a nice town, Rogers thought. A growing town, just the kind of place that needed a good strong man like John Henry Dawes around to make sure it continued to grow and stayed peaceful and friendly.

Rogers had not been a lawman for very long, but he had already learned a great deal from Dawes. He had grown up on a ranch in New Mexico, but the prospect of punching cows for the rest of his life never appealed to him. Drifting into Santa Fe when Dawes was the sheriff there, he signed on as a deputy, teaming up with Cotter and Geraghty. They followed Dawes to Ysleta, then headed to Fort Worth while Dawes came to Kansas in reply to a letter from one of the local businessmen who wanted him to run for sheriff. The wire from Dawes summoning them caught up to them in Fort Worth, and they boarded a stage bound for Arkansas, where they made connections with the railroad. It had been a long journey, but it was starting to look as though all the arduous travel was going to be worth it.

Rogers knew one thing—he would have gone to hell and back for another chance to work with John Henry Dawes. There was no one in the world he admired more.

A bell over the door tinkled prettily as Rogers entered the Sunrise Café. He took his hat off and looked around at the homey room. Tables covered with cheerful, red-checked cloths were arranged around the room. There were booths along the front wall and a counter at the rear. The place was doing a brisk breakfast business. All the stools at the counter were occupied, as were most of the tables and booths.

"Good morning, sir. There's a table right over there. Why don't you have a seat, and I'll be right with you."

Rogers turned to see who had spoken and saw a young woman wearing a brown dress and white apron. She was holding a tray laden with food and was heading toward one of the tables. But as she glanced back at Rogers, she smiled, and he suddenly felt as if someone had punched him in the belly. Lord, she was pretty!

Lush red hair tumbled to her shoulders, and she had large green eyes that reminded him of a lake high in the mountains. Her cheeks were rosy, probably from the heat of the kitchen, but the color only made her more beautiful. The apron did little to conceal the ripe curves of her supple body. She was around twenty years old, Rogers guessed, and so lovely that he was still having trouble catching his breath.

She delivered the food to the table and came back to the spot where he was still standing. Frowning slightly, she asked, "Didn't you hear me, sir? You can sit down. I'll be right with you."

"Uh, thank you, ma'am," he managed to say, twisting his tan hat in his hands. "I . . . I'll do that."

Looking slightly perplexed, she went around the counter and through a door that had to lead to the kitchen. Rogers threaded his way among the tables to the vacant one she had indicated, bumping into one on the way because he was watching the doorway, waiting for her reappearance. He glanced down and muttered an apology to the people he had jostled, then went and sat down. As he placed his hat on the other chair at the table, he thought once again that he was certainly going to like Abilene now more than ever.

The redheaded waitress emerged from the kitchen a few minutes later, bearing another tray of food. She smiled at Rogers as she passed his table. He returned the smile, then forced his eyes off her and turned to look at the menu chalked on a large blackboard behind the counter. By the time she came back to his table, pad and pencil in hand, he had decided what he wanted to order.

"Now, then," she said, "what can I get for you?"

Rogers swallowed and had trouble finding his voice for a moment. He was usually not this awkward in the presence of a pretty woman, but this one was something special. Finally he managed to say, "I'll have sausage and hash browns and a double stack of flapjacks."

She cocked an eyebrow quizzically and commented, "That's a lot of food."

Rogers patted his flat stomach and grinned. "Always have had a big appetite. Reckon I'm still a growing boy."

"I'll get it for you." She started to turn away.

Rogers stopped her by saying quickly, "Ma'am?" When she looked back, he went on, "My name's Linwood Rogers, ma'am, but my friends call me Lin." He put a slight questioning inflection on his words to let her know that he was waiting for a response.

"Well, I'm pleased to meet you, Mr. Rogers," the waitress replied noncommittally. She was still smiling, however. "I'm Agnes Hirsch, and I'll be right back with your food."

"Thank you, ma'am."

As she disappeared into the kitchen, Rogers leaned back in his chair and sighed. *Agnes* . . . The name suited her.

Gradually he became aware that several people in the café were stealing glances at him. The story of the fight in the Bull's Head had no doubt gotten around town, and they were probably wondering if he was one of Dawes's deputies. Soon, after the election was over, he would get to know most of these people as he settled in at his new job. And there was no one he wanted to know better than Agnes Hirsch.

When she set the platters down in front of him, he said, "Thank you kindly, Miss Hirsch." He breathed in deeply, savoring the delicious aromas wafting up from the hot sausage, hash browns, and flapjacks. "Smells mighty fine. There's just one more thing I need."

"What's that?" Agnes asked.

"I need you to sit down and have breakfast with me, ma'am."

Agnes looked surprised for a moment, then shook her head. "I'm sorry, Mr. Rogers, I can't do that. I have to work." She nodded toward the other customers. "You can see that we're busy."

"Yes, ma'am. But it's a shame. There's nothing a fella likes better than good food and a beautiful woman across the table from him."

Her cheeks glowed red again, but this time it was from the blush that washed over her. Surely she had been told before that she was beautiful, Rogers thought.

"I understand you've got to do your job, though. You go right ahead. And I thank you for not taking offense at the words of a man who's been struck almost dumb just from watching you." Now that he was over his initial discomfiture, his easygoing charm was asserting itself again. He meant every word he said, and that sincerity came through in his voice.

"Well, thank you, Mr. Rogers," Agnes began.

"Lin," he told her again.

Agnes smiled. "Lin. Will I be seeing you again?"

"Yes, ma'am." Rogers picked up his fork, took a bite of the flapjacks, and chewed. He swallowed and went on, "I can guarantee it."

Just as Cotter and Geraghty had said about the election. Well, Rogers thought, now he had an even better reason to want John Henry Dawes to win. A redheaded reason named Agnes.

# Chapter Seven

———◆———

ELECTION DAY DAWNED BRIGHT AND CLEAR, WITH A BRISK tang of fall in the air. After the sun had been up for an hour, though, the day began to turn warm. It promised to be pleasant, and that would mean a large turnout for the election. The polling place, which was located in the town hall, opened at nine o'clock, and people were already standing in line to vote then. The voting would continue until six that evening.

School was not in session, and all the bars were closed until the election was over. Sitting at a long table inside the town hall were Orion McCarthy and Thurman Simpson, two of the people affected by those closures. Both of them were serving as election judges. The third judge, sitting beside Simpson, was Mason Kincaid.

Travis's mouth tightened as he stepped into the building to cast his own vote around midmorning. He had known that Kincaid was going to serve as one of the judges, but seeing the land agent waiting there with a smirk on his face still grated on him.

"Good mornin', Lucas," Orion said as he got up and came over to shake Travis's hand. "Ha' ye come t'vote?"

"That's right," Travis said. "Good turnout so far?" He looked around. The stream of voters had slacked off to a trickle, but he knew it would pick up later. Many of the farmers and ranchers in the outlying reaches of the county would want to do their chores before they came into town to vote. The election could well be decided in the late afternoon.

"Aye, 'tis been busy at times," Orion answered. He glanced at Simpson and Kincaid, then lowered his voice and went on, "Dinna ye worry, Lucas. I'll see t'it tha' th' election is conducted fairly an' th' ballots counted right. 'Twill be an honest count, I kin promise ye tha'."

Travis smiled at his friend. "I'm not worried about that, not with you on hand. And while Thurman Simpson and I may not always get along too well, I believe he's an honest man."

Orion nodded grudgingly. "Aye, I suppose ye be right about tha'. An' Kincaid is so sure his man will win, he will no' bother t'cheat."

Travis's grin broadened, and he clapped Orion on the shoulder. "Well, I'd better cast my vote." He walked over to the table, nodded to Simpson and Kincaid, and continued, "Good morning, gentlemen."

"Here to vote, Marshal?" Kincaid asked with a smile.

"That's right."

Thurman Simpson sniffed and said, "You swear that you're a lawful citizen of Dickinson County?"

Travis did not let his irritation show on his face. Simpson was just following the rules by asking the question. "I do," Travis replied.

Simpson pushed the polling list across the table to him. "Sign this."

Travis signed as required, then received his ballot from Kincaid. Orion had resumed his place at the table, behind the big wooden box where the completed ballots were to be placed. The box was sturdy, and its top was fastened with a heavy lock. Only three men had keys to that lock, Travis knew—the three election judges. When the voting was finished, Orion, Kincaid, and Simpson would lock the doors of the town hall, unlock the ballot box, and count the votes. The system was a good one, Travis thought. It had worked for a long time, and regardless of the outcome of this particular election, it would continue to work.

As several more voters came in, Travis took his ballot to another table and picked up one of the pencils lying there. His name and that of John Henry Dawes were written on the piece of paper. Quickly he circled his own name, folded the ballot, and returned to the first table. He dropped the ballot through the slot in the top of the wooden box and nodded to the judges. "Thank you, gentlemen," he said.

Travis walked out of the town hall and paused on the boardwalk to take a deep breath. He had done all he could. From here on, it was out of his hands.

Cody Fisher and Nestor Gilworth had already voted. In fact, Cody had been one of the first to cast his ballot that morning. That left the two of them free to keep an eye on the streets of Abilene during the day, along with Augie, the young blond bartender from Orion's Tavern. With the tavern closed until that evening, Augie had volunteered to help out as a deputy, a duty he had taken on a few previous occasions. The youngster looked up to Travis, Cody, and Nestor, and while he was happy working for Orion, his real ambition was to become a lawman.

"Lots of folks in town today," he said as he stood on the boardwalk with Cody and Nestor, surveying Texas Street.

"Everybody's coming in for the election," Cody replied. "It'll be busy all day."

As on any other occasion when an unusually large number of people crowded into Abilene, a festive air pervaded the town. The last time this many folks had come in was the Fourth of July, but Cody had been out of town and missed this year's festivities.

Election Day was probably not going to provide much reason for celebration, though, at least not for Luke Travis's supporters. Cody hated to admit it, but the odds were good that John Henry Dawes was going to win. That was a bitter pill to swallow, but Cody told himself that if Travis could accept it graciously, so could he.

As Cody looked across Texas Street, a flash of red hair caught his eye. He had been leaning against one of the posts that supported the awning over the boardwalk. He straightened as he saw Agnes Hirsch emerge from the Sunrise Café on the arm of a young, slender, brown-haired man.

Cody caught his breath. The man with Agnes was Lin Rogers, one of Dawes's deputies. Cody had seen Rogers and the other two, Cotter and Geraghty, around town a few times since the brawl in the Bull's Head. The three would-be deputies seemed to be staying out of trouble, but Cody still did not trust them any more than he trusted Dawes. What the devil was Agnes doing with Rogers? Cody wondered.

Nestor nudged him in the side and nodded toward the opposite boardwalk. "Take a look over yonder," he rumbled.

"I see," Cody said tightly, watching Agnes and Rogers stroll down the boardwalk.

Augie had noticed the pair, too. "Why, that's Agnes Hirsch," he said in surprise. "I thought she was sweet on you, Cody."

"So did I." Ever since Agnes had arrived in Abilene with her younger brother, Michael, she had had a crush on Cody. Michael Hirsch looked up to him and wanted nothing more than for his sister to marry the handsome young deputy someday. But while Cody was genuinely fond of both of them, he had never thought seriously about a romantic relationship with Agnes. At first she seemed to be too young for him. Now he had to admit she had grown into a beautiful woman, but he was still unsure about letting their friendship develop into anything stronger.

In that case, he asked himself, why did it bother him so much to see her walking with Lin Rogers, smiling and laughing and talking?

He was not jealous, he decided. He simply did not trust Rogers. The man was a troublemaker, after all.

Nestor was grinning as he said, " 'Pears the gal's traded one deputy for another, don't it, Augie?"

"It sure looks that way to me, Mr. Gilworth."

Cody glared at them. "You two go ahead and joke about it all you want. I don't like that Rogers fella, and I'm not sure an innocent girl like Agnes ought to be getting involved with him."

"Why don't you go over there and tell them that?" Nestor asked.

Cody took a deep breath. "Agnes may be a little innocent, what with living in that orphanage for so long, but I never said she wasn't grown up. She can make her own decisions. Nothing says I have to like them."

"Suit yourself." Nestor shrugged. "If I took a shine to a pretty gal like that, though, I reckon I wouldn't want her carryin' on with some other feller."

"Who said I took a shine to Agnes?" Cody demanded.

"Hold on. Nobody said that. You hear anybody say that, Augie?"

Augie shook his head. "No, sir, Mr. Gilworth, I didn't hear anybody say that."

"You two go ahead and make your jokes," Cody snapped. "I'm going to take a turn around town." Without waiting for a reply, he strode off.

But as he left, a glance told him that Agnes and Rogers were still walking together and seemed to be having the time of their lives.

Agnes Hirsch saw Cody Fisher stalking along the boardwalk on the other side of Texas Street. It was difficult to see his face; several wagons and riders were making their way along the thoroughfare. But from his rapid gait and the stiff way he was holding himself, he seemed to be upset about something.

Had he seen her walking with Lin Rogers? And if he had, would that bother him?

Agnes had done everything a respectable young woman could do to let Cody know she was interested in him. She had even considered doing some things that were not so respectable, although she never would have admitted that to anyone. But nothing seemed to get through to Cody and make him aware of how she really felt about him. That had always bothered her.

Not that she was lacking for suitors. There were any number of young men in Abilene who would not have minded courting her, ranging from those horrible Barlow brothers to Emmett Valentine, the newspaper reporter. But no one had been able to arouse the feelings in her that Cody Fisher did—until Lin Rogers came along.

"You look like you're concentrating on something mighty hard," his voice came from beside her.

Agnes glanced at Lin and smiled. "I'm sorry. I guess my thoughts did drift off. It's just that today is such an exciting day. My mind is all awhirl."

That was true enough. Ever since Lin had come into the café several mornings earlier, she felt as though she had been swept along on a current that she could not control. He had begun taking every meal there, and after a couple of days, his compliments and charm and good looks had started to win her over. When he invited her to have dinner with him at the Alhambra, she accepted. That was the first time she had ever eaten at the restaurant, and she was tremendously impressed by it. But she was even more impressed by Linwood Rogers.

Was it possible, she found herself wondering, that she was falling in love with him?

She did not know much about Rogers, but as they spent more time together, she learned about his background. He was easygoing, had a gentle wit, and could play a guitar and sing better than anyone she had ever heard. She supposed he could use the gun he carried on his hip if he had to and handle himself well in a fight—he had been a deputy in some tough towns, after all—but she never saw that side of him.

"There's plenty of folks in town today, all right," he was saying. "I guess most of them came to vote, or at least to watch the goings-on."

"I suppose so. I'll really have to go back to the café later. We're probably going to be very busy."

"Sure. I'll walk you back. I just thought you might like a look at the excitement."

Agnes glanced at the traffic on the street. The boardwalks were crowded, too. "It is exciting," she admitted. "Sometimes Abilene seems like such a sleepy little town, even though I know it really isn't."

"It's a good town," Lin said. "I'm going to like working here—for lots of reasons."

Agnes felt herself blushing as he looked at her meaningfully. She knew perfectly well what he was getting at. To change the subject, she said, "You sound convinced that Mr. Dawes is going to win."

"Of course he is," Lin declared. "John Henry has won every election he's ever been in. Didn't know that, did you?"

Agnes shook her head. "No, I didn't."

"He'll beat Marshal Travis, too. You just wait and see. It won't even be close, I'll bet."

Agnes made no reply. She caught at her lower lip with her teeth and chewed it for a second. This unexpected attraction she felt for Lin Rogers had really put her in a quandary. She had never paid much attention to politics, but if anyone had asked her before meeting Lin whom she was supporting in the election for sheriff, she would have said Luke Travis. Her admiration for Travis and her affection for Cody would have prompted that unequivocal response. But if Travis won, John Henry Dawes would surely leave town, taking his deputies with him. That meant she would never see Lin Rogers again. Agnes was not sure she could stand that.

Even though she felt disloyal for thinking it, she hoped that Dawes would win the election. If that happened, then Lin would be around Abilene for a long time. And that was exactly what Agnes wanted.

Travis found his nerves stretching taut as the day went on. He told himself not to worry about the election; the outcome would not be known until evening. After the polls closed, it would take Orion, Simpson, and Kincaid a couple of hours to count the votes. Until then, there was no point in concerning himself with it.

But he still found himself glancing toward the town hall as he walked along the boardwalks, keeping an eye open for trouble.

He had heard that some of the cowboys who came into town to vote were unhappy that the saloons were closed. The punchers had been given a little time off to cast their ballots, and they probably figured they ought to be able to get a drink while they were at it.

Travis saw Cody, Nestor, and Augie coming down the boardwalk toward him. He nodded to them and said, "How does everything look?"

"Peaceful, Marshal," Cody replied. "Folks seem to be behaving themselves."

"Heard anything about how the vote's goin'?" Nestor asked.

Travis shook his head. "No, and we won't until it's over. That's the way it works, Nestor. Not even the election judges have any idea which way the vote is running."

Augie spoke up. "Well, we know which way it's going to come out, don't we?" The young man's voice was enthusiastic.

Travis knew Augie was just trying to be optimistic, but there was a touch of pessimism in his own voice as he said, "Yes, I reckon we do, Augie. Dawes is going to win."

"Now, you shouldn't say that, Marshal. You've got just as good a chance as he does. *I* voted for you."

Travis clapped the youngster on the shoulder. "Thanks, Augie. I appreciate that."

"Reckon all of us voted for you, Marshal," Nestor said. "Don't you go givin' up. You might be surprised how it comes out."

"We'll see," Travis replied.

He was about to suggest that they go back to the office for a cup of coffee when he noticed a commotion across the street. A group of men was standing in front of the locked doors of the Old Fruit Saloon, and one of them started pounding on the doors and shouting, "Hey, open up in there! Can't a man get a drink around here?"

Travis frowned as the man's companions echoed his demand. The marshal could hear the loud, angry words plainly, even at this distance. All the men were dressed in dusty range clothes and battered hats. Travis nodded toward them and asked Cody, "You recognize those boys?"

Cody looked across the street, where one of the men was still banging on the doors and yelling. "I think they ride for the Rafter D," the deputy said.

"Hunter Dixon's spread," Travis murmured. The marshal knew the powerful rancher had endorsed Dawes for sheriff, leading many of his fellow cattlemen to do the same. Dawes promised to put an end to rustling in the county. The pledge was going to be almost impossible to keep, Travis knew, but it sounded good, and that seemed to be what mattered to the ranchers.

"We'd better go over there and tell them to move on," Travis continued. "I don't want any ruckuses. Some of those hotheaded cowboys might claim we were harder than necessary on them because Dixon's been supporting Dawes."

"That's ridiculous," Cody snorted. "We wouldn't do anything like that."

"We know that," Travis said. "Other folks might not."

The deputies nodded in agreement, and Travis stepped from the boardwalk and led them across the street.

The cowboy who had started the racket was now kicking at the saloon door and cursing loudly and profanely. Another puncher drew his gun, growled at the first one to step aside, and moved up to hammer on the door with the butt of his pistol.

"That'll be enough of that!" Travis said sharply from behind them. Several men started in surprise, and all of them looked around to see who had spoken. Travis went on, "The saloons are closed during the election; you men ought to know that. They'll be open again tonight. You can get your drink then."

"But we wan' drinks now!" one of the punchers cried. From the way he slurred his words and swayed unsteadily, Travis guessed he had already been drinking somewhere.

"Yeah, we're out of booze," another man said, holding up an empty flask.

Cody frowned. "What do we do, Marshal?" he asked softly.

"There's no law against drinking," Travis replied, "just against selling the stuff during an election. As long as they came by it legally, before the election started, there's nothing we can do about that." He raised his voice to address the cowboys. "But you men are going to have to stop creating a disturbance. Move along now. If you want something to do, go down to the town hall and vote."

"Already did," one of the cowhands said with a harsh laugh. "Voted for that Dawes feller. Reckon now you'll try to throw us in jail 'cause we didn't vote for you."

Travis shook his head. "Nope, that's your own business. I don't want to throw you in jail. I just want you to stop cussing and trying to knock that door down."

The Rafter D rider who had first knocked on the door shook his head. "Hell with this," he said disgustedly. He turned back to the door and lifted a foot. "I'm gettin' me a drink."

Before anyone could stop him, he slammed the heel of

his boot against the locked door, shattering the facing and causing the panel to burst open.

"Dammit!" Travis muttered. He stepped forward quickly as the man started into the saloon. Grabbing the cowboy's shoulder, Travis said sharply, "Hold on—"

"Look out, Marshal!" Cody shouted.

Travis jerked around in time to see one of the men swinging a fist at him. He moved smoothly aside and let the blow go past him. But the distraction allowed the first man to spin around and throw a punch. The cowhand's knobby fist caught Travis on the side of the head, staggering him for a second.

With an angry roar Nestor lunged past Travis, gathering up the man who had hit the marshal in a bear hug. Then Cody and Augie leapt into the fray as the other cowboys surged forward angrily.

Within seconds the boardwalk in front of the Old Fruit Saloon was crowded with battling men. There were eight cowboys facing the four lawmen, but the punchers were drunk. That made quite a difference. Travis drove a blow into one man's stomach, doubling him over, while Nestor squeezed the air out of the man he held and then flung him into the path of two more men, spilling them both. Cody blocked a punch, then threw a hard right that spun his opponent and dropped him to the planks. Augie was the only one having trouble. Three of the cowboys rushed him, forcing him to give ground. As Augie backed up, his right foot slipped off the edge of the boardwalk. He threw his hands in the air and yelled as he tumbled into the street.

Nestor's blunt fingers caught the collars of two of the men who had attacked Augie and jerked them back. A hard shove sent one of them staggering toward Cody, who was waiting to knock him off his feet with a well-timed blow. Nestor whirled the other man around and backhanded him. The man bounced off the saloon's wall and pitched onto his face.

Meanwhile, Augie had scrambled back to his feet and

was meeting the charge of the final combatant. He lowered his head and dove, slamming his shoulder into the cowboy's midsection in a vicious tackle that sent both men flying off the boardwalk. All the air whooshed out of the man's lungs when he landed heavily in the dusty street. Augie climbed to his hands and knees first, and he cracked his fist against the cowboy's jaw as he tried to get up.

Travis took a deep breath and slipped his Peacemaker out of its holster. The fight had drawn quite a crowd; the circle of onlookers surrounding them was four or five people deep. Travis said in a loud voice, "All right, folks, the show's over. Go on about your business."

One of the townsmen indicated the cowboys, all of whom were shaking their heads groggily as they tried to get to their feet. "What about them, Marshal? I heard one of them say you were going to put them in jail because they voted against you."

Travis felt a surge of anger. Were these people blind? he wondered. But he made an effort to control his temper. "Nobody's going to jail," he said evenly. "These boys are going to have to pay for kicking in this door, but if they're willing to do that, I think they'd be better off riding out to their spread to cool off."

"What about the fight they started?" Cody wanted to know.

"Everybody's a little tense today," Travis replied. "I say we let it go as long as they behave themselves from here on out. What about it?" He looked at each of his deputies in turn.

Slowly Cody, Nestor, and Augie nodded, although their expressions plainly showed they were not happy about the decision. Travis knew he was bending over backward in order to appear fair to the cowboys, and he hoped this move would not come back to haunt him.

The fight had been knocked out of Dixon's punchers. Grudgingly they came up with the money to repair the door and handed it over. As they trudged away, a few of them cast hostile glances over their shoulders.

Cody said, "They're liable to find a bottle somewhere else and start all over again."

"If they do, we'll deal with it," Travis told him. "I don't think they'll cause much trouble—"

He broke off as he heard someone calling his name from down the boardwalk. Turning, he saw Sheriff Roy Wade hurrying toward them, an agitated look on his face. Travis frowned.

"There's been some trouble, Marshal," Wade said as he reached them, puffing slightly. "I just got word that Whitson feller and his gang hit Possum Wells a little while ago." The settlement Wade named was a tiny hamlet northeast of Abilene.

Travis stiffened. He had been certain Whitson had left the area; this was the first report of a raid by the gang in quite a while. "Was anybody hurt?" he asked.

"Don't know," Wade said. "One of the settlers rode in and told me Whitson's bunch shot up the place pretty bad."

"Why are you telling us about it, Sheriff?" Cody asked.

Wade took a deep breath. Looking at Travis, he answered Cody's question by saying, "I thought maybe you could take a ride out there and try to pick up Whitson's trail while it's fresh, Marshal."

Travis looked surprised. What Wade was suggesting was exactly the sort of thing he had done for quite a while after becoming the marshal of Abilene. Wade had never objected in those days, and Travis always figured that whatever happened in the surrounding countryside affected Abilene itself. Only in recent months had Wade become touchy about jurisdictional boundaries.

Nestor snorted. "Well, that's a fine howdy-do," he began. "First you tell us we ain't got no authority outside the town limits, then—"

"Nestor," Travis said sharply, cutting him off, "Sheriff Wade has made a request of us, and as fellow lawmen, I think we ought to honor it." That decision made, Travis went on, "Cody and I will ride out to Possum Wells and take a look around. Nestor and Augie can keep an eye on things here in town." He fixed Nestor with a level stare. "I'm counting on you and Augie."

Nestor nodded. "Sure, Marshal. We'll do like you say."

"Don't worry about a thing, Marshal," Augie added, grinning now. He was obviously pleased that Travis trusted him with part of this responsibility.

Cody looked baffled by Travis's compliance, but he went along without complaint as Travis strode toward the livery stable where their horses were. The deputy said, "Wonder why Wade didn't ask Dawes to chase Whitson?"

"Dawes isn't the sheriff yet," Travis said grimly. He was wondering what they would find when they reached Possum Wells.

# Chapter Eight

To call Possum Wells a wide place in the road would have been generous. The settlement consisted of a church, a general store, a tavern, and a cluster of houses. Two wagon roads intersected here, which was the only reason the little community existed at all.

And it was a safe bet that that was the entire population of Possum Wells standing around on the porch of the store, Travis thought, as he and Cody rode up. The group of angry-looking citizens regarded the two lawmen somewhat suspiciously. Several men had crude, bloodstained bandages tied around arms or legs. The storekeeper, identifiable by his apron, had a cloth wrapped around his balding head. He glared up at Travis and demanded, "Where's the sheriff? I sent for the sheriff."

"Sheriff Wade asked me and my deputy to ride out and find out what happened," Travis replied, swinging down from his horse.

"What happened?" the storekeeper repeated queru-
lously. "I'll tell you what happened. That no-good bunch
of desperadoes came in here and pistol-whipped me and
stole all my money! Not to mention carrying off a couple
of weeks' worth of supplies."

"They robbed everybody they saw on the street, too!"
cried another man. "Made us fork over our valuables,
then started shootin'. If we hadn't all dived for cover,
somebody would have got killed, sure as hell!"

Travis spotted the fresh bullet holes in the wall of the
general store. From the looks of it Whitson and his men
had sat on their horses and blazed away at the building
before galloping out. Travis looked back at the storekeeper and asked, "How do you know it was Whitson?"

"He told us so!" the man exclaimed. "Said we'd always
remember the day Mike Whitson came to town. He had
the look of a mad dog as he said it, too. It's just pure luck
they didn't kill all of us!"

The other settlers angrily called out their agreement.
Travis nodded and held up his hands to quiet them. "All
right, did anybody see which way they went when they
left?"

"They headed north," one man said. "Or at least that
was the way they were going when they rode out. No
telling which direction they wound up going."

Travis nodded. The man was right; Whitson and his
gang could have headed in any direction once they were
out of town, but at least he and Cody had a starting place.
"Thanks," he said as he mounted up again. "We'll see if
we can pick up their trail."

He turned his horse away from the store and slowly
walked the animal around the building, Cody falling in
alongside him. They spotted the tracks within moments,
the marks of a large group of riders leaving Possum Wells
in a hurry. The autumn rains had not yet come, so the
ground was relatively dry but not so hard that it would
not take tracks. The two lawmen were able to follow the
trail at a brisk trot, leaving the settlement behind them.

"Something strike you as funny about this, Marshal?" Cody asked after a few minutes.

Travis nodded. "It doesn't seem like Whitson could make enough of a haul in Possum Wells to make the raid worth his while. Judging from the way they shot the place up, they may have burned almost enough ammunition to make up for what they stole."

"It doesn't make sense," Cody agreed. "What could Whitson have been thinking?"

"I don't know," Travis said, "but we'll ask him when we catch up to him."

Back in Abilene the election was proceeding smoothly. The polls would not close for several hours, and voting was still brisk. According to Thurman Simpson, who had served as an election judge before, today's turnout was going to be perhaps the largest ever in the area.

Eight voters were marking their ballots in the town hall when the door suddenly burst open. The townsman who stuck his head through the opening shouted, "Fire! There's a fire over at the Cunningham warehouse!"

Orion surged to his feet. "How bad is't?" he demanded.

"Plenty! Looks like it might spread!"

With that, the man rushed away, leaving confusion and anxiety behind him. Orion frowned as he looked at Simpson and Kincaid. The men who were voting rushed over to the table, stuffed their ballots into the box, and ran out.

"Well?" Orion said to his fellow judges. "Be we going or no'?"

"We can't go!" Simpson exclaimed. "We have to stay here and watch the ballot box!"

Kincaid got to his feet. "Thurman's right, we should stay. But . . ." His voice faded, leaving unspoken the things that the other two men knew as well as he did.

The Cunningham warehouse, located near the Kansas Pacific depot, was used primarily for storing cotton. It would burn rapidly and fiercely, and there were other buildings nearby that might catch fire unless the blaze was put out quickly. Abilene had a volunteer fire department with its own water wagon, but this fire might be too much for it to handle. Bucket brigades to pass water from the public well on Cedar Street would probably be needed.

Frontier communities lived in dread of fire. When a blaze started, it could easily spread, burning a whole town to the ground. If that happened here, Abilene might never be able to recover.

"Sorry," Orion grunted. "I can no' stay, no' while tha' fire be burning. I'm going t'help." He headed for the door.

"Wait a minute!" Mason Kincaid called, shoving his chair back. When Orion looked over his shoulder, Kincaid surprised him by saying, "I'm going with you."

Thurman Simpson's hands fluttered anxiously as he watched Orion and Kincaid hurry out. He muttered to himself, "No one but the three of us has keys to the ballot box."

Simpson regarded his job as an election judge as part of his civic duty, but helping to prevent the town from being consumed in a fire was even more important. Snatching up the keys to the town hall from the table, he pulled down the window shades, locked the back door, then hurried out the front, locking that door behind him as well. The town was in an uproar, people everywhere streaming through the streets toward the spot where thick black smoke billowed into the clear blue sky. A long line of men was already forming into a bucket brigade, and Simpson hurried to join them, leaving the town hall quiet and empty and deserted behind him.

It stayed that way for perhaps ten minutes, then a slight scratching sound came abruptly from the back door. After a few moments the lock yielded, and the door swung open. A man slipped through, closing the door behind him and pausing to make sure he was alone before he continued on the errand that had brought him skulking here.

When he was certain he was alone in the building, Buff Cotter walked over to the table on which the ballot box sat. There was a grin on his red-bearded face. So far, this job had been easy. The lock on the alley door had been no trouble to pick, and he felt sure he would be able to relock it the same way.

The heavy padlock securing the lid of the ballot box was a different story. He knew he could probably pick it, too, given enough time undisturbed. Fortunately that would not be necessary. He withdrew a key from the pocket of his leather coat, thrust it into the padlock, and turned it. The lock sprang open, and Cotter's grin widened. The plan was working perfectly.

He scooped out several large handfuls of the ballots and began going through them rapidly. The ones that had been marked for Luke Travis went into one pile, those for Dawes into another. The pile for Dawes grew much more quickly than Travis's did. From the looks of it, Dawes was going to win this election quite handily.

"Reckon it's goin' to be a landslide," Cotter chuckled to himself. "Ain't no point in takin' chances, though."

He kept sorting the ballots until he had them all separated. Then he took a folded burlap bag from his coat pocket and shook it open. Making a quick count of the ballots cast for Travis, he slid about half of them into it. Pulling the bag shut, he then brought another one from his coat, this one stuffed full. He emptied it onto the table—all ballots marked for John Henry Dawes.

Moving a little more quickly now, Cotter shuffled through all the ballots, mixing the genuine ones in with the fraudulent. He picked them up and shoved them back into the ballot box. When all the ballots had been replaced, he quietly closed the lid and clicked the lock shut.

"No way John Henry can lose now," he muttered as he placed the bag with the stolen ballots inside his coat. He went to the front of the room and eased one of the window shades back just enough to allow him to peek out. He could see that the smoke coming from the warehouse fire was now drifting lazily up in thin streamers, indicating that the blaze was almost fully extinguished. The election judges and the voters would be returning to the town hall shortly. Cotter had to hand it to the man who had planned this—the timing had been just right.

Cotter went to the back door and slipped into the alley, using his lock pick and the skills acquired over a long, unscrupulous career to throw the latch back into place. The election could continue now with its outcome no longer in doubt—if it ever had been—and no one the wiser.

Cody Fisher frowned at the tracks on the ground and commented, "It sure doesn't look like they're trying to cover up their trail."

"No, it doesn't," Travis agreed. "Could be Whitson and his men are so sure nobody is going to catch them that they're not bothering to hide their tracks."

"Or they could be trying to lead us into a trap," Cody pointed out.

Travis nodded. "Could be."

The two lawmen were riding through the flat, open country north of Possum Wells. They had left the little settlement over an hour earlier. Mike Whitson and his gang had continued heading due north, which was a surprise to Travis. He had expected them to be a little evasive—unless, as Cody suggested, they were preparing to ambush anyone who pursued them.

"Keep your eyes open," Travis added, knowing that the advice was not really necessary. Cody was just as aware of the possible danger as he was.

On the horizon ahead of them was a line of scrubby trees, and Travis knew the brush marked the wandering course of a small creek. The outlaw gang's trail led directly toward the trees. Travis frowned as he and Cody drew within a hundred yards of the brush.

"Better slow down," he cautioned. "There's no telling—"

A glint of sunlight suddenly flashed off something in the scrub, and Travis broke off his warning as he started to whirl his horse around. Cody was following suit. Something whined past Travis's head, and an instant later he heard the crack of a rifle.

"There's that ambush!" Cody called out.

Travis waved at a small rise to their left. "Over there!" he barked. "That's the only cover around here!"

More slugs screamed past them as they galloped toward the grassy hillock. Neither man pulled his gun; the range was too far for pistols, and they had no time to break out their Winchesters. Besides, even the finest marksman could not shoot accurately from the back of a running horse.

Bullets kicked up dust both in front of and behind them. Travis grimaced when he saw the dirt spurting up ahead of him, then glanced back and saw the same thing. The ambushers had them bracketed, and that was bad. It was only a matter of time—

Cody yelled as his horse suddenly plunged out from under him. The deputy flew through the air but had the presence of mind to tuck his shoulder under and roll as he slammed into the ground, lessening the impact. He came up on one knee, hatless, dusty, and shaken, as Travis sharply drew rein.

"Come on!" Travis called, extending a hand.

Cody shook his head. He scurried over to his fallen horse. Blood was streaming out of a wound in the animal's neck. The horse had fallen with the Winchester's saddle boot on the top side, leaving the rifle easily accessible. Cody yanked it out of the scabbard and levered a round into the chamber.

"Get out of here!" he said savagely to Travis. "I'll cover you!"

Bullets whizzed by on either side of them as Travis replied, "I'm not leaving without you!"

Cody slammed a shot toward the trees, then surged to his feet and ran toward Travis's horse. He caught the marshal's outstretched hand and vaulted lithely up behind him. Travis dug his heels into the flanks of his horse and sent it leaping forward again, running fast despite its double burden.

They were less than a hundred feet from the rise, and the horse covered it quickly. The ambushers' bullets were still coming close, but none of them had struck anything since Cody's horse had fallen. As Travis's mount reached the slope, the marshal threw himself off its back and hauled on the reins to make it lie down. Cody was already off, his boots hitting the ground a split second after Travis's had. He sprawled in the short grass at the crest of the rise and began firing toward the creek.

Once the horse was down and out of the line of fire, Travis dropped to the ground beside Cody. Both men were excellent shots with the .44 -.40 Winchesters. They peppered the trees along the creek, firing as fast as they could work the levers.

"Look at that!" Cody cried a few minutes later during a lull in the shooting.

Peering through the screen of trees lining both banks of the creek, Travis spotted what Cody was pointing at. Men on horseback were pulling out, galloping away as fast as they could on the other side of the little stream.

"They're giving up the fight," Travis said, squinting into the gunsmoke hazing the air. "At least that's what it looks like. We'd better wait a few minutes just to make sure it's not another trap."

He and Cody lay still for several minutes; no more gunfire came from the brush. Finally Travis stood up, inviting a shot if one was going to come. None did.

"They're gone," he said disgustedly.

Cody got to his feet and gazed at his horse lying motionless on the prairie. "They slowed us down, all right," he said heavily. Carrying the Winchester, he trudged toward the fallen animal's body.

Travis's face was bleak as he followed his deputy. Cody had ridden that pinto pony ever since Travis first met him. A good horse was special, and Travis understood the pain his friend had to be feeling.

Kneeling beside the dead horse, Cody ran a hand over its shoulder, gently patting the black and white hide. "I've heard folks say they'd never have a paint horse in their string," he said quietly. "They say pintos don't have enough stamina. Well, I've never seen a horse with more heart than this one. He was a hell of a pony."

Travis dropped a hand on Cody's shoulder and squeezed. "I know. I'm sorry, Cody. But we've got to get back to Abilene."

Cody glanced up sharply. "What about Whitson?" he demanded.

"There's nothing we can do about him now," Travis said with a shake of his head. "We can't track him riding double. We'd never catch up. About all we can do is head back to town."

"You could leave me here and ride after Whitson," Cody suggested. "I can walk back to Possum Wells and find a horse there, then come after you."

Travis shook his head again. "You wouldn't reach the settlement by nightfall, not on foot. It's too dangerous out here for a man without a horse. Come on."

Cody sighed and stood up. "Guess you're right." He looked down at the pinto and went on, "But I've got a score to settle with Whitson now."

"You'll get your chance," Travis promised. "Now that we know he's still around here, it's going to be different next time. You can count on it."

# Chapter Nine

———◆———

**T**RAVIS'S HORSE WAS STRONG AND RELIABLE, BUT THE MAR-
shal held it to a slow pace since the mount was carrying
double. As a result, dusk was settling in when the two
lawmen reached Possum Wells. Travis's mouth tightened
as he heard laughter coming from some of the bystanders
loafing in front of the tavern. He supposed it was a rather
humorous sight—Abilene's marshal and deputy returning from their pursuit of outlaws, empty-handed and
with one less horse than they had when they started out.
They had tied Cody's saddle onto Travis's horse's back
behind them.

As Travis drew rein in front of the store, the storekeep-
er stepped onto the porch. He frowned at them and said,
"Looks like you didn't have any luck catching up to
Whitson."

"Some of his men ambushed us," Travis said shortly.
"We need to borrow a horse."

The storekeeper sighed and nodded. "I don't have a saddle horse, but you're welcome to borrow one of my wagon team."

Travis looked over his shoulder at the deputy. "That all right with you, Cody?"

"Reckon it'll have to be," Cody answered. His expression was still as somber as it had been when they left his pinto behind.

Travis refused the storekeeper's offer of some food, and the man fetched his wagon team from the barn behind the store. The horses were large, sturdy draft animals, as different from Cody's fleet little pony as they could be. Cody picked out one of them and saddled it, saying little as he did so.

The two lawmen set off immediately for Abilene. The borrowed horse was slow, so slow that they might as well have been riding double. When they finally spotted the lights of Abilene brightening the night horizon, Travis found himself leaning forward in the saddle in anticipation. The voting had ended at least an hour ago; soon the results would be announced, if they had not been already.

As Travis and Cody rode down Texas Street, Leslie Gibson hailed them from the boardwalk. The marshal veered his horse toward him.

"I'm glad you're back, Luke," the schoolteacher told him. "I was afraid all the votes would be counted before you and Cody got here."

Travis swung down from the saddle and tied his horse at the hitchrack. "They don't know who won yet?" he asked.

Leslie shook his head. "Not yet. Orion, Kincaid, and Mr. Simpson have been locked up in the town hall for nearly an hour counting the ballots. We should have the word soon." Glancing in puzzlement at the unfamiliar horse Cody was riding, Leslie went on, "What happened? Did you find those outlaws?"

"They found us," Travis grunted. "We weren't able to bring them in, Leslie. Don't reckon it would have made much difference in the outcome, but maybe it's a good thing this didn't happen before the election."

"Don't be pessimistic, Luke. You might be surprised at how many people weren't taken in by Dawes."

Travis shrugged. He turned to Cody and said, "Come on. I want to find Nestor and make sure there was no trouble while we were gone."

After Cody tied the borrowed horse next to Travis's mount, they walked down the block to the marshal's office, accompanied by Leslie Gibson, who was both excited and apprehensive. That was the way Travis himself felt. He cherished no great hope of winning, but until the results were official, there was always a chance.

The saloons were open now that the polls were closed, and they were doing a booming business. The hitching posts in front of all of them were full, and the sounds of music and laughter drifted out on the cool evening air. After holding it in all day, the cowboys who had come to town to vote were letting go of all their rowdiness. There would be some fights and some arrests before the night was over, Travis thought as they reached the office.

Nestor was alone inside when Travis, Cody, and Leslie entered. He looked up from the desk with a grin and said, "Howdy, Marshal. Have any luck chasin' them owl-hoots?"

Travis hung his hat on one of the pegs and shook his head. "Not really," he said. "We trailed them for a while, but then they ambushed us."

Nestor's eyes widened. "Anybody hurt in the shootin'?"

"They killed my horse," Cody said, his dark eyes somber and his mouth in a tight line. He went to the stove and started to pour himself a cup of coffee, his hand shaking ever so slightly.

"Dammit!" Nestor exclaimed. "I'm sorry, Cody."

"Whitson will pay for it," Cody said quietly. Everyone in the room knew what he meant. Anybody who had ridden the same horse through hard, dangerous times could understand.

Nestor got up to give Travis the seat behind the desk. "Where's Augie?" Travis asked as he settled down in the chair.

"Went back to Orion's," Nestor replied. "Since Orion was still busy countin' them ballots, somebody had to open up the tavern. I told Augie it'd be all right for him to take care of it."

Travis nodded. "Sure. Were there any problems while we were gone?"

"Just the fire."

"Fire?" Travis glanced up sharply. "What fire?"

"Started over at one of them warehouses by the depot," Nestor explained. "Looked for a while like it might get out of hand and start spreadin', but the whole town pitched in and we got 'er under control. Cunningham's place is pretty much a total loss, but that was all the damage."

"Too bad we weren't here to help," Cody commented. "We could've done more good here than we did chasing Whitson."

Travis leaned back in his chair and ran his thumb along his jaw. "You say the whole town helped put out the fire?"

"That's right," Nestor replied with a nod. "You know how folks are when it comes to somethin' like that."

Leslie put in, "Even Thurman Simpson and Mason Kincaid were out there passing buckets from the well with everybody else."

Travis's thoughtful expression deepened into a frown. "I thought they were running the polling place."

"Well, the voting was suspended while the election judges helped put out the fire," Leslie explained. "I talked to Orion for a minute during all the confusion, and he said they decided it was more important to make sure the blaze didn't spread. Don't worry about anything irregular happening, Luke. They locked up the town hall before they left, and besides, only the three judges have keys to the ballot box. No one could have tampered with it."

Travis directed his gaze at Nestor again. "How did the fire start? Anybody know?"

Nestor shook his head. "I took a look around after it was out but didn't see no sign that it was started a-purpose. Could've been some kids playin' or somebody who tossed a cigarette down where they shouldn't have." He shrugged his massive shoulders. "Didn't figger it really mattered. The important thing was we got it put out in time to save the town."

"That's right," Travis agreed. "That's the important thing."

But the wheels of his mind were still turning. Taken separately, a mysterious fire and Whitson's illogical raid on Possum Wells seemed to have no connection. It was strange, however, that both events had occurred on the same afternoon. Plenty of things in life did not make sense, but Travis had learned to take a second look at seeming coincidences. For the time being, he would keep his suspicions to himself, but he wanted to take a look at that burned-out warehouse as soon as he got the chance.

That task was going to have to wait. The door of the marshal's office opened, and Orion McCarthy stuck his tousled red head in. "Th' ballots ha' all been counted," he said. "Th' winner's about t'be announced over on th' courthouse lawn."

Leslie sprang forward eagerly. "Blast it, Orion, go ahead and tell us," he demanded.

Orion shook his head. "I can no' do tha', Leslie. 'Tis bound we be no' t'say anything 'fore th' official count be read. I just come t'let ye know."

"Well, let's go on over there," Travis said, shoving back his chair and standing up. "I'm ready to get this over with."

"Aye," Orion rumbled gloomily. Travis and Leslie exchanged glances. The Scotsman's lack of enthusiasm was a dead giveaway that the outcome was the one they had been expecting. Dawes must have won handily.

The five men trooped down the boardwalk toward the

courthouse. About halfway there, Aileen Bloom crossed the street and joined them.

"Hello, Luke," she said to Travis. "I just heard that the ballots have been counted."

"That's right. We're on our way to find out the tally now," Travis told her.

Surprisingly, she linked her arm with his. "I'll go with you, if you don't mind."

"Don't mind at all," he said with a shake of his head. "It was you and Leslie and Orion who got me into this. All of you ought to be there."

The lawn surrounding the courthouse was ablaze with light from torches carried by some of the many citizens who had gathered to learn who had won the election. Once the word had been passed that the outcome was about to be announced, the saloons had emptied, and so had most of the businesses and homes in Abilene. Almost all of the townfolk, along with many of the voters from out of town, were crowded in front of the courthouse.

Sheriff Roy Wade stood on the steps of the large building with Mason Kincaid and Thurman Simpson. Orion pushed his way through the crowd and joined them. The townspeople parted slightly when they saw Travis, allowing him, Aileen, Cody, Leslie, and Nestor to make their way to the front. When they got there, Travis saw that John Henry Dawes was already present, along with his three erstwhile deputies.

Dawes grinned broadly when he spotted Travis. Several people separated them, but Dawes leaned forward to offer his hand to Travis. "Looks like it won't be long now," he said cheerfully, raising his voice over the babble of the crowd. "Good luck to you, Marshal."

Travis hesitated only an instant before gripping Dawes's hand. "Good luck to you, too," he heard himself saying.

Sheriff Wade was still deep in discussion with the three election judges, and as Travis watched, Thurman Simpson handed a piece of paper to Wade. The sheriff glanced at it, nodded, then turned toward the crowd. He raised his big hands and called out, "Here now! Hold it down, folks! We got us a winner and a new sheriff!"

A premature cheer went up. Wade gestured for the celebrants to quiet down, and as they did, an expectant hush fell over the crowd. Every face was turned toward Wade, all eyes wide with anticipation. Travis could hear his own heartbeat, pounding loudly in the pregnant silence.

"All the ballots from today's election have been counted and recounted, and I've got the official results right here, folks," Wade said in a loud, ringing voice. "In the race for sheriff of Dickinson County, we have five hundred and twelve votes for Luke Travis and two thousand three hundred and thirty-eight votes for John Henry Dawes!" The crowd roared as they heard the totals, and Wade shouted over the noise, "John Henry Dawes is hereby declared the new sheriff of Dickinson County!"

Travis grimaced as the noise swept over the courthouse lawn. The outcome was exactly what he had expected—Dawes winning in a landslide—but still, hearing it put into words and numbers stung slightly. Suddenly Aileen slipped her hand into his and squeezed. Travis looked down at her and saw her lips moving. Even though he could not hear her over the tumult, he knew she was saying that she was sorry. He pressed her fingers in return and shook his head, summoning up a smile and saying, "It's all right."

A smiling, confident Dawes was ascending the courthouse steps to accept his victory, trailed by Cotter, Geraghty, and Rogers. As Travis watched Dawes, Leslie and Nestor slapped him on the back and offered their condolences. Cody managed a faint smile and just shook his head as he met Travis's gaze. The lawmen understood each other. The loss hurt, there was no denying that. But Travis hoped they could put all this behind them and get back to the business of maintaining law and order in Abilene. After all, that was what he had been hired to do.

He had had a taste of politics, and that one taste, Travis decided, was more than enough.

Mason Kincaid applauded vigorously as Dawes started up the steps. He was unsure what Dawes was going to say in his acceptance speech, but it did not really matter. The election was over. John Henry Dawes was now the sheriff of Dickinson County. And Mason Kincaid was well on his way to becoming its real ruler.

Suddenly Dawes stopped when he was halfway up the steps and turned to wave to someone in the crowd, summoning whoever it was to join him. Kincaid frowned and his applause faltered as Faith Hamilton detached herself from the throng and hurried up the steps to take Dawes's hand. Faith's lovely face was radiant.

*Damn!* Kincaid thought. Even now, at the moment of his greatest triumph, Faith had to appear and remind him of the hold she had over him.

Dawes reached the top of the steps and greeted Roy Wade, pumping the former sheriff's hand and accepting his congratulations. Then Dawes turned to Kincaid, thrust out his hand, and said, "Well, we did it, Mason!"

Kincaid hesitated just slightly, glancing at Faith, who stood next to Dawes. Her very presence made Kincaid uneasy, but still, he would not allow her to ruin the moment. He grinned and took Dawes's hand.

"That's right, John Henry," he said. "We did it!" He hoped Dawes caught the slight emphasis he put on the word "we."

Dawes would not be here savoring this moment of triumph had it not been for him, Mason Kincaid. And Dawes would do well to remember that fact.

Turning to face the cheering crowd, Dawes lifted his hands in acknowledgment of the accolades. After a few moments the sound began to die down. Dawes waited patiently until it was quiet enough for him to be heard.

"Thank you! Thank you, my friends! I want all of you to know how much I appreciate the honor you've given me tonight. Because it is an honor, a great honor, to be chosen as your sheriff! I know that you're putting your trust in me, and I promise you I will not violate that trust! With your help and with the help of the fine men who will serve as my deputies, I vow that I will do my best to clean up this county and bring anyone who breaks the law to justice!" More shouts of approval went up, and Dawes waited for them to die down before concluding, "Thank you again, ladies and gentlemen! I promise you'll never forget the day you elected John Henry Dawes!"

There was something in Dawes's voice, Mason Kincaid suddenly thought, an undercurrent that he could not quite identify. But whatever it was, that and the look in Dawes's eyes as he swept his gaze over the crowd sent a shiver of unease down Kincaid's spine.

For the first time in his life, he wondered if he had set in motion events that he could not control.

Several people came up to Travis and shook his hand as he and his friends made their way out of the still-celebrating crowd. One man asked, "What are you going to do now, Luke?"

Travis grinned. "Keep on being marshal, I suppose. I don't intend to leave town just because I lost an election." There was a slight edge to his voice, despite the smile on his face.

"Oh, no, I didn't mean that," the citizen hastily assured him. "I just meant—"

"Don't worry about it, Phil," Travis told him, clapping him on the arm. "I know you didn't mean anything."

When he and his companions reached the edge of the crowd and stepped onto the boardwalk, Travis heaved a sigh of relief. As they strolled toward the marshal's office, Leslie said, "I thought we had a chance. I really did."

"I'll tell you the same thing I told that townie," Travis said. "Don't worry about it, Leslie. I'm not going to.

Shoot, I never planned on being sheriff. I just didn't want Kincaid railroading his own candidate in." He chuckled ironically. "Looks like I didn't do much to even slow down that express, did I?"

"You could always run again in a couple of years when Dawes's term is up," Cody pointed out.

Travis shook his head. "I don't think so. Somebody else can try to beat him next time." Aileen was walking beside him, and he looked down at her as he went on, "If you'd like to go back and join the celebration, it's all right with me. I know that you and Kincaid . . ." That was the closest he had ever come to mentioning anything to her about her relationship with Kincaid.

Aileen shook her head. "Mason and I aren't seeing each other anymore, Luke. I'd much rather be with you this evening."

Travis felt a warm glow inside him. He had not known what to expect, but he was pleased to hear that she and Kincaid were no longer involved. That was almost as good—no, it was even better, he told himself, than winning an election.

"I think we should all go to Orion's and have a drink," he said. "We can do some celebrating of our own."

"What have we got to celebrate?" Leslie said gloomily.

"That everything is going to get back to normal now," Travis declared.

He just hoped he was right.

John Henry Dawes's first official act as sheriff was to swear in his deputies. The ceremony was a short one. While Buff Cotter, Jim Geraghty, and Lin Rogers were pledging to do their duty, the crowd began to disperse, many of them heading to the saloons.

When the ceremony was over, Cotter jerked a thumb toward the people still in the streets and asked, "Want us to patrol tonight, John Henry? The way folks're drinkin', could be a ruckus or two before mornin'."

Dawes shook his head. "Keeping the peace in town is up to Marshal Travis and *his* deputies. You boys go and do some celebrating of your own if you'd like to. Just don't get too rambunctious."

Geraghty grinned and said, "You know us, boss. Meek as little lambs."

"Right," Dawes snorted, then grinned and waved as his men departed. He slipped an arm around Faith and said to her, "What say we celebrate this victory in private?"

"That's exactly what I had in mind, John Henry," she said, flashing a smile at Mason Kincaid, who was standing near enough to have overheard the exchange. It was clear from Faith's expression that she hoped he had heard her reply.

As Cotter, Geraghty, and Rogers reached the bottom of the courthouse steps, Agnes Hirsch stepped out of the small knot of people that remained and greeted Rogers with a smile. "Hello, Lin," she said. "Congratulations."

"John Henry's the one who deserves the congratulations, not me," Rogers replied with a grin. "He's the one folks voted for. I'm just a hired hand."

"Comin' with us, kid?" Cotter asked. "Jim and me are headin' down to the Old Fruit."

Rogers glanced at Agnes's smiling face and shook his head. "You fellas go on. I'll catch up with you later."

"Sure," Geraghty said, his tone making it plain that he did not expect to see Rogers again tonight.

When the two deputies were gone, Rogers said to the lovely young redhead, "Will you take a walk with me, Agnes? I'm pretty excited. Maybe a stroll would calm me down."

"Of course, Lin," she said, slipping her arm through his. He was not the only one who was excited. Agnes's face was flushed, and her heart was pounding in her chest.

Although she still felt slightly disloyal to Luke Travis, Agnes was glad Dawes had won. That meant Lin Rogers would be around Abilene all the time from now on. Whatever was growing between them would have a chance to develop. Arm in arm, they walked down Texas

Street, turning before they reached the busy saloons and ambling along a quieter side street.

"Are you happy with the way the election turned out?" Rogers asked her after a moment.

"Of course," Agnes replied.

"So am I. It means I'll get to see a lot more of you." He stopped and turned to face her, putting his hands on her shoulders. Agnes caught her breath, unsure what would happen next but eager to find out. Rogers went on, "I really like you, Agnes."

"I . . . I like you, too, Lin." They were standing in front of a store that was closed for the night, and Rogers gently drew her into the darkened doorway. Agnes felt a slight surge of nervousness, but she forced it down. Lin Rogers would never hurt her, she was sure of that.

"I've been . . . thinking about you more than I have the election," Rogers went on. "Thinking about doing this."

His lips found hers in the darkness. The kiss was tender, almost tentative at first, but it grew quickly in passion. He pulled her more tightly against him.

Agnes moaned softly, feeling a confusing, urgent mixture of emotions cascade through her. When she took her mouth away from his, she said breathlessly, "I—I think we'd better go over to the café."

"The café?" Rogers sounded surprised. "What for?"

"I . . . I'd like a piece of pie"—the words tumbled from her lips. "We have some really good apple pie left over from supper."

Rogers laughed quietly, understanding her hesitation and her unexpected suggestion that they go have some pie. "Sure," he said. "A piece of apple pie sounds mighty good." There was no need to rush, he told himself. He was going to be in Abilene for a long time.

Linking arms again, they started toward Texas Street, laughing as they talked about the election and Rogers's new job. Neither of them noticed the figure who was watching them from the other side of the street.

\* \* \*

Michael Hirsch, Agnes's teenage brother, stepped out of the shadows of the alley and shook his head in disgust. He had never been a snoop—well, not much of one, he told himself—but when he spotted his older sister strolling along with that Rogers fellow, Michael decided to follow. And he had seen exactly what he was afraid he would.

How could Agnes be interested in Rogers when there was somebody like Cody Fisher around? True, Cody had never seemed romantically interested in Agnes, but that did not make any difference. Sooner or later, Michael was certain, Cody would have come around. Everything would have worked out all right.

"But now it's all going wrong," Michael muttered. He was going to have to do something about this.

# Chapter Ten

——◆——

**E**ARLY THE NEXT MORNING A WEARY CODY FISHER STEPPED out of the marshal's office and leaned on the boardwalk rail to survey Texas Street.

If Election Day seemed like a holiday, with all the visitors in town and the accompanying festivities, today clearly resembled the morning after. The streets were littered with trash, and the hitchracks and livery stables were full. Some of the people who had come to vote and stayed overnight were starting to straggle out of the hotels. Those who could not afford to rent a room had spent the night in alleys and barns. Some men groaned, staggered, and held their heads as they took their leave, paying today for the binges of the night before.

It had been quite a day, all right, Cody thought. It was a shame it had not turned out better.

The cells in the jail behind Cody were full, occupied by

cowboys arrested during the night for getting drunk and causing trouble. Travis, Cody, and Nestor had been busy until just before dawn. During the night they had slept when they could, then gone out again to break up another fight. Finally things quieted down enough for Travis to return to his rented room, Nestor to head for the orphanage, and Cody to crawl into the bunk in the back room of the jail. Not even the raucous snoring of several of the passed-out prisoners had kept him awake.

But his sleep did not amount to much more than a catnap; too soon his instincts nudged him awake, warning him that it was growing light. His eyes felt gritty as he started the coffee brewing and then stepped out onto the boardwalk. A cool breeze blew out of the north, and that helped to wake him. Feeling more alert, he noticed several men come out of the town hall carrying burlap bags. Cody knew the town council had hired the loafers to clean up the debris from the night before. He watched them as they began their work, picking up trash and stuffing it into the bags. Then he turned and went into the office. The coffee smelled as though it was ready.

Cody filled a tin cup with the strong black brew and carried it to the desk. He sat down, leaned back in the chair, and wrapped his fingers around the cup to warm them as he sipped the coffee. After a few minutes he felt even more human and decided that he could make it through the day after all. He glanced up when he heard footsteps on the boardwalk outside.

The door of the office opened, and a sturdy, redheaded, freckle-faced youngster came in carrying several schoolbooks tied together with twine. He said brightly, "Morning, Cody."

"Hello, Michael." The deputy nodded. "Looks like you're on your way to school."

"Yeah, but I wanted to come and see you first," Michael Hirsch said. "I'm glad you're here and not out making rounds or something. I've got something important to tell you."

Cody sat up straighter and placed the coffee cup on the desk. He pulled his watch out of his pocket, flipped it open, and frowned at the face. "You'd better hurry, or you'll be late for school. Mr. Simpson won't like that."

"This is more important than what old Mr. Simpson likes or doesn't like," Michael told him, his smile gone now.

Cody ignored the disrespect for the teacher in Michael's voice. He himself felt the same way about Thurman Simpson. He said, "Well, spit it out."

"I saw Agnes last night," Michael told him as he rested his books on a corner of the desk.

"I should hope so. She's your sister, and you live in the same place."

"No, I mean earlier. Right after they announced who won the election." Michael looked vaguely uncomfortable, as if he did not like carrying tales but considered this urgent enough to warrant it. "She was with some fella. I think he's one of those deputies the new sheriff hired."

Cody's eyes narrowed. "What did he look like?"

"He was about your age, maybe a little older. Not real big but not little, either. I think he had dark hair, and he was wearing a light-colored hat."

"Lin Rogers." Cody nodded. "He's one of Dawes's deputies, all right. What the devil was he doing with Agnes?"

"They took a walk together after things broke up at the courthouse." Michael made a face. "I followed them."

Cody shoved back his chair and stood up. For a moment he considered telling Michael just to skip the rest of it and go on to school. Agnes Hirsch was a grown woman, and what she did was her own business. Against his better judgment he told Michael, "Go on. What happened then?"

"He kissed her!" Michael exclaimed.

Cody took a deep breath, hollows appearing in his lean cheeks. "What did Agnes do?"

"Nothing! It looked to me like she was enjoying it!" Michael shook his head in bewilderment. "Then they went over to the café and had some pie like nothing had happened."

Well, at least things had not gone any further than a kiss, Cody thought. He told himself to relax. He had no right to get upset about this. Agnes was not his girl, after all. But he did not trust Lin Rogers for a second. To Cody, any man who worked for John Henry Dawes was automatically suspect.

He clapped the redheaded boy on the shoulder. "Thanks for telling me, Michael."

"But what are you going to do about it, Cody?"

"I don't know," Cody answered honestly. "Your sister's pretty much grown up. She has a right to see whomever she wants to. But maybe I'll have a talk with that fella, just to make sure he intends to treat Agnes the way she ought to be treated."

"You mean you're not going to go gunning for him?" Michael sounded disappointed.

Cody chuckled and shook his head. "Afraid not. There're enough desperadoes around for me to worry about. I don't need to get into a fight with another lawman."

"I just thought—"

"I know," Cody broke in. "But you'd better get to school now. I may have stopped Simpson from giving you a hiding once, but I can't always be around. Now scoot!"

Looking disgruntled and dragging his books behind him, Michael left the office. Cody watched him go and knew that the boy had expected him to react differently. Michael had wanted gunplay, or at least some fisticuffs.

There would be a confrontation, though. Cody reached for his hat, intending to look up Lin Rogers and ask him a few pointed questions. It was entirely possible that Rogers would not take the interrogation well.

Cody almost hoped that would be the case.

* * *

It was a beautiful morning, Lin Rogers thought as he stepped onto the porch of the hotel and drew in a deep lungful of clean, cool air. He felt good, vibrant with the memory of kissing Agnes Hirsch the night before. He could almost taste her sweet lips even now.

However, Rogers was a practical young man. He had slept well, undisturbed by romantic dreams. Undoubtedly he was very attracted to Agnes, but he was not going to let that emotion overwhelm him. He still had a job to do.

He glanced down with pride at the badge pinned to his shirt. The unassuming piece of tin cut into a star had letters forming the words Deputy Sheriff pressed into the metal. The badge was not particularly impressive, but it meant a great deal to Lin Rogers. It meant that John Henry Dawes trusted him and relied on him, as did the citizens of Dickinson County.

Rogers knew that this morning Dawes and the other deputies would get together in the sheriff's office inside the courthouse. Dawes would go over their duties, assigning different responsibilities to each man. Rogers had already eaten breakfast in the hotel dining room, and he was ready to get to that meeting. A feeling of impatience ran through him as he wondered what his first assignment would be.

Rogers started down the boardwalk toward the courthouse, smiling and nodding at the townspeople he passed. Soon, as he carried out his duties, he would get to know many of these folks by name.

He had gone less than a block when someone behind him called out, "Rogers! Wait up a minute!"

Rogers halted and looked around curiously. Cody Fisher, one of Marshal Travis's deputies, was hurrying toward him. His face was set in tight, grim lines; clearly something was bothering him.

"Howdy, Deputy," Rogers said as Cody came up to him. "Something wrong?"

"There could be," Cody answered flatly. "I'd like to have a talk with you, Rogers."

"Sure. What about?"

Cody looked around. Quite a few people were walking past them, and the street was filling up with traffic. "Not here," Cody said abruptly. "Let's go someplace where it's quieter."

"All right." Rogers glanced along the street, then suggested, "How about that alley over there?" He indicated an opening between two buildings about ten feet away.

"Fine by me," Cody agreed. He stalked toward the alley, not looking back to see if Rogers was following.

Curious, Rogers trailed Cody into the alley. Ever since the night Cody and Nestor Gilworth had horned in on the fight at the Bull's Head, the two groups of deputies had taken pains to avoid each other. The tension between them had been evident to all concerned. Rogers wondered if Cody was ready to make peace now, but Cody's demeanor was not very encouraging.

When they were about twenty feet into the alley, Cody stopped and turned to face Rogers. Rogers halted, standing with his feet apart and his thumbs hooked behind his shell belt. "You look like you've got a burr under your saddle," he said. "What's this all about, Fisher?"

"You know Agnes Hirsch, don't you?"

The question took Rogers by surprise. He frowned and said, "I reckon I do. What business is that of yours?"

"She's a friend of mine."

Rogers lifted an eyebrow. "Is that so? Funny, she hasn't mentioned you much."

Cody's face darkened. "I've known Agnes for a long time," he said. "She's a good friend. I don't want to see her hurt."

"That makes two of us, mister." Rogers had come back here thinking that the other deputy wanted to see him on law business; obviously Cody's concerns were personal. Somehow he must have found out about that walk Rogers had taken with Agnes the night before. And if he knew about the walk, he might know about the kiss.

"Listen, I want to know just what your intentions are concerning Agnes," Cody said sharply.

"My intentions?" Rogers echoed. "I don't think you're old enough to be the girl's pa, Fisher—"

"She doesn't have a pa," Cody broke in. "She's an orphan. She and her little brother are the only ones left of the family. Agnes has seen more than her share of trouble, and I don't want you causing her any more."

Rogers took a deep breath and tried to control his rising temper. "I know Agnes is an orphan," he said, forcing his voice to remain calm. "She's told me all about how she lives with her brother out at that orphanage. So if that's all you're worried about—"

Cody interrupted again. "It's not. She's a young girl, Rogers, and she hasn't had a lot of experience. I don't want you taking advantage of her."

"Dammit, all I did was kiss her!" Rogers snapped, his control slipping.

Cody took a deep breath. "That's all you've done so far. But you still haven't told me what your intentions are."

"And I'm not going to," Rogers said. "It's none of your business, and I'm not going to stand here and argue about it with you." He started to turn away, intending to walk out of the alley.

Cody's hand came down roughly on his shoulder, spinning him around to face him again. "Wait just a damned minute!" Cody blazed. "I'm not through with you."

"Yes, you are."

Rage boiled through Rogers at being manhandled. Without thinking, he balled his fists and suddenly brought the right one up as Cody crowded in on him. The blow caught Cody on the jaw, snapping his head to the side and staggering him. Cody put out a hand, slapping his palm against the wall of a building to keep his balance. Rogers backed off a step, keeping his guard up. Cody shook his head, then threw a punch.

Rogers easily blocked the straight left that Cody jabbed at him, but it was only a feint. Cody's right looped around, driving across Rogers's jaw and knocking him into the wall of the building on the other side of the alley. Before Rogers could regain his balance, Cody was after him, snapping punches into his midsection.

Momentarily groggy, Rogers fought on instinct alone, blocking a few of Cody's blows and trying to shrug off the others. Finally he got his feet set and lunged, wrapping his arms around Cody in a bear hug. Cody rained punches down on Rogers's back, but Rogers ignored them as he forced Cody across the alley. With a shivering impact, he smashed Cody back into the wall.

Gasping for air, Cody slammed his fists into Rogers's temples. The blows were rather weak, but they were strong enough to make Rogers loosen his grip. Cody writhed free, shoved Rogers away from him, and stepped back to catch his breath.

Rogers was doing the same thing. Holding his fists in front of him, he said between gulps of air, "Come on—blast it! This is—what you wanted!"

Glaring, Cody rushed him again. Rogers met the charge. For a long moment the two young men stood toe to toe in the alley, slugging it out. Rogers fought desperately, feeling his strength ebbing. Cody looked as if the same thing was happening to him, but Rogers could not count on that. If one of them collapsed first, the other man would surely be the winner.

The fight could not last much longer, though. Rogers gathered what energy he had left and channeled it into one last punch. He was putting everything he had into it; if the blow was not successful, he would certainly go down to defeat. Even as the punch sped toward the other deputy's head, Rogers suddenly realized that Cody was doing the same thing. This was a last-ditch effort for both of them.

Both blows missed cleanly.

As his fist whizzed past Cody's head, Rogers staggered, thrown off balance by his momentum. His feet tangled with Cody's, and he felt himself falling. He sprawled headlong in the dirt of the alley. Frantically getting his hands under him, he tried to push himself up and turn around, but when he did, he saw that Cody was in the same predicament. Rogers let himself slump into a sitting position against the wall of a building. Cody was doing the same thing across the alley.

Rogers closed his eyes and leaned his head against the wall for a moment. He did not hurt too badly; that would come later when the bruises began to appear. He had given as good as he received, though, and Cody would have some lumps, too.

Cody spat blood and asked harshly, "Had enough?"

With his head still lolling against the rough wood, Rogers began to laugh. "I could . . . ask you the same thing," he said. "Reckon we're both a little . . . done in." He paused, then looked across at Cody and added bitterly, "I suppose you're going to arrest me now."

Cody was holding his jaw, working it back and forth to make sure nothing was broken. He frowned at Rogers and replied, "Arrest you? What the devil for?"

"Oh, disturbing the peace, resisting arrest, whatever. I figure you can think of something, some reason to throw me in jail."

For a long moment Cody regarded Rogers with a bewildered look, but then understanding dawned on his face. "You mean use the law for my own ends? Arrest you to even the score?" He shook his head. "It doesn't work that way around here, mister. This was personal business, and it's going to stay that way."

Now it was Rogers's turn to stare in puzzlement. His experience was limited, admittedly, but still, he was accustomed to Buff Cotter and Jim Geraghty and even, to a certain extent, John Henry Dawes using their positions as lawmen to get whatever they wanted. Cody Fisher seemed offended by the very idea of arresting a man because of a personal grudge, even though a legitimate case might be made against Rogers.

Cody hauled himself to his feet, picked up his hat, and used it to slap some of the dust off his dark clothes. Taking a deep breath, he stepped across the alley and extended his hand to Rogers.

Rogers looked at that hand for a long moment, then took it and let Cody help him up. His hat lay a few feet away, trampled during the fight. Rogers picked it up and tried to knock the crown back into shape.

"You're crazy if you think I'm going to apologize," he said without looking at Cody.

"Don't recall asking you for an apology," Cody replied gruffly. "I just want you to understand that I won't have anything bad happening to Agnes Hirsch. If it does, the fight next time will be with guns, not fists."

"However you want it, Deputy," Rogers said.

He waited until Cody had stalked out of the alley, then left it himself and headed toward the courthouse. Some of the people he passed looked at him strangely, their expressions telling him he bore the marks of the fight. Dawes was going to ask what had happened.

A slight smile tugged painfully at Rogers's mouth. Cotter and Geraghty would be surprised to hear about the fight and learn that Cody had not arrested him. These Abilene lawmen viewed their duties a little differently than did the lawmen in other towns where Rogers had been.

But that would change. With John Henry Dawes in charge plenty of things would change.

# *Chapter Eleven*

Now that the hoopla of the election was over, Abilene began settling down to a routine, just as Travis had hoped it would. A week passed quietly with no trouble in town and no more raids by Mike Whitson's gang anywhere in the county.

Travis had been puzzled by the bruises that appeared on Cody Fisher's face the day after the election, but Cody was closemouthed about them, dodging the questions Travis and Nestor asked. The marshal was willing to respect his deputy's privacy. Knowing Cody's hot temper and his eye for a pretty woman, Travis assumed there had been trouble over some female. If that was the case, it was none of his business.

Several times, Travis ran into John Henry Dawes on the street, and Dawes always greeted him in a friendly fashion. Travis tried to be civil. So far, there had been no reason for Travis and Dawes to work together, but such circumstances were bound to come up sooner or later.

One afternoon, as Travis was walking along Railroad Street in front of the row of saloons across from the Kansas Pacific depot, he saw Harvey Bastrop hurrying out of the large, redbrick station building. Low gray clouds had moved in during the morning, bringing a cold mist with them, but the stationmaster was hatless. Travis frowned as he watched Bastrop angle across the street, and he picked up his own pace to intercept him.

"What's wrong, Harve?" he called as the stationmaster reached the boardwalk.

"Whitson," Bastrop answered curtly, holding up a piece of paper that was beginning to go limp in the moist air. "We just got this wire. Whitson's gang stopped a westbound train, stole the express pouch, and robbed the passengers. Happened just a little while ago. The engineer and the fireman put up a fight, and they were killed. After the gang was gone, the express agent shinnied up a telegraph pole and cut in to let us know what happened. He's trying to get steam back up and come on in."

Travis's mouth tightened in a grim line as he listened. "And Whitson got away?" he asked when the stationmaster paused.

Bastrop nodded. "As far as I know. I was just on my way to tell the sheriff about it."

"I'll go with you," Travis said abruptly. He was curious to know how Dawes would handle this and wanted to see the sheriff's reaction firsthand.

Bastrop hurried along beside Travis, his short legs pumping to keep up with the marshal's long-legged stride. He said, "Every time I start thinking Whitson's left this part of the country, he pops up again. I hope Dawes can run him down."

Travis thought back to Election Day when he and Cody had tried to catch up to Whitson's gang. It was a bitter memory—all that had come out of it was the loss of Cody's horse.

Maybe Dawes would have more luck. Travis found

himself hoping that would be the case. Whitson had to be brought to justice, no matter who did it.

Side by side, Travis and Bastrop ascended the steps to the courthouse, pushed through the heavy front doors, and went down the long main hall toward Dawes's office. Among the many county offices and suites they passed along the way was Judge Homer Davenport's courtroom. The doors of the big room were open. Travis glanced inside and saw that the judge was conducting a sparsely attended trial, probably a civil matter from the looks of it. Dawes was not there.

The two men strode to the end of the hall and stepped through a door; the gilt lettering on its pebbled-glass panel read SHERIFF—DICKINSON COUNTY. Inside was a small reception room with a railing dividing it. The gate in the railing was open as was the door into the office beyond. Travis smelled cigar smoke drifting out of that room and saw John Henry Dawes sitting behind the desk, booted feet propped on the scarred surface. The cigar was in Dawes's mouth.

As Travis and Bastrop entered the office, the sheriff swung his feet to the floor and removed the stogie. He nodded and said, "Hello, gentlemen. What can I do for you?"

"I just got this message," Bastrop replied, waving the limp piece of paper. "Whitson's gang held up a train about ten miles east of here."

Dawes surged to his feet. "What?" he exclaimed.

"Mike Whitson and his men—" Bastrop began again, sounding impatient.

"I heard you," Dawes cut him off. "Sorry, Mr. Bastrop, this just took me by surprise." He lifted his voice. "Buff, Jim, Lin! Get in here!"

A side door in the office opened a moment later, and the three deputies hurried in. Cotter was in the lead, and he had his hand on the butt of his gun as he entered, his eyes darting around nervously. "What is it, John Henry?" he asked.

"There's been a train robbery," Dawes said, taking a

Winchester from a rack on the wall behind him. "That Mike Whitson and his bunch hit a Kansas Pacific train east of here. Grab some rifles—we're riding out there!"

The deputies nodded and pushed past Travis to get to the rifles in the rack. Dawes opened a desk drawer and took out a box of shells. He spilled the cartridges onto the desktop and began loading the weapon he held.

The others followed suit. As Geraghty thumbed shells into his Winchester, he glanced coldly at Travis and asked, "What are you doing here, Marshal?"

"I just walked over here with Mr. Bastrop," Travis replied. "He told me what happened."

Dawes looked at Travis as if something had just occurred to him. "Were you wanting to ride with us, Marshal?" he asked.

Travis shook his head. "It looks like you're on top of things, Sheriff. I'll stay here and do my duty in town."

"All right," Dawes said with a shrug. He turned to the stationmaster and went on, "Don't you worry, Mr. Bastrop. We'll get right on the trail of those desperadoes. They won't get away from us."

"I hope not," Bastrop said, pulling a handkerchief out of his pocket and mopping the sheen of dampness on his forehead. "This Whitson seems to think he can commit whatever outrages he pleases without anyone challenging him."

"He'll learn different," Dawes promised grimly. Swinging to face his men, he asked, "Ready to ride?"

All three deputies nodded.

As Travis glanced at Lin Rogers, he thought he saw some fading bruises on the young man's face. That reminded him of the marks he had noticed on Cody, and he suddenly wondered if there was a connection between them. Surely Cody had not gotten into a fistfight with Rogers, a fellow lawman. Stranger things had happened, though. Whether it was prying or not, Travis decided he was going to ask Cody a few questions.

"Let's get saddled up," Dawes said as he grabbed his hat from a hook and settled it on his head. He led the way out of the office. The three deputies trailed down the hall behind him, all four men carrying loaded rifles.

Travis and Bastrop stood in the doorway of the sheriff's office and watched them depart. "I wouldn't want to be in Whitson's boots," Bastrop commented. "I've heard Dawes has quite a reputation as a manhunter."

"That he does," Travis admitted. "I hope he catches up to that gang. I'd like to see Whitson behind bars."

"Well, I'd better get back to the station and advise the main office of the holdup." Bastrop sighed. "I hate being the bearer of bad tidings."

Until Whitson and his gang were corralled, Travis thought, there were liable to be plenty more of those bad tidings.

Dawes and his men had not returned to Abilene by nightfall. Shadows cloaked the town a little earlier than usual because of the overcast skies. Not long after dark the mist that had lingered in the air all day turned into a chilly drizzle, driving most people off the streets and into the warmth of homes and businesses.

Around eight o'clock Travis and Cody were crossing Texas Street, heading for Orion's Tavern. Both lawmen wore yellow oilskin slickers and had their hats pulled low over their eyes. Cody glanced down the street toward the eastern end of town, then stopped suddenly and caught Travis's arm. "Isn't that Dawes?" he asked, pointing toward the courthouse.

Travis turned and peered through the rain. Four riders had just reined in at the courthouse. They were silhouetted against the lights shining through the building's windows, but in this weather it was difficult to distinguish anything else about them. Travis thought Cody was right, though, given the number of men and their general appearance.

"Come on," he said. "If it is Dawes, he didn't bring Whitson back with him. Let's go find out what happened."

They returned to the boardwalk and strode toward the

courthouse. The rain began to beat down harder as they crossed the lawn and hurried to the side door on Court Street. Travis knew the front entrance would be locked at this time of night.

The two men went down the short side corridor, then swung into the main hall toward the sheriff's office, their footsteps echoing hollowly in the empty hall. Before they reached the door, Buff Cotter appeared in the doorway, a scowl on his bearded face and a rifle in his hands. His clothes were soaked, and he looked cold and miserable. "What the hell do *you* want?" he demanded as he glowered at them.

"We just happened to see you and the others ride in," the marshal replied. "Did you have any luck finding Whitson?"

"You'd better ask Sheriff Dawes about that," Cotter growled. He lowered the rifle, which he had been pointing vaguely toward the two lawmen, and gestured curtly with the barrel. "He's in his office."

Cotter moved aside to let Travis and Cody walk into the office. As they stepped in, Travis saw that Dawes was sitting behind the desk, a furious expression on his face, while Geraghty and Rogers were standing close by. Rogers was saying, "—get them next time, John Henry."

The young deputy broke off when he saw Travis and Cody. Travis sensed Cody stiffening, and he caught the hostile glance that passed between the two young men. His earlier suspicion of some trouble between them certainly seemed valid now.

Dawes glanced up at Travis and asked in a surly voice, "What do you want?" The smooth manner he had displayed in all their previous meetings was gone now.

"Looks like you didn't find Whitson," Travis said.

Dawes's frown deepened. He leaned forward in his chair and placed his palms on the desk. "I'm wet and cold and hungry, Marshal, and I'm damned frustrated, too. So if you've come to gloat, I'd rather you'd just move on."

Cody started to frame an angry reply, but Travis put a

hand on his arm to silence him. "I'm not here to gloat, Sheriff," Travis said. "I just wanted to know what happened."

"We picked up Whitson's trail and followed it for a while, but then it started raining. That washed out all the tracks. There was nothing we could do about it."

Travis nodded in understanding. He had lost more than one trail due to circumstances he could not control, like the weather. It was very frustrating, as Dawes had said, but a lawman had to live with such things.

"That's bad luck," Travis told Dawes. "Whitson seems determined to stay in this area, though, so maybe you'll have another chance to round him up."

"I hope so," Dawes said, slipping his Colt from its holster and laying it on the desk. "I'd like to see that bastard in my sights, just long enough to pull the trigger."

Travis's mouth quirked slightly. Dawes was living up to his reputation. Clearly he would prefer killing Whitson to bringing the outlaw in to face a trial for his crimes.

"Anytime we can give you a hand, just let us know," Travis said, realizing it would serve no purpose to debate ideas on law enforcement with Dawes.

The sheriff nodded. "Thanks, Travis. That's mighty white of you. But we'll handle Whitson and any other owlhoot who tries anything around here. You just wait and see."

That was exactly what Travis intended to do.

During the next two weeks, Mike Whitson's gang struck three more times in locations scattered throughout Dickinson County. They held up another train and raided the two small communities of Shady Brook and Enterprise. None of the crimes netted large hauls for the bandits, but Whitson was probably accumulating a good-sized stash of loot. Each time word reached Abilene that the Whitson gang had struck, Dawes and his deputies thundered out of town on horseback to launch a pursuit. Whitson, however, gave them the slip every time.

Abilene's citizens were growing discernibly uneasy. Whitson seemed to be robbing and killing at will, despite John Henry Dawes's campaign promises to eradicate crime in Dickinson County. Of course, Luke Travis, among others, had never believed that Dawes would be able to keep those promises. There would always be outlaws of one sort or another plaguing the law-abiding folks of the county. All the sheriff could do was try to keep the bandits from getting out of hand. So far, Dawes had not been able to accomplish even that.

He did, however, put in an appearance at the monthly meeting of the county commissioners to ask that more money be allotted to the sheriff's office. When one of the commissioners asked why he needed more funds, Dawes replied, "This is a big county. I can't cover all of it with only three deputies. I want to hire more men and establish regular patrols."

After some discussion among themselves, the county officials agreed to the request—somewhat grudgingly, it seemed to those attending the meeting. Emmett Valentine was one of those, and his story in the *Clarion* the next morning painted Dawes's request for more money as being very reasonable under the circumstances. Something had to be done to eliminate the menace of Mike Whitson and outlaws like him.

The new deputies began arriving less than a week later. They drew surprised stares as they rode into Abilene. Lean-faced, hard-eyed men, they could have been taken for outlaws themselves—if not for the fact that they rode to the courthouse and went in only to emerge wearing badges.

People were still talking about the sheriff's new deputies when the town council met a couple of nights later. As Mason Kincaid sat at the council table in the town hall scanning the agenda, he tried not to listen to the buzz of conversation among the spectators and his fellow council members. More than once in the last two weeks, he had been asked what Dawes was up to. People assumed he would know, since he had been so closely connected with the sheriff's campaign, had in fact been the one to bring Dawes to Abilene.

The truth was, Kincaid did not know what Dawes was doing. Dawes had been cold and distant the few times Kincaid had tried to talk to him. "I appreciate what you've done for me, Mason," Dawes had told him, "but the election's over now. Let me do the job the way I see fit."

Kincaid sighed, the words on the paper in front of him blurring as he thought about the situation. The only thing more disturbing than the sheriff's newfound independence was the fact that Dawes and Faith Hamilton were still carrying on their affair, and they were not being very discreet about it.

"Hello, Mason," someone said, and Kincaid glanced up to see Aileen Bloom taking her seat at the table. Kincaid forced himself to return the smile. Even though he and Aileen were no longer romantically involved, he wanted to keep her friendship. Having the town's leading physician on his side could prove advantageous in the long run.

When all the council members were seated, the mayor called the meeting to order and then said, "We're going to depart from the agenda tonight, because someone wants to make a special statement to us. Sheriff Dawes, I'm turning the floor over to you."

Kincaid frowned and straightened in his chair as Dawes stood up and strode from the back of the room. The sheriff was carrying his big cream-colored hat, and he had a solemn expression on his face. As usual, a small lectern had been set up in front of the table from which citizens could address the council.

Dawes placed his hat on it, then leaned forward. "Thank you for letting me speak like this, Mr. Mayor," he began affably. "I realize it's a bit irregular, but I think what I've got to say is important enough to warrant the change."

Dawes glanced at Kincaid, and the councilman raised his eyebrows as if to demand to know what was going on.

No one had said anything to him about Dawes speaking to the council, and that made Kincaid furious. In the space of a couple of weeks, he had been transformed into an outsider.

Except for that fleeting glance, Dawes paid no more attention to Kincaid than he did to the other members of the council. He went on, "As you know, there's been too much lawlessness in the county of late. We've got a band of outlaws running loose and terrorizing the countryside. Trains have been held up, banks and stores robbed, innocent folks gunned down. It's got to stop."

"Excuse me, Sheriff Dawes," Aileen spoke up, "but as you've said, we know all this. Do you have anything specific to ask us or tell us?"

"Yes, ma'am, I do," Dawes answered. "I came to ask the town council to help me corral these outlaws."

"How can we do that?" Kincaid snapped, suspecting that he already knew the answer.

"Money," Dawes intoned. "I'd like the town council to contribute funds to the sheriff's office."

That was exactly what Kincaid had expected him to say.

The council and the spectators began to murmur in surprise, the sound rapidly growing louder. After a moment, the mayor cracked his gavel against the table.

"Keep it down, folks!" he ordered. "This is a council meeting, not a saloon argument!" When the hubbub had quieted somewhat, the mayor looked at Dawes and continued, "I think I speak for everybody when I say we're behind you, Sheriff, but your office is supported by the county. You'll have to ask the commissioners if you need more funds."

Dawes grimaced. "I've already spoken to the commissioners, Mayor. They've given me as much as they can, and I've used the money to hire more deputies. But we need more guns and horses, and when you come down to it, more men." His voice was earnest as he went on, "You've got to understand, this outlaw rampage in the county is hurting the town, too. Folks don't want to come

# The Lawman

to Abilene when they hear about a desperado like Whitson running loose. He's keeping the town from growing, and he's hurting the businesses that are already here. It seems to me it's only fair that the town pay part of the cost of running these owlhoots to ground."

Kincaid cursed silently. What Dawes was saying made sense, but the sheriff should have discussed it with him first, before coming to the council with his hand out. That way, Kincaid could have laid the groundwork and possibly persuaded the council to go along with Dawes's request.

One of the other councilmen said, "That's an interesting idea, Sheriff, but I'm not sure it's legal for us to give you any money. Like the mayor said, your office is supposed to be supported by the county."

"Well, I've looked into the legalities," Dawes admitted. "I'd like to establish a Sheriff's Law Enforcement Fund. Folks could contribute however much they wanted to it. There wouldn't be anything illegal about the town council donating to a fund like that, would there?"

"That sounds straightforward enough—" Aileen began.

"It sounds like an excellent idea," Kincaid cut in. "That way, we could help fight these outlaws in a totally legal, aboveboard manner."

Dawes's gaze darted to him, and Kincaid saw that they understood each other. He would help Dawes as much as he could now, but in the future Dawes would be well advised not to forget this assistance, as he seemed to have forgotten Kincaid's role in the election.

Aileen turned toward him. "Do you really think this is a good idea, Mason?"

Kincaid nodded and said, "I do. Sheriff Dawes is right about the outlaws hurting the town. I can testify to that. Land sales are down right now, and I attribute it to the fact that people are afraid to come to Abilene, afraid of being robbed or killed. If this keeps up, our town could be in for some very rough times."

Kincaid's voice was sincere, and he saw several council

133

members nod in thoughtful agreement. Pressing his advantage, the land agent went on, "We could always start by making a relatively small donation to the sheriff's new fund, then increase it later as the need arose." He looked at Dawes. "Is that agreeable to you, Sheriff?"

Dawes's dark eyes flashed in anger at the way Kincaid had modified his plan, but his voice was smooth as he said, "Why, sure, Councilman. Any help you folks can give us will be greatly appreciated, I can promise you that."

"I move that the town council donate"—Aileen hesitated slightly—"one hundred dollars to the Sheriff's Law Enforcement Fund."

"Second," Kincaid said promptly.

"All in favor say aye," the mayor ordered.

The vote was unanimous. The mayor rapped the gavel and said, "Motion carries. I'll instruct the town treasurer to issue you a bank draft, Sheriff Dawes."

"Thank you, Mr. Mayor. And thanks to the rest of you council members. I assure you, the money is going to a good cause."

A good cause indeed, Mason Kincaid thought. He had a strong suspicion the money would go directly into John Henry Dawes's pockets. Dawes was becoming more of a problem than Kincaid had anticipated, but he had to admire the man's gall. But if Dawes kept this up, sooner or later there would be trouble. People would begin to see through him, and some of those people would blame Kincaid for bringing Dawes to Abilene in the first place.

Before that happened, he would have to do something about Dawes, Kincaid told himself. The question was—what?

After the meeting ended, Luke Travis waited just outside the door of the town hall. When Aileen Bloom emerged, he stepped up to her, touched the brim of his hat, and asked, "Walk you home, Aileen?"

She smiled, not hesitating at all. "I'd like that, Luke."

He took her arm, and they started down the plank walk

toward the boardinghouse where she rented a room. The rains had moved out, and the weather was turning unseasonably warm for autumn in Kansas. He should have been happy with a mild breeze in his face and a lovely brunette on his arm, Travis told himself, but something was gnawing at him that would not let him appreciate the pleasant evening.

"Dawes sort of threw everybody for a loop in there tonight," he said.

"You were at the meeting?" Aileen asked. "I didn't notice you."

"I slipped in right after things got started and stayed at the back," Travis replied. "I heard Dawes's little speech."

"What he said made sense, you know," Aileen pointed out. "Lawlessness in the county does hurt the town."

Travis nodded. "I've been saying that for a long time. That's why drifting out of my jurisdiction now and then never worried me much as long as Roy Wade wasn't upset by it. John Henry Dawes is a different story, though."

"Yes, I imagine he wouldn't want you helping him," Aileen agreed.

"He's doing all right for himself," Travis replied dryly. "He may not have caught Whitson yet, but he's building up a nice little protection racket."

Aileen stopped short at Travis's words. She turned toward him, her face bathed in the light coming from a nearby window, her eyes searching his intently. "What are you saying, Luke?" she asked quietly.

Travis's mouth twisted bitterly. "I've seen it before, Aileen, but never on this scale. It's usually a small-timer's dodge. A thug says to a storeowner, 'You've got a nice place here. Be a shame if something happened to it. Why don't you pay me to protect you and see that it doesn't?' " The marshal shook his head. "It's nothing but extortion, plain and simple. Dawes is just trying to pull it on a whole county."

"I have a hard time believing that. He has a reputation as an honest lawman."

"He's carried a badge in a lot of different places," Travis pointed out. "Who knows what all he's done? Maybe he's just turned bad now." He paused for a moment, then went on, "Maybe Mason Kincaid had something to do with it, too. A share of the extra money Dawes is getting could be going to Kincaid."

Aileen paled. "You don't really believe that, do you, Luke? I know you've had your differences with Mason, but I'm sure he wouldn't be involved in anything like that."

Travis shrugged. "I'm just thinking out loud. But I intend to keep an eye on Dawes and Kincaid."

"I hope you're wrong," Aileen said with a sigh. "I hope you're wrong about both of them. What sort of place has Abilene become if . . . if the sheriff and a town councilman are both criminals?"

Travis wished he knew the answer to that question.

# Chapter Twelve

❧

"Riders comin', boss."

The words drifting through the open door of the ranch house made Hunter Dixon look up from the ledger on the desk in front of him. The burly, gray-haired owner of the Rafter D saw one of his cowhands on the porch. "You recognize any of them?" Dixon called to the man.

"One of 'em looks like one of those deputies from town."

Dixon frowned, slipped his pen into its holder, and stood up. He was puzzled, but he was also glad to have an excuse to abandon the paperwork for a few minutes. It was a beautiful autumn day, and a man needed some fresh air after he had been bending over a desk for a while.

Dixon strode out the doorway and onto the porch. In his brown whipcord pants, gray shirt, and black vest, he did not look very different from the cowboys who worked his ranch. His clothes were of better quality, perhaps, but not much. Hunter Dixon was not a man to waste money on frills. He had devoted his life to building this ranch. The Rafter D had originally been a farm, but Dixon had never enjoyed grubbing in the dirt. The growth of the cattle market had suited him perfectly, and through his hard work the ranch had become one of the most productive in the state. A widower for many years, Dixon had thrown himself even more into his work after the death of his only son a couple of years earlier. The Rafter D was all he had, and he was learning to be content with it.

Four men were approaching the ranch headquarters on horseback. Dixon squinted, trying to make out their features. The one in the lead had a scruffy, reddish-brown beard. Dixon recalled seeing him in Abilene. The man was one of Sheriff Dawes's deputies, just as Dixon's puncher had said. Cotter, that was the man's name, Dixon remembered.

The men rode past the barns and corrals and brought their horses to a stop in the small yard in front of the ranch house. Cotter cuffed his hat back slightly, rested his hands on his saddle horn, and nodded to the rancher. "Afternoon, Mr. Dixon," he said. "Don't know if you recollect who I am—"

"I know you," Dixon said. "You work for the sheriff."

"That's right." The red-bearded man grinned. "Name's Buff Cotter. These boys here are some of our new deputies." He indicated his companions with a jerk of his head.

Dixon glanced at the other three men. He had heard Dawes was hiring more deputies. They were all of a kind, hardened, rough-looking individuals who looked as if they would be quite competent with the guns they carried. But they each wore a badge, and Dixon supposed that made a difference.

"What can I do for you, Cotter?"

Cotter was still grinning. "It's a long ride out here from

town, Mr. Dixon. We could do with a drink of water, and so could our hosses."

"I'd rather you stated your business first," Dixon said flatly. He had supported John Henry Dawes in the election, but he had to admit he was not very impressed with Cotter or the other deputies.

Cotter's grin faltered a little. "We just come by to see if you've been havin' any trouble, Mr. Dixon. You probably heard there's been a heap of rustlin' goin' on lately."

Dixon frowned; he had heard about the rustling, all right. Recently several of the neighboring spreads had been hit; among them, the ranchers had lost several hundred head of cattle. The rustlers had been daring, raiding well-guarded herds, and they were quick to shoot if they were opposed. Several punchers had been wounded in the exchanges, although Dixon had not heard of anyone being killed, but it was only a matter of time before that happened.

"I know about the rustling," Dixon said. "So far we've been lucky, I suppose. I've got extra men guarding my stock—"

"From what I've heard," Cotter interrupted him, shaking his head, "that ain't goin' to do you much good. The sheriff's had us deputies patrollin' as much as we can, but we can't be everywhere. We need more men, and for that we need more money."

"What's that got to do with me?" Dixon demanded, his frown deepening.

"Well, we figgered this would be a good time to see if you wanted to make a donation to the Sheriff's Law Enforcement Fund." Cotter shrugged. "Otherwise, you can't never tell what's goin' to happen. Them rustlers might take it in their heads to hit you next."

Dixon stared at the man in surprise, not sure he was hearing correctly. He glanced at his ranch hand, who had remained on the porch. The cowboy looked as shocked as Dixon felt. Dixon took a deep breath, his nostrils flaring angrily.

"You're saying that unless I give you some sort of payoff, rustlers are going to hit my spread," Dixon accused.

Cotter gave him a look of wounded innocence. "Now that's not what I'm sayin' at all. If it was like that, it wouldn't be no ways legal. I'm just sayin' that for your sake it might be a good idea to help us look after you."

Dixon's hand twitched. He wanted to reach for his gun, but he was not wearing one. In a voice that shook with rage, he said, "I want you off my place."

Cotter leaned forward in the saddle. "Now, I ain't so sure that's a good idea—"

The Rafter D puncher put his hand on the butt of his gun. "The boss said for you four to get off. Reckon that's what you'd better do."

One of the other deputies spoke for the first time. "There's four of us and only two of you, and the old man's not packin' iron. Don't seem to me you're in any position to give orders, mister."

Slowly Dixon lifted a hand and pointed toward one of the barns. "Take a look over there," he said.

Four ranch hands emerged from the barn, each of them holding a rifle. They stopped and stood casually, but their presence changed everything. Cotter glanced at them, eyes narrowing to slits, then said quickly to the deputy who had just spoken, "Take it easy, Henson. We came out here on law business, not to make trouble."

"But—"

"No buts about it," Cotter snapped. As he darted a nervous glance at the four ranch hands, Dixon could see the cowardice in his eyes. Then Cotter lifted a hand, rubbed his bearded jaw, and said slowly, "We never did get that drink of water."

"No, you didn't," Dixon replied. "There're creeks between here and Abilene. You can water your horses at one of them—as long as it's not on my spread."

"It ain't goin' to help you to be hostile to the law like this, Dixon," Cotter complained as he took up the reins of his horse. "Could be you'll regret it."

"I doubt that. Now I want all four of you off my place, or I'm not going to be responsible for what happens."

"Oh, you'll be responsible, all right," Cotter muttered, but he yanked his horse's head around savagely and kicked it into a trot. "Come on!" he called to the other deputies.

Dixon and his cowhand stood on the porch, watching the lawmen ride away. The puncher looked at Dixon and frowned. With an anxious edge in his voice, he said, "Might've been trouble if the boys hadn't come out of the barn to see what was goin' on."

"Yes, there might have been," Dixon agreed. "I don't care what Cotter said, I know a threat when I hear one."

"You reckon them rustlers'll be after our herd now, boss?"

"Let them try it," Dixon murmured. Silently he vowed never to step out of the house without a gun on his hip as long as John Henry Dawes was sheriff. "Let them just try it."

Cold morning air blew in Hunter Dixon's face as he emerged from the ranch house two days later and walked quickly toward the barn. He hunched his shoulders inside the sheepskin coat he wore. At this time of year, a man could freeze in the morning and burn up in the afternoon. Work went on regardless of the weather, though. This morning Dixon planned to ride out to one of his north pastures to check on the stock.

He glanced up abruptly as the sound of thundering hoofbeats reached him. Someone was coming in a hurry. When he spotted the rider, he recognized him as one of the Rafter D hands. The man was using his hat to slap his horse's hindquarters and urge the animal on to greater speed.

A tingle of alarm went through Dixon. Nobody rode that fast unless there was trouble somewhere behind him. He called to the cowboys working in the corral, made sure that his Colt was loose in its holster, and then ran to meet the rider.

The man thundered into the yard, hauled back on the reins, and skidded the lathered horse to a stop. Hanging onto the reins, he slid out of the saddle. Dixon saw the crimson stain on his shirtsleeve; the puncher was wounded.

"My God, what happened?" Dixon demanded as he grasped the cowboy's other arm and held him up.

"Rustlers hit us . . . right before sunup," the man gasped. "We heard 'em . . . drivin' the cattle off. . . . When we come out of the line shack, they . . . they opened up on us."

Dixon's weathered face was grim as he said, "Was anybody hurt?"

"Two of the boys went down with bullets in 'em. Don't know how bad they was hit." The cowboy looked down at his own injury. "This here's just a crease. Don't trouble yourself with it, boss——"

His knees gave out at that moment, and if it were not for the men crowding around him, he would have fallen. But strong hands caught him and carried him toward the bunkhouse, his fellow punchers handling him with surprising gentleness. Dixon trailed behind, his features bleak, his hand on the walnut butt of his gun.

The wounded cowboy had been staying at a line shack in one of the northern sections of the ranch. Dixon knew he could not visit the area alone today, as he had planned.

"I want a couple of men to stay here and keep an eye on the place," he said as the wounded man was eased into his bunk. "Get that bullet crease cleaned up and bandaged. If it looks like it needs more attention, send Cookie into town for the doctor. The rest of you come with me."

He turned and stalked out of the bunkhouse, heading for the corral to saddle his own horse.

It was almost noon when Hunter Dixon rode into Abilene. He was alone, having left his hands on the Rafter D to make sure the rustlers did not strike again.

Everyone was even more alert than before, riding the range with their rifles drawn.

Dixon estimated that at least two hundred head of cattle had been stolen in the predawn raid. That was bad enough, but worse, two men were dead. The rustlers had also run off the horses of the men staying at the line shack, preventing the two survivors from giving chase. If the hand who had carried news of the raid to Dixon's headquarters had not grabbed his mount as soon as he ran out of the shack, he, too, would have been horseless.

The rancher and his men had spent most of the morning trailing the stolen herd. The tracks had gradually played out, diminishing each time the cattle crossed a creek or a stretch of rocky ground. Dixon realized that the rustlers were splitting up the herd into smaller groups and riding off in different directions so the pursuers would have no chance of catching up to all of them. Eventually Dixon and his men had lost the trail entirely. Sooner or later, an embittered Dixon knew, the rustlers would regroup with the stolen animals. He would be able to do nothing about it—except head for Abilene and report the crime. That was what he was doing now.

When Dixon reached the county courthouse, he reined in and swung down from his saddle. As he tethered his horse at the hitch rail, he saw his hands were still trembling with the rage that burned inside him.

There were a few people in the main corridor of the building, but they moved out of Dixon's way as he strode toward the sheriff's office. His grim expression would make anyone step aside; Dixon looked more than ready to use the big revolver holstered on his hip.

He slapped open the door of the sheriff's office and stepped inside. As Dixon burst in, a deputy he had never seen before rose from the chair behind the desk in the anteroom. His hand drifted toward the gun he wore.

"Hold it right there, mister!" he snapped. "You can't come bustin' in here like that—"

"Where's Dawes?" Dixon barked.

The deputy stopped with his hand on the butt of his

pistol. He frowned, his eyes darting toward the door of the inner office. "What's your business with him?" he demanded.

Dixon forced himself to take a deep breath and try to calm down. He was glad that Cotter was not on duty in the office. Seeing the red-bearded deputy might have been too much to take; Cotter's veiled threats still echoed vividly in Dixon's mind. And the raid by the rustlers had come too soon after that visit to be entirely coincidental.

"I want to report a crime," Dixon said slowly, imposing his iron will on the fury that threatened to consume him. "I need to see Sheriff Dawes."

Before the deputy could reply, the door of the inner office opened, and Dawes himself stepped out. "I couldn't help overhearing what was going on out here. Hello, Mr. Dixon." Smiling broadly, he extended a hand toward the rancher.

Dixon ignored it, brushed past the sheriff, and pushed into the office. He was too agitated to sit down so he stood behind a chair, gripping its back.

Dawes stepped behind the desk, sank into the big leather chair, and regarded him with one eyebrow raised quizzically. "What's the trouble, Mr. Dixon?" he asked.

During the election campaign Dixon had spoken with Dawes several times because the rancher felt he needed to know the man better before he announced his support for him. But Dixon could see now that he had never really gotten to know him at all. On that handsome, mustachioed face was a mask, a mask of smooth amiability that concealed—what?

"Rustlers hit my spread this morning, just before dawn," Dixon rasped. "Killed two of my men and made off with a sizable bunch of cows. I want to know what you're going to do about it." Dixon took a deep breath and told himself to give Dawes a chance to answer. The rancher was convinced that Buff Cotter was somehow tied in with the outlaws, but that did not mean Dawes had to be. The sheriff could be unaware of what his deputies were doing.

"Well, I'm mighty sorry to hear that, Mr. Dixon," Dawes said, although he did not sound particularly sorry, in Dixon's opinion. "Did you try to track the thieves?"

"Yeah, but we lost them."

Dawes shrugged and spread his hands. "I'm not sure what you expect me to do."

Dixon stared at the lawman for a moment, wishing that his eyes and ears were lying to him. Then he abruptly slammed his open palm down on the desk. "I want you to find those rustlers, dammit!" he roared.

Dawes, his eyes growing cold, the affability gone, pushed his chair back and stood up. "I told you there's nothing I can do, Mr. Dixon. Getting upset isn't going to help anything. I don't have the manpower to send a bunch of deputies out to track down some rustlers." A shrewd look appearing on his face, Dawes went on, "It's probably Whitson's gang. Reckon he's left off robbing banks and trains and such and gone into the cattle rustling business. If I had more men, I could run him down. But that takes money, plenty of money. . . . Has anybody mentioned the Sheriff's Law Enforcement Fund to you, Mr. Dixon? This would be a perfect opportunity for you to make a donation."

Dawes had brass, all right; Dixon had to give him that. The rancher fought the urge to snatch his gun out and put a bullet in that smirking face. He knew about Dawes's reputation with a gun. Even if he tried to draw first, there was little chance he could beat Dawes. And if he did, that deputy was right outside; undoubtedly more of Dawes's men were elsewhere in the courthouse.

"I may have to take this pill, but I damn sure don't have to like it," he grated. "You haven't heard the last of this, Dawes."

"I reckon you won't be contributing to the fund, then," Dawes said dryly.

Not trusting himself to say anything else or even to remain in that office for one more minute, Dixon turned on his heel and stalked out, slamming the door behind him. He strode through the anteroom, stormed into the corridor, and pulled the door behind him with a rattling of the pebbled glass. But the gestures were futile. He was still as angry as ever. This visit had done nothing but confirm his worst suspicions. He still had to deal with two dead punchers and a couple of hundred stolen cattle. And there did not seem to be a thing he could do about either of those facts. If Dawes was not going to help him, who was?

Luke Travis and Cody Fisher looked up in surprise as Hunter Dixon stormed into the marshal's office. Travis had been writing a report for the town council, but he put down his pen when he saw the expression on Dixon's face. Anger was etched into the rancher's rugged features, but Travis thought he saw grief, too.

"What's wrong, Hunter?" the marshal asked.

As Dixon tugged his hat off, embarrassment joined the other emotions on his face. "I'm not sure I've got any right to bring this to you, Marshal, not after the way I told everybody I was going to vote for Dawes. . . ."

Travis shook his head. "I don't hold grudges. If you've got trouble, I'll do what I can to help."

"Rustlers hit my place this morning," Dixon said heavily. "Killed two of my punchers and ran off some stock."

"I'm sorry to hear that," Travis told him sincerely. "You have any idea who they were?"

Dixon nodded his head jerkily. "That may be the worst of it. I think they were working for the sheriff."

"What?" Cody exclaimed.

Travis's eyes narrowed. "You'd better be sure before you go saying things like that, Hunter. Several other spreads have been having trouble with rustlers lately. I think maybe Whitson has started stealing cows."

"Dawes tried to pass it off as Whitson's work, too, but I'm not convinced." Dixon's voice was harsh and stubborn. "I just went to Dawes's office and told him about it, and he refused to do one damn thing. Said he didn't have enough men or money."

That was a familiar refrain, Travis thought. But it did not mean Dawes was connected to the rustlers.

He was about to say as much when Dixon went on, "That's not all, Marshal. A couple of days ago, one of Dawes's deputies—that Cotter fella—came out to my spread with some of those cold-eyed gents Dawes brought in. Cotter said he was there to warn me about the rustling, but what he was really after was a donation to that so-called law enforcement fund Dawes set up. Said if I didn't kick in, the rustlers might hit me, too, like they have the others. It's nothing but plain and simple black-mail, dammit!"

"Extortion, actually," Travis muttered, leaning back in his chair. What Dixon was saying put a new light on things. Travis wondered if any of the other ranchers who had been raided had been visited first by Cotter or one of Dawes's other deputies. If that was the case, he had not heard about it. Of course, it was always possible that the ranchers were reluctant to come forward with accusations against Dawes and his men.

"Can you do anything about this, Marshal?" Dixon asked, his tired eyes boring into Travis's.

The marshal glanced at Cody and saw that he was looking at him intently, waiting to hear his answer. Travis sighed. "Not a whole lot, I'm afraid. You've got your suspicions and frankly I do, too, but there's no proof of anything."

Dixon glowered at him. "So you're going to sit on your rear end just like Dawes and let honest citizens be robbed and killed?"

Travis forced back the surge of anger he felt by reminding himself that Hunter Dixon had always been stubborn and blunt. "You can look at it that way if you want, Hunter," he said quietly. "But until there's some proof of wrongdoing, any lawman's hands would be tied."

Dixon stared at him for a moment, then turned without another word and walked out, his back ramrod-stiff. The door shut behind him with a slam.

"There goes one mad fella," Cody said into the silence that followed the rancher's angry departure.

"I know," Travis murmured and sighed again. "And I don't blame him. What did he expect me to do, though—march over to the courthouse and arrest Dawes?"

"Sounds like a good idea," Cody replied. "We might as well admit it, Marshal. John Henry Dawes is as crooked as they come."

"Of course he is," Travis agreed wearily. "But like I told Dixon, there's not enough proof to do anything about it. I reckon Cotter was careful enough about what he said to Dixon that none of it would stand up in court to incriminate Dawes, or even Cotter for that matter." The marshal shoved his chair back and stood up. "Which means that we're going to have to *find* some proof."

A grin tugged at Cody's mouth. "That sounds more like it. You just didn't want to tell Dixon we were going to investigate."

"The fewer people who know about this, the better." Travis took his hat off its peg. "I'm going to take a turn around town and try to think this thing through. You coming?"

"Sure." As Cody got his own hat, he went on, "What do you reckon happened to Dawes? I thought he was supposed to be a good lawman."

"Maybe he was once," Travis said. "But maybe being in power got to him after a while. Could be he was a low-down thief all along and just covered it up. None of that really matters now." The marshal's face settled into grim lines. "What's important is that somebody's got to stop him."

# Chapter Thirteen

MASON KINCAID HAD A MAP OF THE COUNTY SPREAD OUT
on his desk and was studying it with an expression of
concentration on his handsome face. With a fingertip he
idly traced the rough outlines of the areas he now
controlled, either personally or through the land development company he had formed with Eugene Croft. The
size of his holdings was growing rapidly, but not fast
enough to suit Kincaid. Within a few weeks, though, he
would be ready to make another move, the most lucrative one so far for him.

The door of the land office opened, breaking into
Kincaid's musings. He glanced up in annoyance and then
frowned when he saw that his visitor was Hunter Dixon.
What the devil was the rancher doing here?

"Good day, Mr. Dixon," Kincaid said, forcing his
voice into pleasant tones. "What can I do for you?"

"I got no time for small talk, Kincaid," Dixon snapped. "I'm here about that sheriff you brought in."

Kincaid blinked and leaned back in his chair, regarding the cattleman's taut, angry face. "I'm not sure I know what you mean," Kincaid said slowly. "Sheriff Dawes was elected by the voters. You supported him yourself, if I remember correctly."

"Yeah, well, we all make mistakes," Dixon said. "I reckon we both made one. That bastard Dawes is nothing but an outlaw himself."

Kincaid stood up. "You can't make accusations like that, Mr. Dixon. Sheriff Dawes has always had a reputation as a fine, upstanding lawman—"

"He's in cahoots with a bunch of rustlers!" Dixon broke in. "I already went to the marshal, but Travis said there wasn't anything he could do about it. I thought maybe you could, since you and Dawes used to be so thick . . ." Dixon's voice trailed off, and suspicion lit his eyes.

Quickly Kincaid said, "I know what you're thinking, Mr. Dixon, but I assure you it isn't true. I don't have the slightest idea what you're talking about. I know there's been some rustling in the area lately, but this is the first I've heard about Sheriff Dawes being involved."

"He is," Dixon said flatly. "If you're telling the truth, then you don't know about Cotter coming out to my spread and threatening me."

Kincaid stared at Dixon in bafflement, then sat down heavily. "You'd better tell me all about this."

While Dixon explained what had been happening to the area's ranchers, the land agent listened in silence. As the details were described, Kincaid could draw only one conclusion—John Henry Dawes was running a protection racket.

A protection racket! It was all he could do not to snort in disgust and contempt. With all the money that could be made, all the opportunities just waiting for the right man to seize them, Dawes had to threaten everything by getting mixed up in something as low-class as this crude extortion scheme. If no one stopped Dawes, the sheriff's activities could disrupt Kincaid's own plans. As his mind reeled, Kincaid realized he would have to convince Dixon that Dawes was not directly involved.

"This is serious," Kincaid said solemnly when Dixon had finished his angry speech. "But I can assure you, Mr. Dixon, Sheriff Dawes has no connection with this deputy's misconduct. Cotter himself must be the one behind it."

Dixon frowned. "You really think so?"

"I'm sure of it," Kincaid declared.

He was sure of one thing: To salvage this situation, Dawes would need a scapegoat. Cotter was perfect. Now all Kincaid had to do was make Dawes see how logical it all was.

"I'm going to have a talk with the sheriff right now," Kincaid continued as he stood up. "I know you gave him all the facts, but he probably didn't want to believe that Cotter could be doing such a thing. They've worked together before, you know. Naturally Sheriff Dawes would be more inclined to believe in Cotter than he would in your story. But he'll believe it from me."

"What if he doesn't?" Dixon prodded.

"You let me worry about that."

Grudgingly Dixon nodded. He rubbed his jaw and said, "Sorry about stomping in here like an old bull, Kincaid. It's not losing the stock I mind so much—even though that's bad enough—it's the two punchers those bastards gunned down. They were both good youngsters. No wives or kids left behind, thank God."

"Thank God," Kincaid echoed. He took Dixon's arm and steered the rancher toward the office door. "You just let me handle everything. I'll see that it's put right."

As Kincaid closed the door behind the rancher, he heaved an irritated sigh. He supposed he should have let Dawes in on his plans from the very beginning. That might have prevented the sheriff from acting on his own.

It had all seemed so simple when the idea first occurred to him, Kincaid thought. His own veneer of respectability was well established. With a tame sheriff in his pocket it would have been so easy to launch the empire that had been his dream for such a long time.

That dream would still come true. Mason Kincaid would not let anything—or anyone—stand in his way.

He rolled up the map he had been studying, stored it in its case, then took his soft felt hat from the hat rack beside the door. The sooner he disposed of this problem, the better, he thought as he left the office and walked toward the courthouse.

When Kincaid arrived at the sheriff's office, he found Lin Rogers on duty in the anteroom. The young deputy smiled and said, "Afternoon, Mr. Kincaid. Something I can do for you?"

"Is the sheriff here?"

"Sure is. He just got back from lunch. You want to see him?"

Kincaid bit back a sarcastic retort. He just nodded and said, "If he's not too busy."

"No, I don't think so." Rogers stood. "Wait just a minute."

The young man went to the door of the inner office, rapped on it, and disappeared inside when Dawes responded. A moment later he came out and told Kincaid, "Go right on in."

Dawes was standing behind the desk when Kincaid entered the office. He waved a hand toward the visitor's chair and said, "Have a seat, Mason. You here on business or just dropped by to pass the time of day?"

Kincaid closed the door firmly behind him. "I'm here to find out what the hell you think you're doing," he said as he sat down.

The cheerful grin vanished from Dawes's face. "I'm not used to people talking to me like that, Mason," he said as he sank into his chair. He plucked a cigar from a box on the desk and put it in his mouth without offering one to Kincaid. "If you've got something to say, spit it out," he growled.

"I don't like the way you're using this law enforcement fund to extort money from the local cattlemen."

"Extort—? Who the devil told you that?" Before Kincaid could reply, Dawes answered his own question. "Never mind. Had to be that son of a bitch Dixon. He was in here earlier, tracking manure on the floor and making all kinds of crazy accusations."

"Do you deny that Cotter went to him and asked for money?" Kincaid asked.

"Deputy Cotter may have asked him if he'd like to make a donation." Dawes shrugged. "Reckon that was all it amounted to, though."

Kincaid did not believe Dawes for an instant. He could tell that the sheriff was laughing at him, could see the mocking amusement in Dawes's eyes. Dawes thought he was putting something over on the whole town, Kincaid included.

The land agent took a deep breath. "Listen, Dawes, I've got plans for this town and this county. And I won't have anybody interfering in them, not even—"

"Just a damn minute!" Dawes interrupted, his teeth clenching savagely on the cigar. "In case you've forgotten, Mason, I am the duly elected sheriff of this county. I'll run this office the way I see fit, and *I* don't want any interference from you."

"You would never have been elected if it hadn't been for me!" Kincaid shot back.

To his surprise, Dawes chuckled. "Reckon that's true. After all, it was you who had the key to the ballot box."

Kincaid frowned in consternation. "Key . . . ? I don't know what you're talking about. That election was conducted fairly and honestly."

"I'll bet now's one of the few times you can say that about something you're mixed up in and mean it," Dawes said, grinning again. "You never even knew I lifted that key while we were having dinner the night before the election. I passed it to Cotter, he made an impression, and I put the original back in your pocket less than an hour after I'd taken it. Smooth as silk, Mason, that's what it was."

Kincaid's eyes widened in shock. "You mean you—"

"No point in keeping it a secret from you now," Dawes went on expansively. "Geraghty set that warehouse on fire to draw everybody's attention. Then, while the town hall was empty, Cotter slipped in and . . . adjusted the votes a little. Of course, I reckon I would've won anyway, but it never hurts to make sure, does it?" He lit a match and held it to the tip of the cigar, puffing it into life as he regarded the stunned Kincaid with a smug expression on his face.

Kincaid sat in shocked silence for a moment. When he finally recovered his voice, he said, "You . . . you can't get away with such high-handed behavior!"

"Shoot, I'll bet you've pulled trickier deals yourself, Mason," Dawes replied lazily. "Nobody knows about it but me and Cotter and Geraghty. And now you. But you can't say anything about it to anybody, because if you do, I'll claim you were in on the scheme with us right from the start. You can't bring me down without taking yourself along."

As Kincaid listened to the boasting, he felt a shiver go through him. Dawes was right. Kincaid could not *force* him to do anything. But perhaps he could persuade Dawes to give up these dangerous, penny-ante plots and bide his time for a bigger payoff. Dawes was intelligent enough to see the sense in that. Kincaid was almost starting to admire the man.

"All right. I won't try to tell you how to run the sheriff's office. But if you'll just work with me, John Henry—"

Dawes shook his head. "I'm running things now. I don't need some pasty-faced Easterner telling me what to do." His tone was harsh and angry again. These sudden shifts in attitude worried Kincaid almost as much as Dawes's refusal to listen. The sheriff went on, "You'd better leave now, Mason. I don't think we have anything else to talk about."

"But I just want to explain some things to you!" Kincaid exclaimed, his frustration building.

"So now I'm too dumb to understand things unless you explain them to me, is that it?" Dawes asked coldly. "Get out, Mason, while you still can."

Kincaid stared at his implacable visage for a long, tense moment, then sighed and shook his head. He stood up. "I'm going," he said. "I won't bother you anymore, John Henry."

"Reckon that'd be a good idea. Don't get me wrong, Mason—I appreciate everything you've done for me. But I'm running the show now, and that's the way it's got to be."

"Of course," Kincaid muttered. He opened the door, walked past Lin Rogers, and strode out of the building without looking back.

When he reached the front steps of the courthouse, he paused and drew a deep, ragged breath. His heart was pounding with anger and—whether he wanted to admit it or not—fear. Dawes could ruin everything. Besides that, Kincaid would not tolerate being under another man's thumb. He had never allowed that before, and he could not begin now.

Somehow, Kincaid vowed, he was going to turn the tables on John Henry Dawes.

Lin Rogers watched Kincaid leave the courthouse. Kincaid had left the door open behind him, and Rogers could see all the way down the long corridor that led to the front entrance of the building. He could tell from the stiff set of Kincaid's back that the land agent was angry about something.

Rogers frowned. He had a pretty good idea what was bothering Kincaid. It was not his nature to eavesdrop, but he had not been able to avoid overhearing some of the heated conversation coming from the sheriff's private office. From the sound of the argument, Kincaid had been accusing Sheriff Dawes of some sort of wrongdoing.

That was hard to believe. Dawes had always seemed

like an upstanding lawman to the young deputy. Oh, Dawes might cut a few corners now and then, just to make sure that justice operated more smoothly, but that did not make him a criminal. And it was true that Dawes had never been one to refuse favors from the grateful citizens of the towns he had cleaned up. Again, such things might not have been strictly "by the book," but they had never seemed really wrong to Rogers.

What about Cotter and Geraghty? Thinking back on it, Rogers had seen them taking advantage of their positions before, using their power as deputies to settle personal grudges, for instance, or hinting that it might be wise for local merchants to offer them whatever they needed or wanted. But that was only fair, Rogers decided, since the deputies put their lives on the line daily for the citizens. Rogers himself had always paid for whatever he needed, but he was not going to condemn a couple of fine men like Cotter and Geraghty for accepting gifts.

Suddenly he remembered his battle with Cody Fisher and his comment when the fight was over that Cody would probably arrest him. "The law doesn't work that way around here," Cody had said.

Rogers shook his head. It was too much for him to puzzle out by himself. He would talk it over with Agnes, he decided. She was levelheaded; she could help him make some sense of things. But he knew one thing for sure: He believed in John Henry Dawes, and *nothing* was going to shake that belief.

# Chapter Fourteen

WHEN LIN ROGERS STEPPED INTO THE ALAMO SALOON that evening, he was wearing his badge even though he was off duty. During the weeks since the election, people had come to know him, and they would have recognized him as one of Dawes's deputies even without the star. The buzz of conversation in the room died down as Rogers paused just inside the batwings.

He glanced around, saw the hostile looks being directed at him, and frowned. What had he done to make these men angry with him?

Then he spotted Hunter Dixon standing at the bar, surrounded by several local cattlemen. The area's ranchers and their cowhands frequented the Alamo. Over half the men in the room either owned or rode for one of the spreads around Abilene. All of them clearly had no use for Lin Rogers.

The young deputy stood there for a moment, then

squared his shoulders stubbornly and headed across the saloon toward a vacant table. He sat down, stared at the bartender, and motioned for a drink. If these men did not feel like being friendly, that was their business. He was supposed to meet Agnes shortly, and he wanted to have a drink first.

When a bar girl approached him and hesitantly asked him what he wanted, Rogers forced himself to smile. No point in taking his anger out on her, he thought. "I'll just have a beer," he told her. She hurried away to fetch it.

The noise in the saloon was rising again. At the bar Hunter Dixon seemed to be doing most of the talking. Rogers could catch only part of the conversation over the tinkling of the piano, but he heard enough to know that Dixon was discussing the sheriff.

"Kincaid told me not to worry . . . won't do any good . . . in cahoots with that bunch of rustlers . . . not a lawman . . . Dawes . . . nothing but an owlhoot himself!"

Cold rage surged through Rogers. Dixon had no right to accuse the sheriff of such things. Rogers had heard that rustlers had hit Dixon's place, killing a couple of his men and running off a herd of cattle. The rancher was understandably upset, but that did not give him the right to slander a man like John Henry Dawes.

The girl brought Rogers's beer. He thanked her and took a sip of the cool, foaming liquid, hoping it would calm him down. But as Dixon's booming voice still holding forth on crooked lawmen reached him, Rogers realized he was going to have to get out of the Alamo if he wanted to control his temper.

He stood up and dropped a coin on the table to pay for the beer, most of which was still in the mug. As he strode toward the door, he could feel the eyes of the men in the saloon following him. He pushed the batwings aside and stepped onto the boardwalk, glad to be leaving that hostility behind him.

It had been a disturbing day, he thought as he strolled

toward the Sunrise Café. Agnes would be getting off work soon, and he had promised to walk her back to the orphanage. He was looking forward to seeing her. Her beauty and sweetness would help soothe the uneasiness gnawing at him.

Rogers saw Agnes emerge from the café when he was still half a block away. Her red hair gleamed in the light streaming out of the window, and she smiled as she noticed him. Rogers thought she was the most beautiful sight he had ever seen. He quickened his pace.

"Good evening, Lin," Agnes greeted him as he came up to her. "How are you?"

"Oh, I reckon I'm fine," he lied. "How about you?"

"A little tired. We served quite a few more suppers than usual tonight. I'll be glad to get home and sit down."

Rogers offered her his arm. "Well, I'm mighty happy to escort you, ma'am."

Agnes laughed lightly and took his arm. They strolled along the boardwalk in silence for a moment, enjoying each other's company. Finally, although he hated to break the mood, Rogers said, "You must have heard about rustlers hitting the Rafter D."

Agnes nodded. "Yes. It was awful the way those two cowboys were killed. I don't really know Mr. Dixon, but I'm sure he must feel terrible."

"I just saw him down at the Alamo. He's pretty upset." Rogers hesitated, then went on, "He came to see the sheriff today. Seemed to think Dawes had something to do with the rustlers."

When Agnes did not reply, Rogers realized he had been hoping she would exclaim that such an accusation was ridiculous. Now he wondered if she agreed with what Dixon had been saying. When he could no longer stand her silence, Rogers asked, "You don't think that's true, do you?"

"I . . . I don't know, Lin," Agnes said reluctantly. "I hear a lot of things in the café. I know that some of the people who supported Sheriff Dawes in the election aren't very happy with the way he's been handling things. It . . . it looks bad that he hasn't been able to catch Mike Whitson."

"Whitson!" Rogers bristled. "Wait a minute! I was part of some of the posses that went after Whitson. We did the best we could. John Henry is a good tracker, but anybody can lose a trail."

"Sheriff Dawes was the one responsible for following the tracks?"

"Of course. You can't think he deliberately lost them?" That idea was almost beyond Rogers's comprehension.

"I didn't say that. I don't know a thing about chasing outlaws, Lin. But there're other things—like the way the sheriff is always asking for more money from the county and the town and the townspeople."

"It takes money to run a sheriff's office."

"I know that. I'm just telling you what I've heard." Agnes smiled at him. "But I've never heard anyone say anything bad about you, Lin."

She obviously had not been talking to Cody Fisher, Rogers thought. But he was glad to know the townspeople did not hate him. Some of the folks who were upset with Dawes were probably tarring him with the same brush, but at least not all of them.

They reached the spot where the railroad tracks angled across Texas Street, and Rogers held Agnes's arm firmly as they stepped over the rails. Then they turned north onto Elm Street. The rising full moon cast a silvery light on the leafless trees and darkened buildings. The night was cold, and a wind was blowing. Rogers felt Agnes shiver.

"We'll be there soon," he told her. "I ought to rent a carriage to take you home, so you don't have to walk in this wind."

"Oh, I don't mind the cold," she replied. "I was thinking about how I would feel if everyone thought you were . . . were a criminal. I don't think I could stand it."

Rogers stopped, turned to face her, and put his hands on her shoulders. Agnes tilted her head back slightly and looked questioningly into his eyes as he asked, "You don't think that, do you?"

"Oh, no," she breathed. "I trust you, Lin. I think I always have, ever since I met you."

Rogers leaned forward, his lips gently touching hers. The long kiss was both passionate and innocent, and it shook him to the core of his being. No one had ever demonstrated such faith in him.

He could not let Agnes down. No matter what happened, he would not allow her innocence and trust to be destroyed.

As Lin Rogers returned to the courthouse later that evening, he felt a strange mingling of joy and trepidation. The time he had spent with Agnes had given him joy. The trepidation came from the doubts he had begun to feel about John Henry Dawes, a man who until today had been his hero.

Rogers could still not bring himself to believe the rumors that were floating around about Dawes and his connection with the crooked dealings in the county. But rumors, even wild ones, often had their beginnings in a kernel of truth. A part of Rogers wanted to confront Dawes and ask him to explain away all those confounded suspicions.

If Dawes was innocent, though, Rogers's doubts would surely offend him. Rogers might find himself without a job and, worse, without a mentor.

Uncertain how to proceed, Rogers let his footsteps take him back to the courthouse. The night was growing chillier, and he wished he had stopped at the boarding-house where he rented a room and gotten his jacket. Well, he told himself, he would not be out much longer. He would stop at the office and make sure he was no longer needed tonight, then head home himself.

The front door of the courthouse was locked, but Rogers knew the side door would be open. As he circled around the building toward that entrance, the sudden nicker of a restless horse startled him. The sound had come from the rear of the courthouse; Rogers went to the corner of the building, some instinct warning him to proceed cautiously, and peered around it.

In the deep shadows cast by the courthouse were the darker shapes of several horses. It was hard to tell how many there were in the darkness. Rogers thought he saw a man, too, holding the reins of the animals.

Suspicion flared inside Rogers. Whoever that was, he had no business lurking back here this way. The first thought that occurred to Rogers was that the strangers might be outlaws who had sneaked into town to ambush the sheriff.

Rogers leaned out a little farther and glanced at the window of the sheriff's office. A light glowed there, and he could see the silhouettes of at least two men moving around.

There were dense shadows all along the rear wall of the courthouse. If he wanted to, Rogers knew he could slip along the wall until he reached that window. Dawes habitually left the sash open a couple of inches for fresh air, even when it was cold.

Rogers remembered the guilt he had felt earlier in the day when he accidentally overheard part of the argument between Dawes and Mason Kincaid. What he was contemplating doing now would be no accident. But he might overhear something that would answer some of the questions that were nagging at him.

He took a deep breath and began to slide silently along the brick wall.

The man holding the horses was smoking a cigarette; Rogers could smell the smoke drifting toward him. But if he was there as a lookout, he was not doing a very good job of it. Rogers could tell that the man's back was half turned toward the courthouse. It was hard to see much in the darkness, but the man's pose seemed rather negligent, as if he felt he had nothing to fear.

Rogers moved under the sheriff's window. It was about a foot above his head, and he could see that Dawes had indeed left the sash open slightly. The sound of voices drifted out to him from inside the office, and although Rogers missed a fragment of a sentence every now and then, he heard enough to make his blood run cold.

"—nothing to worry about, Whitson," Dawes was saying. "I'll take care of Dixon."

"We can't have him stirring up the whole town," a strange voice replied. "Better to take care of . . . before things get worse. . . ."

"You just carry on with the plan." The sheriff's tone was firm. "Before we're through, we'll bleed this county dry. Then I'll resign, and we'll move on. There're still plenty of spots in the West where it'll work again."

The stranger laughed. "You enjoy this, don't you, Dawes? You like playing the upright lawman. Well, just don't ever forget you need an outlaw like me to make everything work."

"Don't worry, Mike. I'm well aware of what an important part you and your men play."

Outside the window, Rogers shuddered. He was not sure whether to cry or laugh. It was almost funny how quickly a man's whole world could fall apart. He had gotten out of bed this morning believing that he was working for the finest lawman in the West. He had been proud to wear that deputy's badge. Now he was hearing with his own ears proof that John Henry Dawes was nothing but a crook, an outlaw just as bad as his accomplice, Mike Whitson. Suddenly a lot of things began to make sense. Too many things . . .

Revulsion racked him as he pulled away from the window. Not all of it was directed at Dawes. He was disgusted with himself, disgusted with the way he had closed his eyes to all the signs of corruption around him. As he thought back to the days in Ysleta and Santa Fe, he could see that Dawes had been mixed up in shady deals in those places, too. None of it had been on the same level as this alliance with Mike Whitson, a vicious killer and bandit, but it had been wrong all the same.

There was no arguing with what he had just heard, no

way to twist things around to make Dawes look better. The question now was, what was Lin Rogers going to do with this newfound knowledge?

He turned away from the window, unsure of the answer to that dilemma, then stopped short as a figure loomed out of the darkness in front of him. The hard round mouth of a pistol barrel jabbed painfully into his belly, and a harsh voice Rogers recognized as Buff Cotter's said, "Well, what the hell we got here? Don't move, boy, or I'll blow a hole in your gut, sure as shootin'."

John Henry Dawes glanced up sharply as Cotter opened the door of the office and shoved Rogers inside. Rogers caught his balance and looked around, feeling like a trapped animal. A few feet to his left, a small man with a narrow, pockmarked face was holding a gun on him. *Mike Whitson,* Rogers thought.

"Hold it!" Dawes snapped to Whitson. "It's one of my deputies."

Cotter strolled into the office, keeping his pistol trained on Rogers's back. "Howdy, boss," he drawled, not seeming surprised by the outlaw's presence. "Look what I found sneakin' around outside the window."

Dawes frowned at Rogers. "What are you doing here, Lin? You've been off duty for a while."

In spite of the shocking revelations of the last several minutes, Rogers's brain was still working. It told him that unless he was very careful about what he said and did in the next few minutes, he would not live to see morning. Not live to see Agnes again.

"I just came by to see if you had any more chores for me to do, John Henry," Rogers said, trying to sound calm. He glanced over his shoulder at Cotter and let some anger creep into his tone. "I don't know what the hell's wrong with Buff. He jumped me like I was doing something wrong."

"What would you call spyin' under the sheriff's window?" Cotter growled.

"I heard some horses behind the courthouse and just walked back to see who was there." Rogers had no idea how long Cotter had been watching him; if the older deputy had been there for a while before making his move, Rogers's next statement would be challenged. There was nothing he could do but continue. "I'd just gotten back there when Buff popped up and started waving a gun at me."

Cotter said nothing, and after a few seconds Dawes looked at him and asked, "Well, Buff?"

"All I know is I found him under your window, John Henry. I knew you was in here talkin' to Whitson, so I figgered I'd better bring Rogers in, too."

Dawes sighed. "Well, if Lin didn't know what was going on before, he does now. You talk before you think sometimes, Buff."

Cotter rubbed at his bearded jaw and looked somewhat sheepish. "Yeah, I guess I shouldn't'a mentioned Whitson, should I? Too late now, though." He did not sound overly regretful.

Rogers glanced at Cotter again and saw the vicious triumph in the man's eyes. And to think he had regarded Cotter as his friend!

Swinging his gaze back to Dawes, Rogers said hotly, "Look, John Henry, I don't know what's going on here, but you know damn well I'm just as loyal to you as Cotter!" He waved a hand at Whitson. "I don't care if this fella is Jesse James himself. If you say you know what you're doing, I'll believe you. I don't know why you didn't trust me to start with."

Dawes leaned back in his chair, a smile quirking his lips and twitching his mustache. He chuckled, then said, "Maybe I made a mistake about you, son. You've always followed orders pretty good—"

"Damn right," Rogers cut in. He was not sure how far to push this act, but so far it seemed to be working.

Dawes looked at Whitson. The outlaw had holstered his Colt, but he was watching Rogers closely. "What do you think, Mike?" Dawes asked.

"I don't trust him," Whitson snapped. "If I was you, Dawes, I'd get rid of him."

The sheriff studied Rogers thoughtfully. Seconds turned into minutes and stretched out agonizingly while Dawes pondered the situation. Rogers felt a fine sheen of sweat break out on his forehead as he waited to see if he would live or die.

Abruptly Dawes said, "You've been a good deputy, Lin. But things are going to have to change now. You know too much." He nodded toward the outlaw. "You know that Whitson is working with us. We're cleaning up, Lin. Another few weeks and we'll have more loot to divide up than you've ever dreamed of. Then it'll be time to move on. I'll resign as sheriff because I won't have been able to catch the outlaws who're operating around here. Then we'll all meet up later, somewhere a long way from here, to divvy up the haul and plan our next move. You understand all that, son?"

"I understand." Rogers nodded.

"So, now you know the whole plan. And you've got a simple choice facing you—join us, or die. Which will it be?"

Rogers took a deep breath. "I'm not a damn fool, John Henry. I was satisfied with a deputy's wages, but if there's a chance for more money, I want it."

"He's lyin', John Henry," Cotter snapped. "You know how lily-white this boy's always been. That's why you never let him in on the scheme before. How the hell can we believe him?"

"Your man's right," Whitson added. "I still say kill him."

Dawes rested his palms on the desk. "Now hold on, men. I didn't say I'd take Lin's word for anything. If he wants to be one of us, he'll have to prove himself. And I know just how he can do it." He smiled broadly. "You know Hunter Dixon, don't you, Lin?"

Rogers nodded slowly. "Sure, I know him. I saw him earlier tonight in the Alamo."

"He was still there a little while ago. He's trying to stir

up trouble, trying to turn the citizens against me. We can't have that, can we, Lin?"

Feeling a ball of coldness begin to congeal in his belly, Rogers shook his head. "No, sir," he managed to say. "I guess we can't."

"Good." Dawes's voice was flat and merciless as he issued the orders. "You find Hunter Dixon, Lin. And you kill him."

# Chapter Fifteen

———————————⊷❦⊶———————————

As Lin Rogers went down the boardwalk on Texas Street, he felt as though he was sleepwalking. He could hardly believe he had made it out of the courthouse alive. He even had his gun; Dawes had ordered Cotter to give it back to him, and the red-bearded deputy reluctantly complied. All Rogers had to do now was use that gun to kill an innocent man.

If he had harbored any stubborn doubts about John Henry Dawes's guilt, that cold-blooded command banished them forever. Dawes was nothing but an outlaw himself, worse than any of the owlhoots he had arrested over the years because he was betraying the trust of the people who had elected him. Rogers paused for a moment and lifted a hand to rub at his eyes, trying to ease the ache that was pounding in his skull. He had to stop Dawes, and as far as he could see, there was only one way to do that.

*The law doesn't work that way around here.*

He would go to the marshal's office, tell Travis and Cody what he had discovered tonight. They would know what to do.

Rogers's step was stronger, firmer, as he headed toward his new destination. He could see a light up ahead, burning in the window of the marshal's office.

As Rogers walked into the office, he saw that Cody Fisher was alone. Cody looked up from the desk and scowled. "What are you doing here?" he asked sharply. Before Rogers could answer, he went on, "I've been keeping an eye on you. You're still seeing Agnes Hirsch, aren't you?"

"Agnes is why I'm here," Rogers said. That was the truth. He was falling in love with her; he could see that now. That was why he had to stop Dawes. Otherwise he could never live with himself, knowing that he had let Agnes down. "There's trouble, Fisher. Bad trouble."

Cody came up out of the chair. "With Agnes?"

Rogers shook his head. "Mike Whitson is down at the courthouse," he said.

"You caught him? It's about time—"

"No. He's not a prisoner. He's down there talking to his boss—Sheriff Dawes."

Cody stared in surprise as Rogers quickly explained everything that had occurred in the last hour. Cody's eyes narrowed angrily as Rogers detailed Dawes's plan for bilking the county.

When Rogers finished, Cody said grimly, "Marshal Travis and I were convinced Dawes was crooked, but I never thought it went that deep. We've got to find the marshal and tell him." Cody frowned suddenly. "How come you told me all this, Rogers? Are you saying that you weren't part of it?"

"I had no idea what was going on," Rogers said, then laughed humorlessly. "Or maybe I did but just refused to see it. I don't know. But we can't let Dawes get away with—"

A rifle cracked wickedly somewhere up the street.

The door of the marshal's office was kicked open at that same moment, and both men jerked around. Cody's hand instinctively flashed toward the Colt Lightning on his hip, but he froze as Jim Geraghty stepped into the room and leveled the twin barrels of a shotgun at him. At this range the shotgun blast would also cut down Rogers, even though the two young men were several feet apart.

"Both of you hold it!" Geraghty barked. "Get your hand away from that gun, Fisher!"

Slowly Cody and Rogers lifted their arms.

"Know what that shot was?" Geraghty asked with a grin. "That was Buff bushwhacking that bastard Dixon. You didn't think John Henry really trusted you, did you, kid?" The heavy-featured deputy laughed. "Hell, he sent me and Buff to keep an eye on you. As soon as we saw you head for the marshal's office, Buff went to do your job for you, and I came on here. Pretty stupid, boy. Now your pal Fisher's going to have to die, too."

Cody's gaze flicked toward Rogers, and Rogers read the message in his eyes. If they leapt away from each other, there was no way Geraghty could down both of them. The scattergun might hit one of them, but the other one would have a chance to return Geraghty's fire. Rogers tensed, ready to move when Cody did—

A boot scraped on the floor behind them. Rogers started to whirl around, but something slammed into the back of his head. His skull seemed to explode, and as he fell, he caught a glimpse of several of Dawes's new deputies—men Rogers realized now had probably been recruited from Whitson's gang. One of the hardcases was clubbing Cody with the butt of a pistol; the same thing had just happened to Rogers. Geraghty must have summoned the men and told them to slip into the marshal's office through the back while Geraghty distracted Cody and him.

Those thoughts whirled through Rogers's mind as his consciousness slipped away. He tried to hold on, but a red current carried him into blackness.

* * *

Luke Travis stood on the front porch of the boarding-house where Aileen Bloom lived. The marshal had just rapped on the glass door panel with his right hand, and while he waited for a response, he tightened the grip of his left arm around the man he was supporting. The lamplight coming from inside the house cast a pale yellow glow on the pain-contorted features of Hunter Dixon.

Less than ten minutes earlier, Travis had been walking along Cedar Street when he saw Dixon emerge from the Alamo. The rancher had gone to his horse and mounted up. As Dixon started to ride away, Travis hailed him from the boardwalk.

"I'm surprised to see you still in town," Travis said, standing on the walk while Dixon glared at him from his saddle.

"I've been trying to find somebody who's willing to do something about Dawes," Dixon shot back. "Kincaid promised to have a talk with him, but the more I thought about it, the more I realized that that wasn't going to do a damn bit of good. It's going to take more than talk to put a stop to what Dawes is trying to pull here. And it looks like the citizens are going to have to do it."

Travis did not want to argue with the man again. Besides, he was certain Dixon was right about Dawes. Still, Dixon was hinting at vigilante justice, and Travis was not going to allow that in his town. He had just opened his mouth to say as much when a freight wagon with a lantern hung beside the driver's seat passed by.

Suddenly Travis's sharp eyes spotted a flash as the lantern light reflected off something metallic in the alley across the street. The marshal's instincts took over. He might be wrong, he thought fleetingly, but he would rather look foolish later than take a chance with a man's life.

He leapt off the boardwalk, lunging at Hunter Dixon and slamming his open palm into the rancher's chest. The hard shove knocked Dixon halfway out of his saddle. Travis landed heavily in the street and went to his knees.

At that same instant, a rifle blasted from the alley. Dixon jerked forward and pitched out of the saddle. His horse, already nervous from Travis's abrupt action, panicked and began to rear up and flail its hooves in the air.

Deftly Travis came to his feet and moved out of the way of the slashing hooves. He palmed out his Colt and lined it on the alley, but before he could squeeze off a shot, he heard the pound of running footsteps. Whoever the bushwhacker had been, he was fleeing after firing that single shot.

Travis glanced at Dixon and grimaced. The cattleman was writhing and moaning from the pain of the gunshot wound. Travis could give chase or help Dixon.

With a sigh the marshal slipped his gun into its holster. There was really no choice at all.

He went to Dixon and knelt beside him, looking at the dark spreading stain high on the right side of the man's jacket. The bullet had gone all the way through and emerged there. Travis glanced at the alley, figuring the angles in his head, and realized that if he had not shoved Dixon, the slug would have caught him dead center.

There was no time now for self-congratulation. Travis slipped an arm around Dixon and lifted the semiconscious man to his feet. Half carrying and half dragging him, Travis started toward Aileen Bloom's.

The door opened less than a minute after Travis knocked urgently on it, although the wait seemed longer. He could hear Dixon's harsh, labored breathing and feel the sticky wetness of the spreading blood.

"Luke . . . Luke, what happened?" Aileen asked anxiously as she peered out at Travis and Dixon. Evidently she had already retired for the night, for she was wearing a dressing gown, but she had her black medical bag in her hand. Old habits, Travis thought. A knock on the door in the middle of the night usually meant trouble.

"Dixon's been shot," Travis grunted as Aileen stepped

back to let him bring the injured rancher through the door. "Don't know how bad it is."

"Bring him into the parlor," Aileen said crisply. "You can put him on the sofa."

"He'll get blood on it," Travis warned.

A single lamp was burning in the parlor. As they moved into the room, Aileen deftly picked up a rug from the floor and spread it out on the sofa. "Let him down gently," she told Travis and reached out to help him.

Together they eased Dixon onto the sofa, and then Travis stepped back as Aileen knelt and began to examine the wound. While she was cutting away Dixon's jacket, shirt, and long underwear with a small knife she took from her bag, Travis glanced over his shoulder and saw the other occupants of the boardinghouse standing on the staircase that led down into the foyer.

Seeing the curiosity on their faces, Travis said, "We've got a wounded man here, folks, but Dr. Bloom is tending to him. There's no need for the rest of you to concern yourselves."

"Who is it, Marshal?" asked old Mrs. Dorsey, the widow who owned the boardinghouse.

"Hunter Dixon. Somebody ambushed him a few minutes ago." Travis turned back to Aileen. "How does he look?"

"Help me lift him so I can see the entry wound," she replied. Travis did so, and after a quick examination, Aileen went on, "It looks like a clean wound, straight through and out. The bullet passed just above his right lung, thank God. It tore some muscle, and he's lost quite a bit of blood, but I think he'll be all right, Luke."

"Glad to hear that," Travis murmured. "Anything I can do to help you?"

"No, I think everything is under control. I'll clean and bandage his wound, then some of the boarders can help me get him into a bed."

Travis nodded. "All right. I'd better go see if I can find the skunk who did this." Travis straightened and began to turn away.

"Luke . . ." Aileen said softly. He stopped, and as he looked back, she murmured, "Be careful."

Travis had to smile at the genuine concern in her voice. "Sure," he said.

His mind was whirling as he strode toward the office. He would pick up Cody, then the two of them would pay a visit to the alley where the bushwhacker had lurked. With any luck they would be able to follow the man's tracks and at least see which way he had gone. The rifleman had probably had a horse waiting somewhere, so he might have a good lead already.

Why would anybody want to shoot Hunter Dixon? Travis wondered. The rancher could be pretty abrasive at times, and Travis had had his share of clashes with him, but he respected the man. Most people in the county felt the same way, Travis thought. The only person Dixon had really had trouble with lately had been John Henry Dawes.

Travis almost stopped in his tracks as that thought hit him. If Dixon had been right about Dawes's involvement with the rustlers operating in the area—and Travis believed that he was—would Dawes have resorted to murder in order to silence him? Just before the shooting, Dixon had admitted that he was trying to stir up sentiment against Dawes.

As soon as he and Cody had checked out the alley, they would have to pay a visit to the courthouse, Travis decided.

When he swung open the office door and stepped inside, Cody was nowhere in sight. Thinking that the deputy might be in the back room or the cellblock, Travis started across the office, but the door leading to the cells opened before he reached it. Nestor Gilworth stepped out, a frown on his bearded face.

"Thought I heard somebody out here," the big man rumbled. "Figgered it was Cody comin' back from wherever he'd got off to."

"You mean he's not here?" Travis asked, returning Nestor's frown.

"Nope. Place is empty. I just stopped by to say good night 'fore I headed out to the orphanage." Nestor's look of puzzlement grew. "Say, I heard a shot a little while ago. You reckon Cody went to see what was goin' on?"

"He could have, but I didn't see him. And I was pretty close to that shot. Somebody ambushed Hunter Dixon while I was talking to him."

That news jolted an exclamation out of Nestor. Quickly Travis filled him in on what had happened. "I guess Cody and I could have missed each other in the dark," he concluded. "Get a lantern. I want to take a look at that alley, and then we'll see if we can find Cody."

Nestor nodded and fetched a lantern from the back room. He checked to see that it had oil and then said as the two lawmen were leaving the office, "I ain't much for hunches, Marshal, but I got me a feelin' all hell's about to bust loose."

"I'm afraid you may be right, Nestor," Travis replied grimly. And he wondered again just where the devil Cody Fisher could be.

Cody had been knocked out before, so he realized what was happening as he struggled back to the surface of the dark, oily river. There was a light above him, barely visible through the gloom. He kept pulling himself toward it, fighting off the clutching fingers that tried to hold him back.

Suddenly he was no longer in a river, struggling against the current, but was lying on something hard and unyielding. A floor, he decided after a moment. He was lying on a wooden floor, and his hands and feet were tied. He started thinking about opening his eyes, then decided against it when he heard voices nearby. The words made no sense at first, but after a moment he sorted them out.

"—take 'em out on the prairie and kill 'em. We can bury the bodies where nobody'll ever find 'em. That'd be the best thing to do, John Henry."

Cody recognized the voice as belonging to Jim Geraghty, and the memory of what had happened in the marshal's office came flooding back to him. He was not surprised to hear Dawes's voice reply.

"I reckon you're right, Jim." The sheriff sighed heavily. "I was hoping Lin was telling the truth when he said he wanted in on the deal. We could have used another good man."

"Well, he showed he couldn't be trusted, boss. Better to find out now—" Geraghty paused suddenly, then went on in a more excited tone, "Here comes Buff."

Cody heard a door open and close. Then Dawes snapped, "Well? Did you get him?"

"I hit him," Cotter replied grimly. "But I'm not sure he's dead, John Henry."

"What the hell do you mean by that? Didn't you check?"

"The marshal was there," Cotter replied, a whine in his voice. "He must've noticed me just before I squeezed off the shot, 'cause he reached up and pushed Dixon. I still hit the son of a bitch, but I don't know if I killed him."

Dawes cursed roundly. Then there was a sharp crack of flesh against flesh, and Cody guessed that Dawes had just backhanded Cotter. "You should've put another bullet into Dixon and one into Travis, too, while you had the chance!" the sheriff raged.

"Sorry, John Henry," Cotter said, sounding like a whipped dog. "I . . . I was afraid of attractin' too much attention—"

"You were afraid, period!" Dawes shot back. He took a deep breath, and Cody could hear him trying to calm himself down as he went on, "Well, what's done is done. There's a good chance Dixon will die anyway. Did Travis get a look at you?"

"No, sir. I got out of there in a hurry, and it was mighty dark in that alley. There's no way he could have seen me."

"You'd better hope you're right, Cotter. If you are, we can still come out of this all right."

"What about those two?"

Cody's eyes were still squeezed shut, but he could almost see Cotter indicating him and Rogers as he asked the question.

"They'll be disposed of," Dawes replied coldly. "Once they're dead, there won't be any evidence linking me or the sheriff's office with Whitson's gang. Travis may suspect, but he won't be able to prove anything." Dawes sounded more satisfied as he went on, "All we have to do is behave normally and go on about our business."

Cody fought off the despair that threatened to grip him. Rogers was probably trussed up just as tightly as he was. Putting up a fight was impossible. He was going to feign unconsciousness for a while longer, though, just on the off chance that something might happen to give him an opportunity to escape.

"Take them down and lock them in the storeroom," Dawes ordered. "Later, once everybody's asleep, we'll sneak them out of town and get rid of them."

Cody had to suppress a moan. Dawes had everything covered. In a few hours he and Rogers would be hauled out of the courthouse, taken on horseback into the country far away from Abilene, then presented with a bullet in the back of the head and a hastily dug grave. And for the life of him, he could not see a thing he could do to prevent it from happening.

It was going to take a miracle to save them, Cody realized. A genuine miracle.

# Chapter Sixteen

———◆———

J OHN HENRY DAWES SAT IN HIS CHAIR IN THE SHERIFF'S
office, smoking a cigar and gloomily regarding the top of
his desk. This had been an eventful night, and much of
what had happened had not been good. Dawes just
hoped he could salvage his plan. He would feel a sight
better once those two meddlesome deputies were dead.

There was a hesitant knock on the office door. Dawes
looked up and growled, "What is it?"

Buff Cotter opened the door and stuck his head in. He
had not gotten over the slap and the tongue-lashing
Dawes had given him earlier; fear and resentment were
still visible in his eyes. He said, "You got a visitor out
here, boss."

"A visitor?" Dawes echoed. "Who the hell . . . I told
you I didn't want to be disturbed—"

"I didn't give Mr. Cotter much choice, John Henry," a
new voice said. Faith Hamilton pushed past Cotter. The

deputy gave her an angry glance but did not try to stop her.

Dawes frowned. "Isn't this a little late for a visit, Faith? What are you doing out at this hour?"

"I couldn't sleep, John Henry. Please—I have to talk to you."

Dawes sighed. "Can't this wait, Faith? We're sort of busy here tonight."

"You don't look particularly busy," Faith said. Dawes had to admit that was true enough, but then she had no idea what was going on. "This is important, John Henry," she continued urgently. "I'd think that if I really meant anything to you, you'd want to hear what I have to say."

The sheriff's teeth clamped down on the cigar in anger, almost biting the cheroot in half. Then he forced himself to sound calm and said, "All right, Faith. Of course I'll listen to you. Come and sit down."

As Faith took a seat in front of the desk, Dawes flipped a hand at Cotter, motioning for him to leave and shut the door behind him. Then he looked across the desk at the young woman. Faith looked lovelier than ever this evening, he thought briefly, or at least she would have were it not for the agitation in her face.

"Something's bothering you," Dawes said after she had sat there in silence for a moment. "I can't help you if you don't tell me what it is."

"Do you know how long it's been since we had dinner together, John Henry?" she blurted.

Dawes shrugged. "I'm not sure. A couple of days?"

"It's been over a week! I hardly ever see you anymore—at least not in the light."

Dawes narrowed his eyes at the bitter, complaining tone in her voice. He recognized the signs. Faith thought she was being neglected, and she did not like the feeling. So now she was going to harp at *him* about it, on a night when he already had more than enough troubles. *Lord save us all from whiny women,* he thought disgustedly.

"I don't remember you seeming too upset the last time I came to your hotel room," he pointed out.

Faith flushed warmly. "That has nothing to do with what I'm talking about—"

"It has everything to do with it," Dawes interrupted sharply, pointing the cigar at her. "A woman thinks that once she lets a man into her bed, she has the right to take over everything else in his life. Well, it doesn't work that way with me, girl, and you'd do well to remember it."

She blinked, suddenly looking more stunned and hurt than angry. "How can you talk to me that way, John Henry?" she asked after a moment. "After all we've meant to each other . . ."

"We don't mean anything but a good romp between the sheets, and you enjoy that as much as I do."

A tear trickled down her cheek, and Dawes rolled his eyes. They all resorted to that same weapon sooner or later, but Faith would learn that it did not work on him. She lifted her chin, clearly trying to summon what was left of her pride and dignity, and asked, "Are you saying that you want it to be over between us?"

"I'm not saying that at all," he told her. "I'm just saying that I don't have time for this foolishness tonight. We'll have to talk about it later."

"Foolishness?" Faith repeated, her voice quavering. "If that's all I represent to you, John Henry Dawes, then I'm not sure we have anything to talk about!"

"Fine," Dawes grunted, pushing his chair back and standing up. He came around the desk and took hold of her arm, lifting her from her seat. Faith did not resist as he led her toward the door. As he opened it and took her through the anteroom and into the corridor, he said, "Sorry it had to work out like this, Faith. Maybe you'll feel different about it later."

She turned to face him, her eyes moist. "You're not sorry at all, John Henry. Not at all. But you will be." She turned and stalked down the hall without another word.

Dawes frowned as he watched her go. Suddenly he

became aware of someone looking at him and turned to see Buff Cotter regarding him with something like amusement in his eyes. "What the hell are you laughing at?" Dawes demanded.

"Me? Laughing? I'm not laughing at anything, John Henry." But Cotter had clearly enjoyed seeing Faith tell Dawes off. Cotter had been on the receiving end of some scornful words earlier, and now it was Dawes's turn.

"You'd better not be," Dawes warned and started to go back into the office.

"Sounded to me like that gal was threatenin' you, John Henry," Cotter told him, his tone more serious. "She don't know what we been doin' around here, does she?"

"What kind of fool do you take me for?" Dawes snapped. "Of course she doesn't know anything about it. The only ones who do are those two deputies, and they'll be dead before much longer." Dawes grinned tiredly as he shook his head. "No, Faith may be mad as a hornet right now, but there's not a damn thing in the world she can do to hurt me."

Faith Hamilton's fury carried her out of the side door of the courthouse and down the narrow walk to the street. Her heart was pounding wildly, and the only way she could keep her hands from trembling was to clench them into fists.

For the second time in her life, a man she had trusted betrayed her. The first one had been Mason Kincaid. She had never forgiven him, had not rested until her private detectives traced Kincaid to Abilene. Finding him and seeing his expression when she turned up had given her some satisfaction, but her real revenge was yet to come. Faith was not sure what form it would take, but sooner or later Mason Kincaid would realize that spurning her love had been the worst mistake of his life.

John Henry Dawes was going to realize the same thing.

Dawes was a different sort of man from Kincaid, however. He would never torment himself with worry simply because she represented a threat, the way Kincaid had ever since Faith arrived in Abilene. No, Faith told herself, there was only one way to make Dawes see the error of his ways.

She slipped her hand into the beaded bag she always carried. Her slender fingers closed around the butt of the Rupertus pocket revolver she had bought before leaving Philadelphia. It was a short-barreled .22, a "lady's gun" without much stopping power but wicked enough at short range. Faith Hamilton knew how to use it.

She took a deep breath and threw off the brooding melancholy that had seized her as she stood in the shadows outside the courthouse. Dawes would realize his mistake, all right—about the time she put one of those .22 slugs through his head.

But she had to deal with the deputies. Somehow she would have to get them out of the building. If she came groveling back to Dawes and begged his forgiveness, played up to his strong, passionate appetites, perhaps he would send the other men away so that he could demonstrate his control over her right there in the sheriff's office. There was an overstuffed sofa in the anteroom.

Faith's mouth curved in a smile. It would work; she knew it would. She would get John Henry Dawes alone, then teach him a lesson he would remember for the rest of his life, short though it would be. She had no doubt that she could get him to do what she wanted.

She replaced the gun in her bag, then walked quickly back to the side door of the courthouse and opened it. No one was in sight. She tiptoed down the short passageway and stopped at the corner. A quick glance told her that Buff Cotter was no longer stationed in front of the sheriff's door, and she risked taking a longer look. The sheriff's office door was ajar, allowing light to spill out into the hall, and a small lamp was burning in the big main foyer of the building at the opposite end of the corridor. Faith took a deep breath and started toward the sheriff's office. A faint sound coming from the other direction drifted to her ears. She stopped, frowning, then heard the noise again. It sounded like someone moaning in pain.

Faith no longer considered herself a compassionate person; Mason Kincaid's cruelty had killed that part of her. But she was curious. The sound had come from somewhere along the hallway, from behind one of the doors that lined the corridor. Abruptly she decided that her vengeance on Dawes could wait a few moments while she indulged her curiosity.

The moaning, if that was what it was, had been so low that it probably would not have reached the sheriff's office at the other end of the hall, even with the door open. As Faith walked silently down the corridor, she paused at each door, hoping to hear another sound that would tell her she had found the right place. She had no idea what was behind these doors. Various county offices, she supposed. Some of them had signs on them, but she did not bother trying to make out the words in the gloom.

Suddenly, as she leaned close to one of the doors, she heard a scraping sound from the other side of it, a small noise like someone dragging a booted foot across the floor. Faith waited. A few seconds later, the sound came again. This had to be the right place.

A wave of nervousness went through her. She was not sure why she was doing this. She had returned to the courthouse with a specific mission in mind, and she was neglecting that goal. But some instinct told her that this was important, too, that discovering what had made that sound could have some connection with John Henry Dawes.

There was no sign on this door; it was a plain wooden panel. Faith put her hand down to the latch and felt the key sticking out of the lock. Whoever had come out of the door last had locked it but left the key in place. Summoning up her courage, she grasped the key and twisted it, then turned the knob and shoved the door open.

She peered into the dim room, then jerked back and gasped as her eyes made out the two forms lying on the floor. Both men were tied hand and foot, but they were not gagged, as one of them proved by saying quickly, "I'm not sure who you are, ma'am, but please turn us loose! We're lawmen."

"What . . . what are you doing here?" Faith stammered. She could see them a little better now as a little light from the hallway filtered into the room. It was a storage area, she realized, but practically empty at the moment except for the two prisoners. Faith squinted at them and recognized Lin Rogers, one of Dawes's deputies. She thought the other one was a town deputy whom she had seen around Abilene a few times. Fisher, that was his name. Cody Fisher.

"There's no time for explanations, ma'am," Cody told her. "I'm just glad you heard Rogers moan while he was coming to. If you don't have a knife to cut us loose, then head for the marshal's office as fast as you can and tell Luke Travis there's big trouble down here!"

"But . . . but what about Sheriff Dawes?"

Rogers spoke up, his voice strained. "You can't go to him, Miss Hamilton. He's an outlaw, just like Mike Whitson! Him and the others, they're all crooked. And they'll kill us if we don't get out of here!"

"All right, all right," Faith said, her confusion building even more. Too much was happening too quickly tonight. She could not seem to take all of it in and make sense of it. So for the time being, she decided abruptly, she would free these two deputies and let them sort everything out. After all, that was their job.

"I have a little knife in my bag," she said as she came into the storeroom. "I hope it'll cut those ropes."

She found the clasp blade, opened it, and bent over to saw at the bonds around Cody's wrists, which were tied in front of his body. As she put the knife against the ropes, she saw Cody's gaze shift to something behind her. A shadow suddenly loomed over her.

Cody rapped, "Watch out!"

Faith tried to stand up and spin around at the same time. She caught a glimpse of Jim Geraghty, his heavy features contorted in a grotesque grin. Before she could even think about how to react, Geraghty's left hand closed over her wrist, twisting brutally and making her drop the knife. The blade clattered to the floor.

"What's this?" Geraghty demanded. "Helping prisoners escape? Reckon John Henry will want to know what his lady friend's up to."

"I'm not his lady friend!" Faith snapped. "Let go of me, you oaf!"

"Oaf, is it?" Geraghty asked, his eyes narrowing dangerously. His free hand grabbed her other arm. He yanked her against him and roughly pulled her halfway into the corridor. Hot breath laden with stale whiskey fumes assaulted her senses as he said, "I'll take you to John Henry, all right, but not before I have a little fun with you myself."

As he pawed clumsily at the front of her dress, Faith screamed, then twisted in his grip, her panic giving her strength. She still held her bag tightly in her left hand, and as she wrenched her right arm and shoulder free from Geraghty's grasp, that hand dived desperately into the bag. She snatched out the Rupertus revolver, tilting the barrel up as she pulled back the hammer. Seeing the weapon, Geraghty let out a yelp and grabbed for his own gun.

He never reached it. Faith squeezed the trigger, guided by instinct and blind luck as much as skill.

The crack of the .22 revolver was loud, but Geraghty's scream was even louder as his head snapped back. The cry was short-lived, though, because the deputy's knees folded, dropping him to the floor. As he sprawled out, Faith got a better look at the damage her bullet had done as it entered Geraghty's right eye and bored on through to his brain. She turned away, sickened by the sight. Geraghty was dead, there was no doubt of that.

Worse still, her scream, the sound of the gunshot, and Geraghty's cry would all draw plenty of attention in the quiet courthouse. Stunned, Faith could not move.

From behind her, Cody Fisher said urgently, "Get the knife, ma'am! Cut us loose while you've still got the chance!"

Faith shook her head slightly to brush away the shock. She turned around, her eyes searching the storeroom floor for the fallen knife.

The sound of running footsteps made her jerk her head up. John Henry Dawes had emerged from his office, gun in hand, and was hurrying toward her. As his eyes met hers down the length of the corridor, he faltered.

"Faith!" he exclaimed, his gaze going from her to the body of Jim Geraghty lying on the floor, then to the open door of the storeroom.

Dawes hesitated only a split second, then he was running toward her again. The little revolver was still in Faith's hand, and she knew she had to use it if she wanted to get out of here alive. She tried to raise the gun. Something stopped her, and she realized that it was the horror of seeing what the .22 slug had done to Geraghty. She had never seen anyone shot before, never seen such a hideous wound, and it was almost beyond comprehension that *she* had been responsible for it. That slight pressure of one finger had taken a man's life.

Faith hesitated long enough for Dawes's long legs to cover the distance between them. She was only vaguely aware of Cody and Rogers shouting behind her. Finally, at the last moment, fear took over, and she tried to jerk the pistol into firing position, but she was too late. Dawes loomed in front of her, his left hand slapping the gun to the side. She felt it slip from her fingers. He had holstered his own gun while running toward her, leaving his right hand free to grab her arm and shove her backward into the storeroom.

She let out a cry of pain as she struck the wall of the little room. Dawes held her there, demanding harshly, "What the hell's going on here?"

Faith gasped, unable to answer. Dawes glanced over his shoulder at Geraghty's corpse and continued, "Never mind. I can read the signs pretty easy. Geraghty came along just as you were about to turn these two deputies loose, didn't he?"

Somehow Faith was able to jerk her head up and down in a nod.

"You shouldn't have come back here tonight, Faith," Dawes said, and his voice seemed genuinely regretful. "I don't know why you were messing around down here in this storeroom, but it was a bad mistake. I can't let you make any more of them."

Keeping one hand tightly on her arm, the sheriff bent down and picked up a length of cord from the floor. Roughly he pulled her wrists in front of her and began lashing them together.

Faith finally found her voice again. Sobbing in terror, she stammered, "J-John Henry . . . don't do this! I . . . I wouldn't do anything to . . . to hurt you!"

"Sorry, Faith," Dawes grunted. He finished tying her wrists, then put a hand on her shoulder and shoved her down into a sitting position in the corner opposite Cody and Rogers. "I'd like to trust you, but I don't reckon I ever could, not enough anyway. No, you'll have to die along with Rogers and Fisher."

"You don't think you're going to get away with this, do you, Dawes?" Cody asked, his tone icy.

"Certainly I'll get away with it," Dawes replied arrogantly. He knelt and reached out to pick up the knife Faith had dropped a few minutes earlier. He cut off the extra cord from her bindings and used it to tie her ankles together. "Nobody will ever be able to prove anything against me, Deputy," he went on. "I'm just too damn smart to be caught."

"I've heard you say that outlaws who believe that always wind up tripping themselves, John Henry," Rogers said coldly.

"There's one big difference, Lin. Those were outlaws I was talking about. I'm a *lawman.*"

Cody's lip curled in a sneer of contempt. "You may wear a badge, Dawes, but you're no more a lawman than Jesse James! You're just as big a crook—"

Dawes backhanded Cody, the loud, sharp slap cutting off the angry accusations.

"I'm tired of you people yapping at me," Dawes growled. "If I hear any more out of any of you, I'll finish you off here and now. I don't care who hears what." He dropped his hand meaningfully to the gun on his hip. Rogers glared at him balefully, and Faith moaned. But neither of them said anything.

"Good," Dawes said in satisfaction. He glanced at Geraghty's body, then went to it and grasped the man's legs. Grunting with effort, Dawes pulled the corpse into the storeroom. Faith shrank away from it, her reaction prompting Dawes to grin.

"You shouldn't be so squeamish, my dear," he told her. "You're responsible for Jim's condition, so you shouldn't mind spending a little time with him."

Faith whimpered as she realized that Dawes intended to leave the body in the storeroom with them until he had a chance to dispose of it—and the three of them as well.

"Don't worry, it shouldn't be long," Dawes told her. "I've already sent for all the other deputies in town tonight. Someone will be coming for you in a while. This is probably the last time I'll see you, Faith. I'm truly sorry everything didn't work out between us. You should have settled for what I could give you."

Tears ran down Faith's cheeks, and shudders racked her bound body.

Dawes glanced at Cody and Rogers, both of whom were glowering at him. "Good night, gentlemen. Enjoy what you have left of life."

With that, he was gone, closing the door behind him and cutting off the light. Darkness shrouded the storeroom again, hiding three frightened people and one dead man who no longer felt a thing.

Travis and Nestor were in the alley where Hunter Dixon's ambusher had waited when both of them heard a faint, muffled sound. Travis looked up sharply, his eyes narrowing in the light of the lantern Nestor held, and said, "Was that a shot?"

"Sounded like it might've been," Nestor rumbled. "Couldn't tell for sure where it come from, though. Off down Texas Street somewhere."

"Well, we're not going to find anything here," Travis said in disgust. As revealed by the yellow glow of the lantern, the floor of the alley was a welter of footprints, wagon ruts, and horse tracks. Picking out the marks left by the bushwhacker would be impossible. Travis went on, "Let's go see if we can find out who fired that shot."

"You reckon Cody's mixed up with it somehow?"

"Could be," Travis replied. "He sometimes charges right into things when he shouldn't."

The two men left the alley, walking quickly down Cedar Street, then turning east on Texas Street. Travis's eyes searched up and down the avenue, looking for any sign of trouble. There had been no more shots, at least none that he had heard. It was late; all the businesses except the saloons were closed. Travis saw a few men on the boardwalks, but at the moment no riders or wagons were passing by in the street.

"Let's go to the courthouse," Travis decided. "Maybe Dawes or one of his deputies heard that shot and have already investigated it."

Nestor snorted. "Wouldn't hold my breath waitin' for that bunch to figger out anythin'! Not the way owlhoots an' rustlers been runnin' free around here lately. If Dawes'd just let *us* work on trackin' them varmints down—"

"That's his job, not ours," Travis said. "Although it does rub me the wrong way to see them get away with it."

They were walking quickly, and it did not take long to cover the two blocks to the courthouse. Travis knew that the front entrance would be locked, so he led Nestor toward the side door. As they approached, Travis saw several figures silhouetted against the light coming through the open door. At least four or five men were gathered around the doorway, and all of them seemed to be carrying rifles. Suddenly one of them stepped away from the group and came down the narrow walk toward Travis and Nestor. The other men disappeared into the courthouse.

Travis recognized the man coming to meet them as Buff Cotter. The deputy had a Winchester cradled in his arms, and his cheek was bulging. Probably chewing tobacco, Travis thought. Cotter came to a stop and regarded them through eyes narrowed with suspicion.

"What do you want, Marshal?" he demanded.

"I want to see Dawes if he's here," Travis replied shortly, in no mood to spar with Cotter. He started past the deputy.

Cotter moved slightly to block Travis's path. "Sheriff's office is closed for the night," he said.

Travis frowned. "You mean Dawes isn't here?"

"Didn't say that." Cotter spat into the darkness. "Didn't say he was; didn't say he wasn't. Just said that the sheriff's office is closed. You can come back in the mornin', if you've a mind to."

"This is ridiculous," Travis snapped. "I saw you talking to those other men. They were more of Dawes's deputies, weren't they? Something's going on."

"Reckon you can think whatever you want, Travis. It's a free country."

"Last time I checked," Travis shot back. "It might not stay that way with men like Dawes in office—" He broke off and took a deep breath, biting back his anger. He could sense the tension in Nestor beside him and saw that Cotter also seemed edgy about something. There could easily be trouble unless he was able to reason with the deputy.

"All right," Travis went on. "I had intended to ask the sheriff about this, but I suppose you might be able to help. We heard what sounded like a shot a few minutes ago, and it seemed to come from this direction. Do you know anything about it?"

Cotter shook his head. "Ain't heard no shot lately. You must've imagined it, Marshal."

A low rumble came from Nestor's throat. He took a half-step before Travis put his hand out to stop him.

"We're looking for my other deputy, too," Travis said. "You know Cody Fisher. Have you seen him this evening?"

"Nary hide nor hair," Cotter replied immediately with another shake of his head.

"Don't seem to know a whole hell of a lot, do you?" Nestor asked.

A grin split Cotter's bearded face. "I know what I'm supposed to know, Gilworth," he drawled scornfully. "I know I been right here in this courthouse all evenin', and there ain't been nothin' strange goin' on around here. So why don't you fellers just take your tin stars and move along."

Travis was not accustomed to anyone talking to him that way, especially not another peace officer. He was almost certain that Cotter was lying, that the man did know something about the shot and maybe even about Cody's strange disappearance. But standing out here arguing with him was not going to get them anywhere.

Somehow he and Nestor were going to have to get inside that courthouse.

"All right," he said to Cotter with a curt nod. "We'll be going. But we'll be back to see Dawes in the morning."

"You do that," Cotter replied smugly. As Travis and Nestor started to turn away, the big deputy moving reluctantly, Cotter went on, "Say, before you go, you heard whether or not ol' man Dixon died from that gunshot?"

Travis stopped in his tracks and slowly turned back to face Cotter. "How did you know Dixon was shot?" he asked quietly.

Cotter's rough features suddenly tensed even more. After a moment, he said, "I . . . I reckon somebody must've told me—"

"Who?" This question struck him like a lash.

"I don't recollect," Cotter retorted. "Could've been somebody in town. I . . . I was down at the Alamo a little while ago. Yeah, that's where I must've heard it."

"You said you'd been here at the courthouse all night," Travis pointed out. His eyes never left Cotter's now, and in the moonlight he could see the panic in the man's gaze. There was only one way for Cotter to know about Dixon being ambushed—if *he* had pulled the trigger.

Suddenly Cotter let out a yell and jerked his rifle around. The Winchester blasted, the slug tearing through the space where Travis had been an instant earlier. But the marshal was already moving, throwing himself to the side in a rolling dive that brought him back up onto his feet, his Colt flicking out of its holster and into his hand. Travis triggered a shot of his own.

The bullet whined past Cotter, who was now running toward the side door of the courthouse. Nestor's old Dragoon boomed heavily, but that ball missed as well, thudding into the heavy stone wall of the big building. Cotter moved fast for a middle-aged man; he slammed the door open with his shoulder and disappeared inside the courthouse before either Travis or Nestor could fire again.

Rifle fire snapped at the two men from inside the building, the slugs coming from more than one weapon. Clearly the deputies inside had heard the shots and come to give Cotter a hand.

"Head for cover!" Travis barked at Nestor.

The closest shelter was a wagon parked on the other side of Texas Street. Both men raced toward it, bullets kicking up dust around their feet as they ran. Travis flung himself behind the vehicle, and a cursing Nestor joined him an instant later. The deputy yanked his floppy-brimmed old hat off his shaggy head and thrust a blunt finger through a hole in the crown.

"Look at what one o' them bustards did!" he howled.

"We've got more to worry about than a bullet hole in your hat," Travis grated, crouching lower as the shots from the courthouse knocked splinters from the wagon. "They've got us pinned down here."

"What the hell happened, anyway?"

"Cotter's the one who tried to kill Dixon," Travis told him. "I'm not sure why, but Dawes probably gave the order to do it. When Cotter saw I'd figured that much out, he lost his head. I reckon it's war now, Nestor, but I'd say we're outnumbered. And I've got a hunch Cody's somewhere inside that courthouse, so he won't be coming to help us."

"So what d'we do now, Marshal?"

"All we can," Travis said grimly, "to try to stay alive."

# Chapter Seventeen

———◆———

"**Y**OU DID *WHAT?*" JOHN HENRY DAWES ROARED.

Buff Cotter returned the sheriff's angry glare. "You'd better quit yellin' at me, John Henry," he warned. "I been yelled at enough tonight."

"You couldn't tell it by the way you've acted. Of all the stupid—"

"I told you, Travis figgered out it was me who shot Dixon! There weren't nothin' else I could do!"

"So you tried to kill Travis now when you passed up a perfectly good chance earlier." Dawes drew a deep breath. "Well, this tears it, Buff. It's all out in the open now." A savage grin pulled at the sheriff's mouth. "But I'll tell you this much—I still intend to win, dammit!"

The two men were standing in Dawes's office. The sound of gunshots came clearly to their ears. Cotter had explained the encounter with Travis and Nestor Gilworth, and Dawes felt as if the floor had finally been jerked out from under him. All night he had been struggling to save the situation so that he could keep up his pose as an honest lawman. But Cotter's rash actions had ruined that possibility now.

It was time to cut his losses, Dawes realized. He and Whitson had already stashed plenty of loot.

"We'll have to get out of here," Dawes said, as much to himself as to Cotter. He looked up at the deputy and went on, "In the meantime, if anybody else tries to get into the building—kill 'em!"

The pounding of footsteps coming down the boardwalk behind them made Travis look around. A group of men led by the unmistakable figure of Orion McCarthy was running toward them, their attention apparently drawn by the fusillade of gunfire from the courthouse. Travis lifted himself slightly and shouted, "Orion!"

The burly Scotsman called back, "Lucas! Wha' th' divil be going on here?"

Urgently Travis waved them back. "The courthouse!" he cried. "Gunmen in the courthouse!"

Orion threw out his brawny arms to stop the men with him, many of whom were brandishing weapons. Since the saloonkeeper had worked as a deputy before, Travis knew he could quickly take control of the group. The marshal saw them scuttle back to take cover behind the building that stood on the corner of Texas and Buckeye streets. A moment later Travis heard the tavernkeeper's booming voice.

"Spread out!" Orion ordered the townsmen who had come with him. "There be villains in th' courthouse! Dinna let 'em escape!"

Several men hunkered behind the building at the corner, where they could cover the front entrance of the courthouse at an angle. Others retreated down the short block to Spruce Street and began circling around so that they could surround the big building.

Travis watched what he could see of the maneuvers with approval. The rifle fire from the courthouse was dying away now. If the deputies inside had spotted what the townsmen were doing, they had to realize that the tables were being turned on them. Within a matter of minutes, *they* would be pinned down.

Another yell drew Travis's attention. He turned slightly to see that Orion had commandeered a wagon from somewhere and was whipping its team of mules down Texas Street. Travis's eyes widened as he realized what Orion intended to do. The Scotsman hauled heavily on the reins as the bouncing vehicle reached Buckeye Street. He ducked as more shots came from inside the courthouse, aimed at him this time.

Travis barked at Nestor, "Let's give him some cover!"

Both lawmen raised up, exposing themselves as they opened fire on the courthouse. The distraction they provided gave Orion enough time to bring the wagon to a stop, turned crossways in the street. He leapt down from the seat, pulled loose the pin that fastened the tongue to the body of the wagon, and slapped one of the mules on the rump as hard as he could, yelling at the same time. The spooked mules lunged, dragging the wagon tongue with them as they ran out of the line of fire.

Orion crouched at the side of the wagon and put his brawny shoulder against it. As he slowly straightened his legs, the wagon began to tip slightly, but the strain had to be incredible. Even from several yards away, Travis and Nestor could hear him groan with the effort.

"I'll give him a hand!" Nestor exclaimed. He jammed his pistol back in its holster and ducked out from behind the wagon. As he ran toward Orion, a bullet plucked his hat off, putting yet another hole in it.

Travis emptied his Colt and was forced to crouch again to reload. He could do that without looking, so he leaned over slightly to peer around the wagon wheel. He saw that Nestor had reached the other vehicle and joined Orion in attempting to turn it on its side. Both big men gave a mighty heave, and the wagon went up and over, coming down with a crash. The thick boards of the wagon bed provided excellent cover.

Two men carrying Winchesters darted from the board-walk to join Nestor and Orion behind the overturned wagon. They barraged the courthouse with rifle fire and created enough of a distraction so that Travis could abandon his own position and join the others. The marshal took a deep breath, surged to his feet, and sprinted across the moon-bathed distance.

"Welcome, Lucas," Orion said with a grin as Travis reached his side. The Scotsman was still a little breath-less from his earlier exertion. "Who in th' name o' all th' saints be in there causing such a commotion?"

"Dawes and his men," Travis panted, a little winded himself.

Orion's eyes widened as he stared at Travis. "Ye mean tha' we be fighting th' sheriff an' his deputies?"

Travis realized how that had to look and sound to the other men. Having them oppose a duly elected sheriff just on his say-so was asking a lot. But they did not know all the facts, and he had no time for lengthy explanations. He settled for saying, "I can prove that Buff Cotter ambushed Hunter Dixon earlier tonight and tried to kill him, and I think Dawes was behind it. At any rate, the sheriff's men started shooting at us first. We have to restore order before we can worry about sorting every-thing else out."

Orion studied Travis's face for a long moment, then nodded and rumbled, "Aye. 'Tis good enow f'me, Lucas. Ye never lied t'me yet, an' I dinna believe ye would start now. D'ye want us t'rush th' scoundrels?"

Travis shook his head. "Not yet," he said grimly. "I'd rather try waiting them out. I don't want anybody else to get hurt if we can avoid it."

The deputies inside the courthouse did not seem to be interested in avoiding violence, however. They kept up a steady fire. This had the makings of a standoff, Travis thought, especially when he looked around and saw men bringing more wagons, these loaded with barrels. While Travis and the others provided covering fire, the wagons were rolled up and parked in the middle of Texas Street, creating a formidable barricade after their teams were led away. Travis, Orion, and Nestor were able to crouch down and trot behind the wagons over to the boardwalk, where, well out of the line of fire, they could discuss strategy without bullets singing past their ears.

Augie met them on the boardwalk. "It was my idea to get those other wagons and use them for cover," he said proudly, grinning broadly. "What do you think?"

"That was good, Augie," Travis told him. "Why don't you pass the word for everybody to hold their fire? There's no point in wasting ammunition taking potshots at that building. We're not going to do much damage."

"Sure, Marshal." Still grinning, Augie hurried away to deliver Travis's message.

Orion and several townsmen gathered around Travis and Nestor as the citizens' gunfire gradually slackened. "'Tis no' tha' we be doubting ye, Lucas," Orion said, "but prob'ly 'twould be a good idea t'tell us wha' this be about."

Quickly Travis explained how Cotter had let slip his role in the attempt to kill Hunter Dixon. "I didn't have any real proof," Travis concluded, "but the way Cotter reacted when I accused him, I'm sure he pulled the trigger. However, I suspect Dawes ordered it done. Dixon was becoming a thorn in Dawes's side."

One of the townsmen looked dubious. "It sounds to me like you've turned a political conflict into a shooting war, Marshal, and I'm not sure I want any part of it."

"Then go home," Travis snapped. "It was Dawes's deputies who opened fire on us. If they want to call it off, they're welcome to any time."

The citizen looked slightly shamefaced as he muttered, "I didn't mean anything, Marshal. I'll back your play."

"My only play right now is to wait and see what Dawes wants to do," Travis replied. "But I won't hold it against anybody who wants to leave. The only ones who have any official business here are Nestor and me."

No one in the little group made any move to leave. After a moment Travis nodded grimly but with a certain sense of satisfaction. Quite a few of these people had probably voted against him, but they still believed in him enough to take his side in this battle.

The shooting had roused the whole town, and lamps and lanterns were lit in nearly every building in Abilene. Travis sent men down Texas Street and north and south along Spruce and Buckeye to keep spectators away. Men who were armed and wanted to join the marshal's group were allowed to proceed; women and children were turned back, with one exception.

Aileen Bloom came hurrying down the boardwalk, her black medical bag in hand. Travis went to meet her. "You'd better not come any closer, Aileen," he warned. "There's been a lot of lead flying around."

"What in the world is going on, Luke?" she asked. "It sounds like a war at this end of town."

"That's about what it is. The sheriff's deputies have gone loco for some reason. I have no proof, but I think Dawes is in on it. But I am sure that Buff Cotter shot Dixon. How is Dixon, by the way?"

"He's going to pull through," Aileen said with a slight smile. "He came to a little earlier and heard all the shooting. It was all I could do to keep him from getting up and going to see what it was about. If he hadn't been so weak from loss of blood, I don't think I'd have been able to stop him." She looked past Travis, an anxious frown on her face. "Has anyone been hurt here?"

Travis shook his head. "Nestor's hat has been shot up a little, but that's the only damage so far. I've ordered the men to stop shooting for now, and I think Dawes's deputies have eased off some."

As the marshal spoke, the sporadic gunshots coming from the courthouse ceased entirely. Travis turned toward the building, sensing that something was about to happen. "Maybe Dawes wants to parley. . . ." he murmured.

A moment later one of the townsmen behind the barricade in the street called, "Man with a white flag coming out of the courthouse, Marshal."

"Hold your fire!" Travis bellowed. He cast a glance at Aileen, then hurried into the street as his order was repeated, the echoed murmur buzzing around the blocks surrounding the courthouse. He looked toward the big building and saw a tall, erect figure striding across the lawn, a rifle with a white rag tied to its muzzle gripped tightly in the man's hand.

Travis recognized him immediately: John Henry Dawes.

Dawes stopped about halfway between the courthouse and the street and shouted, "Travis! Luke Travis! You out there, Marshal?"

"I'm here," Travis called back. "What do you want, Dawes?"

"I won't try to claim there's been some sort of misunderstanding, Travis." Dawes's voice had an ironic tone, almost a touch of humor. "We both know things can't go back to what they were before. Too much has happened."

"Like telling your deputy Cotter to kill Hunter Dixon?" At Travis's shouted question, a stir went through the crowd.

"I'm not going to argue with you, Travis," Dawes called. "I'm just telling you how things are going to be. We have three prisoners in the courthouse, and unless you let us ride out of Abilene, we'll kill them. That's a promise."

Someone clutched at Travis's arm, and he looked around angrily to see who was bothering him at this crucial moment. He was surprised to see Mason Kincaid standing there. The land agent was somewhat pale, as if he was much closer to danger than he ever wanted to be.

"This is crazy, Marshal!" Kincaid said urgently. "What can you hope to accomplish by provoking a fight with Sheriff Dawes? I know you resent the fact that he defeated you in the election—"

"Shut up, Kincaid!" Travis cut him off savagely. It was all he could do not to smash a fist into the Easterner's face. "This isn't about politics anymore, you idiot.

Dawes is an outlaw. We know it, and he knows we know it. That's why he just threatened to kill three hostages!"

Kincaid paled even more. He stammered, "I . . . I thought I heard something about that, but I was sure I was mistaken—"

"What about it, Travis?" Dawes shouted. "I'm waiting for your answer. Do we ride out of here, or do we kill those prisoners? Just in case you're wondering, your deputy Fisher is one of them."

Travis turned away from Kincaid, ignoring the land agent now. The knowledge that Cody was Dawes's prisoner hit him hard. He had suspected as much, but a part of him had still hoped that Cody would show up, grinning and ready to pitch right into the fray.

There was still the matter of the other two hostages. "Who else do you have in there, Dawes?" he called. It could not hurt anything to keep Dawes talking for a while.

"No harm in telling you," Dawes replied. "One of my men, Lin Rogers, decided he wanted to change sides. He's a prisoner, too. And the third one is a beautiful lady named Faith Hamilton. You probably know her, Travis. You don't want her death on your conscience, do you?"

Travis heard Kincaid gasp at the revelation that Faith was one of the hostages. Kincaid had seemed to know her fairly well, and when Travis glanced at him now, the man looked as though a mule had just kicked him in the belly. Kincaid turned away and headed toward the boardwalk, muttering to himself.

Travis was glad to see him go. That was one less thing he had to worry about. It was going to be hard enough deciding what to do. Cody had been a good deputy for a long time, but more importantly, he was Travis's friend.

Unfortunately the choice was clear-cut. Dawes was crooked, quite possibly a murderer. Travis could not let him go, hostages or no hostages. Besides, Dawes might well kill his prisoners no matter how the situation developed. But the decision was still a painful one.

Travis raised his voice and called out, "I can't let you ride out of here, Dawes. You and your men throw down your guns and leave the courthouse with your hands in the air. That's your only choice."

Slowly, deliberately, Dawes took a cigar from his shirt pocket and stuck it in his mouth. "Wrong, Travis," he said. "There's one more choice. You can come in and get us—and bury those three prisoners. Up to you." With that, he turned and strolled arrogantly back into the building.

As Travis watched Dawes disappear through the door, he held his breath, hoping that no one would get trigger-happy and drop the sheriff. That would no doubt launch a bloodbath inside the building. Travis still hoped to wait this out. He could send a wire to Governor Anthony asking for troops.

But every instinct told him that this standoff would end badly. People were going to die, maybe a lot of people, and he had a feeling that the showdown would come before the night was over.

On impulse, he reached into his pocket and pulled out his watch, flipping it open and holding it at an angle so that he could see the hands in the light coming from a nearby building. The hour was already past midnight.

"Well, Lucas?" Orion McCarthy asked, voicing the question that nearly everyone in Abilene had to be asking themselves at this moment on this cold autumn night. "Wha' do we do now?"

"We wait," Travis said. "We wait."

# Chapter Eighteen

———◆———

MASON KINCAID STOOD ON THE BOARDWALK ON TEXAS Street, struggling with the mad whirl of emotions that threatened to make him sick to his stomach. Somehow everything had gone wrong. Dawes was obviously as big a criminal as Hunter Dixon had made him out to be. And incredible though it seemed, Luke Travis had uncovered some proof of that. Now Dawes was fighting back, battling for survival rather than wealth this time.

And one of Dawes's weapons was none other than Faith Hamilton.

Above all else that fact hammered at Kincaid's mind. Faith was in deadly jeopardy, a prisoner of what was evidently a bloodthirsty band of outlaws masquerading as lawmen. Dawes had made it plain during his exchange with Travis that Faith, along with the other two prisoners, would be killed if anyone tried to rush the courthouse.

Kincaid smiled grimly. Bringing Dawes to Abilene had not worked out as Kincaid had planned, but the sheriff could still serve a purpose.

Although he hated to get anywhere near the line of fire, Kincaid crouched and trotted out into the street again, seeking Luke Travis. He spotted the marshal behind one of the wagons in the barricade and headed toward him. Travis glanced around, spotted him, and got an irritated look on his face again.

"I haven't come to argue with you, Marshal," Kincaid said quickly. "I've been thinking about the situation, and I believe I was wrong about John Henry Dawes."

"Is that so?" Travis replied, the derision in his voice palpable.

Kincaid flushed but maintained a tight grip on his anger. "I suppose I deserved that. But the important thing now, Travis, is that Dawes be brought to justice."

"That's what I intend to do," Travis told him. "Do you have any suggestions how we can go about it?"

"I think you should rush the courthouse," Kincaid said solemnly. "Dawes can't have any more than, what, seven or eight men in there with him? Surely they can be overpowered."

Travis regarded him for a long moment, frowning in obvious surprise at this change in Kincaid's attitude. Kincaid had always complained about excessive violence. Finally Travis said, "If we did that, we'd lose some men for sure. And Dawes would probably kill those hostages."

"He's going to kill them whatever you do—unless he's stopped first."

Travis nodded slowly. "Could be you've got a point, Kincaid. Reckon I just expected you to be a little more concerned about Miss Hamilton."

"I am concerned," Kincaid said earnestly. "That's why I can't bear the thought of waiting out here while God knows what could be happening to her inside. I say rush the place, Marshal, and do the best we can to save the prisoners."

"I'll keep it in mind," Travis replied. "That's all I can promise."

"I wouldn't wait too long. You never know what a madman like Dawes is going to do."

Kincaid turned and scurried back to the safety of the boardwalk. He had done the best he could. Now it was up to Travis and Dawes.

With any luck, before this night was over, Faith Hamilton would be dead—and one more threat to Mason Kincaid would be gone.

Inside the courthouse John Henry Dawes sat on the floor of the main corridor with his back against the wall, a Winchester across his lap. He was seated only a couple of feet from the short, narrow passageway that led to the side door of the building, where he had stationed one of his deputies. The rest of his men were scattered through out the courthouse, crouched at windows in various offices that overlooked all approaches to the building. They were spread thin, no doubt about that, but it was vital that they cover all the angles. Dawes did not want any of Travis's forces sneaking up on them.

He felt a bit like a general commanding a badly outnumbered army against a wily opponent. He did not really respect Luke Travis—no honest man could ever receive Dawes's respect—but he did give the marshal credit for being a worthy adversary. Dawes held a superior position, but Travis led the stronger force—for the moment.

The marshal had no way of knowing that Dawes had sent for reinforcements.

When he had first spotted men trying to surround the courthouse, Dawes grabbed one of his deputies and barked, "Slip out a back window and grab a horse! You've got to get to Whitson and bring back help!"

The man knew very well where the outlaw camp was, since until recently he had been a member of the gang. "I'll fetch 'em, John Henry!" he answered enthusiastically, then disappeared through one of the windows into the night.

Buff Cotter came along the hallway now, the truculent expression still on his bearded face. He had been given the job of going through the building and checking each man's position, to make sure the citizens were not preparing to rush the place. After each round, he returned to Dawes, apprising the sheriff of what was happening.

"Still quiet out there," Cotter said, dropping into a crouch beside Dawes. "That bastard Travis must be plannin' something. How long we goin' to wait before killin' them hostages, John Henry?"

"I'll let you know when it's time," Dawes snapped, taking the cigar out of his mouth. "They're no protection to us if they're dead. That whole parley was just to buy us some time."

Cotter frowned. "Time for what? Seems like things is just gettin' worse."

Dawes snorted and took a puff on the stogie. He had not told Cotter all of his plans; the man's earlier rash decisions certainly did not inspire confidence. Still, Cotter was here risking his life with the others. Dawes supposed he had a right to know what was going on.

"All we have to do is hold out until help arrives," he told Cotter. "I sent a man to fetch Whitson and the rest of the gang, just after this mess started."

Cotter let out a low whistle. "That was smart thinkin', John Henry. They can bust us out of this damned bottleneck."

"They can do more than that. When Whitson and the boys come boiling in, we'll have the town's defenders in a cross fire." A note of brutal anticipation entered Dawes's voice as he went on, "We'll wipe out Travis and the others, join up with Whitson, loot the banks, clean out the rest of the town, and leave Abilene a long way behind us. It'll be the best haul yet, Buff."

Cotter licked his lips and grinned. "Sounds like it. But

the story'll get out. We won't never be able to pretend to be honest badge-toters again."

"Don't reckon I care about that," Dawes said with a shrug. "I was getting a mite tired of it, anyway. With the loot we take out of here, I'll be able to head for Mexico, find me some hacienda with plenty of those hot-blooded, brown-skinned wenches, and live like a king for the rest of my life." He slapped Cotter on the shoulder. "Doesn't sound half bad, does it?"

"No, sir, it sure don't," Cotter agreed.

Dawes took a deep breath. "Well, Whitson ought to be here soon. No point in waiting until the last minute to do everything. Why don't you go get rid of those prisoners in the storeroom while I check the other men?"

Cotter straightened. "It'll be a pleasure," he said. "Especially Rogers. I never did trust that young pup. Ain't surprised he turned on us."

"Hold on a minute." Dawes's sharp command stopped Cotter. "We don't want three shots giving Travis the idea that the hostages are dead. He might make a move too soon if he thought that." Dawes grinned. "Use a knife."

Cody Fisher could hear Faith Hamilton sobbing quietly in the opposite corner of the dark storeroom. A little light came under the door, and Cody's eyes had adjusted to the gloom enough for him to see the others as shadowy forms in the darkness. Rogers had not said anything for a long time, but Cody heard him shift around occasionally. Every now and then Rogers let out a grunt of effort.

Jim Geraghty, of course, said absolutely nothing.

His curiosity aroused to the point where it would not be denied, Cody whispered to Rogers, "What the devil are you doing?"

"Almost . . . got these ropes . . . loose," came the strained answer from the other young man.

Cody felt hope surge at those words. He had tried to loosen his own bonds, but the effort had been futile. Maybe Geraghty had not tied Rogers quite as tightly.

Cody had heard all the shooting earlier and knew that

Travis and Nestor must have found out what was going on. That no one had come to release the prisoners told Cody that Dawes and his men were still in control of the courthouse.

Now, if Rogers could manage to free them, he and Cody might be able to get some guns and turn the tide in the battle by taking Dawes by surprise.

"I used to . . . play with ropes a lot . . . when I was a kid," Rogers suddenly said, and Cody could tell from his voice that he was still trying to work loose. "My pa said I could . . . tie knots before I could walk."

Cody heard himself asking, "Where are you from, anyway?"

"Grew up on a ranch . . . in New Mexico. Just a little spread. . . . My pa and my brothers ran it. I didn't have the belly for . . . ranch work. Started packing a star for Dawes instead." Rogers laughed humorlessly. "Wish I'd . . . kept punching steers. . . . Ah!"

Cody leaned forward eagerly. "You got it?"

"Got it," Rogers replied. "A couple of fingers, anyway, and that's all I really need. Now all I have to do is undo this knot here. . . ."

Less than thirty seconds later, Rogers's hands were free, and he quickly untied his legs. Cody's pulse began to beat faster. He did not recall that Dawes had locked the storeroom door when he left earlier; they would be able to get out, and then they could jump a couple of Dawes's men and grab their guns—

Cody's head snapped up at the sound of footsteps hurrying down the hall. He had heard other men going by before, but these steps sounded different somehow, as if they were coming in this direction for a purpose.

Rogers heard the sounds, too. He had been about to untie Cody's hands, but he stood up abruptly and moved back against the wall beside the door. "Close your eyes!" he whispered urgently to Cody.

Cody knew why Rogers told him to do that. They had been sitting in this dark room for a long time. Even the relatively dim corridor would seem blindingly bright until their eyes adjusted. Cody wished Rogers had gotten free five minutes earlier.

Just as Cody had feared, the footsteps stopped outside the door. With his eyes squeezed shut, Cody heard the hinges squeak as the door swung open. "Time for you folks to say so long," a rough voice announced cheerfully.

Cody carefully opened his eyes a slit and saw Buff Cotter stepping into the storeroom, a grin on his face and a big knife in his hand. The renegade deputy had come to finish them off, Cody realized. In that same instant he lifted his lashed-together feet and kicked out.

Cotter must not have expected resistance. He tried to jump back, but he was slow. Rogers lunged and threw himself onto Cotter's back at the same moment that Cody kicked the knife out of the man's hands.

Faith Hamilton let out a scream.

As Rogers and Cotter grappled furiously, they staggered backward out of the storeroom. Cody hunched forward to see what was happening. Rogers cracked a hard right across Cotter's face, then suddenly stumbled over a rifle that had appeared under his feet. Cody guessed that Cotter had leaned the Winchester against the corridor wall before opening the storeroom door, and the two men had knocked the gun over during the struggle. Rogers's balance deserted him, and he started to fall. Leering triumphantly, Cotter grabbed for the pistol on his hip.

Rogers's hand landed on the stock of the Winchester. Instantly he snatched up the rifle, his finger finding the trigger. Cody's eyes widened as Rogers tilted the barrel toward Cotter. If there was no round in the chamber, Rogers could never work the lever in time.

Cotter's revolver blasted as soon as it cleared leather. But the Winchester had cracked wickedly a split second earlier, the upward-angling slug smashing into Cotter's stomach and probably barreling through his heart. Dead on his feet, Cotter fired a second shot, this one into the floor, then toppled backward.

"Get the knife!" Rogers called to Cody as he raised himself onto his knees, levered the rifle, and glanced around anxiously in case someone came to investigate the shots.

Cody heaved himself back, grappled for the knife Cotter had dropped, and began awkwardly sawing through the ropes around his ankles. The blade was sharp, and the cords parted quickly. Turning the blade, Cody cut the ropes binding his arms, being careful not to slice his wrists.

His fingers were clumsy and felt twice their normal size after hours of impaired circulation, but he managed to free himself. He turned to Faith Hamilton, who shrank back as he approached her with the knife.

"Take it easy," Cody told her. "I'm just trying to help you. Hold out your hands."

Trembling, Faith did as he told her, and within seconds he had freed her as well. Rogers had retreated just inside the little room. As Cody straightened from cutting Faith's bonds, Rogers suddenly moaned a little. He swayed and would have fallen if Cody had not quickly put a hand on his arm to support him. As it was, Rogers sagged against the wall.

"Damn!" Cody breathed as he saw the spreading red stain on Rogers's side. He had been too busy to notice it until now. Obviously Cotter's hastily fired first shot had hit its target after all. Cody asked Rogers, "How bad is it?"

"B-bad enough. I thought I could just ignore it until we . . . until we got out of here. Now I don't reckon—"

Rogers broke off, bit his lip, and winced. Cody eased him into a sitting position against the wall and said, "What did it look like out there?"

"Didn't . . . didn't see anybody. There's some shooting . . . sounds like from the front of the building . . . south side. . . . Fighting's starting up again. . . . Lord, it's starting to hurt, Fisher!"

"Take it easy," Cody told him, knowing there was

nothing he could do for Rogers here. He had to get him out of the courthouse. Cody could hear the renewed shooting, too. It sounded like a pitched battle, and there was a good chance Luke Travis was leading the other side. Cody went on, "You just stay here with Miss Hamilton. I'm going after Dawes. I'm betting that Travis is outside, and if Dawes is busy in here, that'll give the marshal a chance to bust in from the front."

Rogers caught weakly at his sleeve. "You . . . you'll be killed."

"I'll take that chance." Cody's face was grim. "I already have a score to settle with Dawes, for a mighty good paint pony Whitson's men killed. I'll even things for you, too."

"You . . . do that," Rogers said, managing a tiny smile. "Cody . . . I really do care for Agnes Hirsch. I never wanted to . . . to hurt her."

"I know," Cody whispered. "I know that now."

"You . . . tell her . . ."

"You can tell her yourself once we get out of—"

"No! You do it . . . pard . . ."

Cody took a deep breath. "I'll do it," he told Rogers, even though the other man could no longer hear him. Cody reached out, closed Rogers's unseeing eyes, and stood up.

He lifted the Winchester, turned to Faith, and said, "Stay right here until somebody you know comes to get you." Then he eased himself out into the hall. When no one took a shot at him, he bent down and scooped up Cotter's fallen pistol. He glanced into the storeroom and saw the terror on Faith's face, but there was nothing he could do about it now. Cody started down the hall, the Winchester gripped tight and ready in his hands.

Outside, all hell was breaking loose.

Travis heard the shouts and screams and gunshots behind him and jerked around to see a dozen or more men on horseback charging down Texas Street from the west. In the forefront was a small, pallid man who matched the description Travis had been given of Mike Whitson. As he recognized the outlaw, Travis realized that Dawes must have slipped a man out to go for help.

Now the town's defenders were caught in a cross fire. Whitson's gang presented the most immediate threat. Travis bellowed, "Look out behind! Everyone turn around!"

The men at the barricade wheeled around. Travis noticed that the onlookers who had been standing along the boardwalks on both sides of Texas Street had scattered for cover. Travis hoped a stray bullet had not struck any of the bystanders. Then he saw to his surprise that former sheriff Roy Wade was crouched behind a barrel on the boardwalk, blazing away at the outlaws with his old .45.

A slug whizzed past Travis from the courthouse. Travis threw a glance over his shoulder and saw Dawes's phony deputies surging out of the building, yelling and shooting as they charged across the courthouse lawn. Dawes must have seen Whitson attacking and sent his men out to deliver the finishing punch, the final blow that would wipe out Travis and his comrades and leave a defenseless Abilene in the hands of Dawes and Whitson.

Suddenly a rifle cracked from a courthouse window, and one of Dawes's deputies staggered, threw his hands up, and fell forward limply. Travis's eyes scanned the façade and came to rest on a figure crouched at the window, emptying a Winchester at Dawes's men. When the last bullet was gone, the man tossed the rifle aside, plucked a handgun from behind his belt, and dropped through the opening, heedless of the shards of shattered glass that had to be clinging to the frame. Dawes's men stopped their charge and turned to fire at the man attacking them from behind.

*Cody!* Travis almost smiled. Somehow, Cody had come through after all—

And then he had no time to think about anything but firing the gun in his hand as fast as he could.

With Cody blunting the force of the attack from the courthouse, the citizens of Abilene were able to put up a much stiffer resistance than the outlaws led by Whitson must have expected. Several of them went flying from their saddles, and the charge began to waver. Whitson lifted himself in his stirrups, screamed curses at his men over the din, and waved them on.

Kneeling beside Travis, Nestor Gilworth lifted his heavy, freshly loaded Sharps Big Fifty buffalo gun and settled the sights on Whitson's chest. He ignored the bullets whining past him as he coolly squeezed the trigger. The blast of the big carbine was thunderous, the recoil making the barrel climb a few inches despite Nestor's strength.

The bullet took Whitson dead center, lifting him out of his saddle, a look of stunned surprise on his narrow face. He was dead before he hit the ground and sprawled in the dirt. The plunging horses of the men behind him pounded his body into something that only vaguely resembled a man when they stampeded over him.

With their leader shot down, Whitson's men threw away their guns and desperately thrust their arms into the air in surrender. Led by Travis and Nestor, the townspeople surrounded them, guns cocked and ready.

Roy Wade was one of the men holding guns on the outlaws. As Travis came up to him, Wade grinned and said, "Howdy, Travis."

"Hello, Roy," Travis replied. "I didn't expect to see you here tonight."

"Well, hell, once I heard about what was happenin' with Dawes, I had to come down and give you a hand." The grin slipped from Wade's florid face and was replaced by an unusually solemn expression. "I might've done some things that weren't too smart in the past, but I couldn't sit by and let a dadburn rascal like Dawes make a mockery of the sheriff's office. Reckon this ol' bear's got a little growl left in him."

Travis slapped Wade on the shoulder. "Glad to be on the same side with you again, Roy," he said sincerely.

Leaving the prisoners in the capable hands of Nestor and Orion, Travis hurried toward the courthouse. The shooting from that quarter seemed to have ended as well. When he reached the barricade, Travis hurdled a wagon tongue—

Then he stopped and grinned tiredly when he saw Cody Fisher herding five men toward him. The captives were all that was left of Dawes's deputies, Travis assumed. None of them looked familiar, and the marshal figured that they had been members of Whitson's gang until recently.

"Howdy, Marshal," Cody said calmly. "Here's some more prisoners for you. I'm mighty happy to turn them over, too, seeing as how I brought them over here holding an empty gun on them."

Several of the men stiffened and shot hate-filled glances at the grinning deputy. As weary as he was, Travis had to chuckle and shake his head at Cody's coolheaded recklessness.

Lining his Colt on the prisoners, Travis asked Cody, "Did you see Dawes in there?"

Cody shook his head. "Didn't see him anywhere. Cotter and Geraghty are both dead, and so is Lin Rogers." The young deputy's face became unusually somber. "Rogers saved my life and Faith Hamilton's, too, Marshal. He wasn't part of Dawes's crooked schemes. I'm going to have to let Agnes know, and I'd appreciate it if you'd let other folks in on it."

"I will," Travis promised solemnly. "Is Miss Hamilton all right?"

"Scared out of her wits, but other than that she's not hurt."

"If you don't mind, why don't you go fetch her? I'll turn these men over to Nestor and Orion so they can be taken to jail." Travis slipped some cartridges from his shell belt and handed them to Cody. "Here. Just in case."

Cody nodded and began to thumb the fresh bullets into the pistol he held.

Travis looked again at the courthouse and wondered just what the devil had happened to John Henry Dawes.

The man ran through the darkened alley, his heart pounding wildly in his chest. Everything had gone wrong. *Everything!*

Right up until the last moment, Dawes had thought that somehow he would win this fight, would emerge victorious as he always had in the past. But when he saw Cody Fisher break the back of that last-ditch charge . . . when he saw Mike Whitson blasted out of the saddle . . . Dawes knew it was over. All that was left for him was escape.

With all the confusion around the courthouse, it had been easy for him to slip out a rear window and race into the night. Now the courthouse was several blocks away, and in another minute or two, he would reach a livery stable. The gunfire had spooked all the horses tethered near the scene of the battle, and they had snapped their reins and bolted. So Dawes had come this way, intent on stealing a mount from the stable. He would ride away from Abilene and never look back.

Whitson had stashed plenty of loot, and Dawes knew where to find it. Even though he was panting and sweating, he found himself grinning. John Henry Dawes might lose a battle now and then, but he always won the war.

"Hold it right there, John Henry!"

The sharp command cracked through the darkness. Dawes stopped short as a figure stepped out of the shadows. A little light entered the alley from the street at the far end, and the illumination was sufficient for Dawes to see the gun in the man's hand. Dawes's own Colt was holstered.

He frowned suddenly. "Kincaid?" he said, disbelief in his voice. "Kincaid, is that you?"

"That's right," Mason Kincaid said, his voice trembling slightly. "Don't move, Dawes. You're not going anywhere."

Dawes grinned again. "What is this, Kincaid? I thought we were on the same side."

"You're not on anyone's side but your own, Dawes. I understand that now. But I'm not on anyone's side, either. When I saw you slipping out of the courthouse, I knew I couldn't let you get away."

"What the hell are you going to do, turn me in? You know you can't do that. I told you, if I go down, I take you with me." Dawes took a step toward Kincaid. "Now get out of my way, dammit. We both know you're not going to pull that trigger."

Too late Dawes saw that Kincaid was smiling, too. "You can't spread any lies about me if you're dead," the land agent said coolly, his voice steadier now. "And once the whole truth about you comes out, the man who kills John Henry Dawes will be a hero in this town."

Frantically Dawes tried to jerk his gun from its holster. The heavy weapon had just cleared leather when Kincaid fired. Dawes grunted as a small black hole appeared in the center of his forehead. The gun slipped from his fingers. He swayed for a second, then fell with a crash.

Kincaid was still standing over the body a few moments later when a group of townspeople came running up. Luke Travis was in the lead.

The land agent looked up, met Travis's eyes, and said shakily, "I tried to take him alive, Marshal. I really did. I warned him to drop his gun. . . ." Kincaid fell silent and passed a trembling hand over his face. He turned away from Dawes's body as if sickened.

The citizens gathered around him, slapping him on the back and congratulating him. Travis studied Kincaid for a long moment and then slid his Colt into its holster, his lean face unreadable.

The long night was nearly over. In a few hours it would be dawn.

# Chapter Nineteen

"I'LL BE MIGHTY GLAD WHEN THIS DAY IS OVER," SAID CYRUS Worden, Abilene's undertaker, coroner, and now acting sheriff of Dickinson County. The fussy little man passed a hand over his bald pate. "Yes, sir, mighty glad. I don't know why you couldn't just take over as sheriff from the start, Luke."

"Because that's not the way the law works, Cyrus," Travis said as he leaned back in the chair behind his desk. "Officially, Buff Cotter was Dawes's chief deputy, and with both of them dead, the job goes to the county coroner. That's you."

"I know, I know," Worden grumbled. "I just wish Governor Anthony hadn't taken so long to appoint you as the new sheriff."

"It's only been four days, Cyrus," Cody pointed out; the deputy was perched on the sofa and was watching

Worden with a bemused expression. "That's pretty fast for a politician to get *anything* done."

The other people who were crowded in the marshal's office laughed. Aileen Bloom, Leslie Gibson, Orion Mc-Carthy, and Nestor Gilworth were all waiting with Travis, Cody, and Worden. In a few minutes the group would proceed to the courthouse, where the Honorable George T. Anthony, the governor of Kansas, would swear Travis in as sheriff of Dickinson County. The governor was already on hand, having arrived the previous evening on the train from Topeka. Instead of quietly swearing Travis in, as the marshal would have preferred, Anthony had insisted on a ceremony.

"I'm just glad everything is getting back to normal," Aileen said. "We were very lucky that more people weren't hurt in that battle."

Travis nodded. "It could've been plenty bad," he agreed. "Maybe things will stay settled for a while."

"Augie's mighty excited about being a full-time deputy," Orion put in. "Th' lad will gi' ye his best effort, Lucas."

"I was happy to give him a chance. Now that I've got a a whole county to cover, I'm going to need more deputies." Travis grinned. "But you've lost a good relief bartender, Orion."

The big Scotsman waved a knobby-knuckled hand. "Dinna worry about tha', Lucas. We'll manage down t' th' tavern."

Leslie Gibson had taken his watch out and was studying it. He snapped the cover shut and smiled. "I believe it's time we started down to the courthouse," he announced. "Wouldn't want to keep the governor waiting."

Travis stood up slowly and took a deep breath. Now that the time had come, he felt a little nervous. He had not requested that the governor appoint him to serve the rest of Dawes's term, but he had to admit he was the logical choice. And the town had made its wishes known to Governor Anthony as soon as the smoke and dust of battle cleared, bombarding the state house with telegrams of support for Travis. He could not let everyone down now.

He came out from behind the desk, plucked his hat from its peg, and said, "Let's go."

Quite a crowd had gathered in front of the courthouse, Travis saw as he and his companions walked down the street. The scene reminded him of some of the rallies during the campaign. There were no bands playing now, though. The atmosphere was still solemn enough that such a celebration would have been out of place. After all, although it could have been worse, quite a few men had died during the short reign of John Henry Dawes.

The crowd parted to let Travis and his group through. The marshal spotted Faith Hamilton among the spectators. She still looked a little haggard after her ordeal. But she managed to smile as her gaze moved from Travis to the steps of the courthouse where the governor awaited. Standing next to Anthony was Mason Kincaid, a self-satisfied smirk on his face. Kincaid had been the focus of almost as much attention as Travis during the past few days, and he seemed to be enjoying his new status as a hero.

Travis met Kincaid's gaze as he started up the steps. A look of chagrin flashed through the land agent's eyes. It had to gall him that Travis had won in the end. But the expression was fleeting, replaced in an instant by a forced smile and a hearty handshake as Travis reached the top of the steps. Flash powder went off with a whoosh as the photographer who traveled with the governor captured the moment. Emmett Valentine stood nearby taking notes, no doubt for yet another story about the heroes of the Battle of the Dickinson County Courthouse, as the reporter called it.

"Congratulations, Marshal," Kincaid said, lifting his voice so that Travis could hear him over the applause from the crowd. "I suppose I should say Sheriff, though, shouldn't I?"

"Doesn't matter to me," Travis replied. "The law is what counts, not the title."

He saw the hatred shining in Kincaid's eyes as he turned to shake hands with the governor. The trouble between them was not over yet, Travis thought, not by a long shot.

For one thing he wondered what had really happened in that alley between Mason Kincaid and John Henry Dawes.

But there would be time for that later. Right now, with his friends and most of the town looking on, he wanted to concentrate on getting this right. He placed his left hand on the Bible the governor held, raised his right hand, and began, "I, Lucas Travis, do solemnly swear . . ."